THE
Caroline
PAINTINGS

ALSO BY
ARTHUR D. HITTNER

<u>FICTION</u>

Artist, Soldier, Lover, Muse

*Four-Finger Singer and His Late Wife, Kate: A Novel of Life,
Death & Baseball*

<u>NON-FICTION</u>

*Honus Wagner:
The Life of Baseball's 'Flying Dutchman'*

*At the Threshold of Brilliance:
The Brief but Splendid Career of Harold J. Rabinovitz*

*Cross-Country Chronicles:
Road Trips Through the Art and Soul of America*

THE
Caroline
PAINTINGS

An Art Novel

ARTHUR D. HITTNER

Apple Ridge Press
Oro Valley, AZ

ISBN 978-0-9989810-7-9

Cover Design by Pure Fusion Media
Formatting by Polgarus Studio

Cover painting on easel: *The Dreamer* by Stan P. Poray, 1935. Author's collection.

Chapter One

Fort Myers, Florida
April, 2010

Dressed incongruously in worn-out flip-flops, plaid shorts, a vintage Hawaiian shirt, and a sweat-stained Red Sox baseball cap, Jerry climbed into the driver's seat of his '98 Chevy Blazer and cruised down Cleveland Avenue toward KeepSafe Storage. Gus, one of his ballpark buddies and the owner of the storage facility, had telephoned Jerry the night before, reminding him of his auction of the contents of four abandoned storage units. "There's one with some paintings," he'd informed his pal, suggesting he stop by in the morning, well in advance of the three o'clock auction.

Spring training had ended and the snowbirds had flown the coop. Jerry was relieved. The absence of traffic pleased the transplanted Bostonian nearly as much as the thrill of the chase. He parked near the office at the west end of the sprawling metal building, opened the driver-side door, and grimaced as he extracted his generous frame from its perch behind the wheel.

A portly, seventy-one-year-old widower with replaced hips, Jerry Deaver passed his time attending baseball games and peddling antiques and old paintings from a stall in Barnacle Bill's Antique Emporium, a dealers' cooperative in a run-down strip mall on the outskirts of Fort Meyers. His late wife, Blanche, had been the collector in the family. After he'd retired from his job as an IRS auditor and they'd moved to

Florida, it was she who cajoled him into starting the "little business on the side." With little else to amuse him, he found the hunt for treasure surprisingly fulfilling. When Blanche passed away unexpectedly three years ago, he redoubled his commitment to the business, both as a tribute to her and to stave off his loneliness. Florida, he'd concluded, was ripe for the picking, with retirees like him moving into the Sunshine State in droves, carting with them paintings and furniture their kids didn't want. If he looked hard enough, Jerry figured, he'd find that occasional needle in the haystack; but even if he didn't, he still felt a rush when some undiscerning tourist shelled out three bills for something he'd snatched for a C-note.

Gus greeted him with a smirk and his trademark dead-fish handshake. He led Jerry along the perimeter of the building to a small unit on the north end, one of the few equipped with air conditioning. He unlocked the padlock and rolled up the squeaky overhead door.

Jerry had played this game before, so he knew the rules. By the afternoon, each of the units would be opened, though roped off to prevent entry. You brought a flashlight and perused the contents from a distance. If you thought what you saw looked promising, you placed a bid on the contents of the entire unit; if not, you moved on. For Jerry, Gus would stretch the rules—but only so much.

The unit Gus unveiled was small and cramped. Stacks of cardboard boxes cluttered the front portion, obscuring what lay behind. "Go on, take a look in the back," Gus urged. Jerry flipped on his flashlight and squeezed his ample torso through the narrow space between rows of boxes. An old computer collected dust atop a battered metal desk on his right. Random pieces of office furniture were strewn haphazardly on his left.

Jerry directed his flashlight toward the back right corner. What he saw was encouraging: a dozen or so canvases stacked vertically, all facing toward the rear. He wound his way into the corner. The stack was wedged between a gray metal file cabinet and the back wall, offering little room to maneuver. Jerry leaned forward, tilting the first canvas backward as far as he could, hoping to catch a glimpse of the painted surface.

Gus observed from outside the dusty locker. "Whaddya think?" he wheezed.

"Tough to tell," Jerry replied. "Okay if I move some of this crap out of the way for a better look?"

"No can do, buddy," Gus said. "I'm already pushing the envelope just letting you in there." Jerry muttered something unflattering under his breath.

Given the awkward angle, Jerry couldn't locate a signature, but the surface of the painting suggested an artist of some ability. It appeared to be a portrait of a young woman or girl. At least it wasn't another of those "abstract" fiascos painted by some dilettante with a six-inch brush and a bucket of house paint. He ran his finger gently across the painting's surface. He could feel the delicacy of the brushstrokes under a thin layer of varnish.

"Okay, Jerry, gotta close it up now. You were never here. Got it?"

"Sure, Gus. Got it." Mildly annoyed, Jerry slithered back through the maze of furniture and boxes.

Although frustrated by his inability to properly assess the artwork, Jerry was intrigued. Viewing the backs of the few accessible canvases, he noticed their consistency. The raw canvas surfaces revealed only minimal discoloration, suggesting the works were of similar vintage, probably not more than fifty years old. As none were framed, it suggested the output of a single artist rather than the cache of a collector.

"Who rented it?" he asked Gus.

"Some retired lawyer," Gus said, declining to elaborate.

"Why'd he abandon it?"

"Guy croaked. Four years ago, turns out. Paid in advance for the first two years and then nada. Took a while to track down someone to confirm the fate of the poor bastard."

"Hmmm."

Though it would have been nice to learn more, Jerry knew he'd be back later to bid. In a way, it was more exciting to gamble on what he *didn't* know.

Jerry returned at three o'clock—along with a dozen others. Most were the types you'd see astride slot machines in the casinos clutching coffee cups filled with quarters. What did that say about him, Jerry wondered?

The unit he'd previewed was the last on the docket. Four potential bidders had dropped out by then, leaving a pack of eight. They stood there glaring, like coyotes salivating over a carcass.

Gus took a position in front of the rope barring access to the storage locker while several of the bidders leaned over, hoping to spot something they might have previously missed. Gus scrounged for an opening bid of $100 for the contents of the unit. "What, are you all bashful?" he chirped.

"Hundred bucks," cried the fat man on Jerry's left.

"Thanks, Eddie," Gus said, acknowledging the bid. Eddie, it appeared, was one of Gus's regulars.

"One fifty" belched a generously tattooed woman with bleached blond hair, her bust threatening to burst out of her ill-fitting tube top.

Jerry held back, content to jump in when the bidding slowed.

"One seventy-five." A third bidder had entered the sweepstakes.

"Two balloons," yelped Eddie.

Gus surveyed the motley crew for an advancing bid. No one stirred. He eyed Jerry, his stare an unambiguous call to action.

"Two and a quarter," Jerry chimed in.

"Two fifty," drawled the Tube-Top Diva.

"Two seventy-five," Jerry countered.

Eddie scratched his chin. "Three bills," he said.

"Three fifty," Jerry called out, hoping to stem the bidding then and there.

"Four bills!" Eddie boomed.

You'd've been lucky even to discern the presence of the canvases from behind the ropes, Jerry thought, so he wondered if Gus had "pushed the envelope" for Eddie as well. He did some quick math: even if they only brought a hundred bucks each, a dozen or so canvases would gross twelve hundred bucks. But then you'd have to factor in the time, trouble, and potential cost of transporting, sorting through, and otherwise dealing with the remaining contents of the storage locker. And were he inclined to be enterprising, he'd need to shell out more to frame the pictures. Was he edging a little too close to the possible breakeven point? He resolved to stop at five hundred.

"Any advance on four hundred or are we done?" Gus again peered at Jerry.

"Four fifty!" Jerry barked.

"Five hundred!" Eddie shot back.

Fuck it, Jerry thought. One more bid. "Six hundred!" he yelled with feigned confidence.

"You can fuckin' have it," growled Eddie, waving his hand dismissively as he stomped off in disgust.

Chapter Two

Longmire, Virginia
September, 1968

No one ever accused Caroline McKellan of reticence. She marched right up to the studio door and rapped loudly, like the wolf in the nursery rhyme. Irritated at the interruption, the artist sighed. He deposited his brush in the paint-splattered coffee can he'd used for decades, rose as quickly as his arthritic knees would allow, and opened the creaky wooden door.

"Caroline?" he stammered. The visit from his young next-door neighbor was unexpected; she'd been in grade school the last time she'd appeared at his door. Wearing cowboy boots, a tight pair of blue jeans, and a low-cut sweater, her lips painted a lush ruby red, she looked every bit of her sixteen years—and then some.

"Hi, Mr. Elliott," she said breezily, whisking into his studio as if entering her own living room.

Caroline McKellan had known Grant Elliott all of her life. Growing up on the small Virginia farm that had been in her family for generations, her parents had often hosted intimate dinners with their famous neighbors, Becky and Grant Elliott, whose eighteenth-century fieldstone farmhouse stood a mere two hundred yards from their own, nestled in the ancient ridges of the Shenandoah Valley in the rural climes of northern Virginia.

The McKellans traced their ancestry back to a hardy couple

of Scottish descent who'd emigrated on the eve of the Revolutionary War, settling in Longmire, on the very plot of land on which their early nineteenth century farmhouse now stood. They'd been there ever since, passing the farm down, as was the custom, to the eldest son. But the enduring chain of patrilineal descent had come to a crushing halt.

"To what do I owe the honor?" Grant inquired, a smile spreading across his well-chiseled face. Tall, broad-shouldered, and ruggedly handsome, he looked more like the Marlboro Man than a world-famous artist. But his advancing arthritis, the deepening lines on his face, and the random specks of gray intruding upon his unruly mantle of black hair bore testimony to his fifty-eight years.

"I'd like to be your muse, Mr. Elliott," she said bluntly.

Her boldness amused him. "My muse?" He laughed heartily. "It's not that simple." She stared at him, undaunted, her eyes blazing with determination.

Ever since she was a child, Caroline had reveled in her proximity to the artist celebrated for his poignant studies of the denizens of the Shenandoah Valley, ordinary people to whom the verdant valley was a cherished birthright. When she was eight, Grant had produced sketches of each of her parents, presenting them as framed gifts to the family that Christmas. Four years later, he'd contributed another portrait to the family collection, a sketch of her brother done from a photograph. But he'd never drawn Caroline.

Caroline had long admired the glossy reproductions in the lavish books displayed with pride on the coffee table in her living room, imagining her own image gracing the cover of some as yet unpublished volume. She'd longed to become his muse, aspiring to the recognition and acclaim reserved for inspirational subjects in the oeuvres of famous artists. It was a self-indulgent dream, perhaps, but the only one that had survived the ravages of her shattered life.

It happened quickly, four years ago, on one of those brisk autumn days Grant had often captured in paint, the foothills of the Blue Ridge Mountains magically illuminated by the scarlet sunset, awash with the shimmering reds and yellows of the changing leaves. Trent, Caroline's older brother, rode atop their ancient tractor, plowing under the detritus of the recent harvest. Encountering a hidden boulder, the tractor suddenly seized, overturning and spilling him into the unforgiving jaws of the machine.

In addition to her own grieving, Caroline bore the burden of her parents' devastation. They dwelled on their loss instead of their daughter. The tragedy soured her on the agrarian life that was her legacy. She rebelled. By her own reckoning, she'd sooner end her life than spend a day more than necessary on the family farm. During the winter of her fourteenth year, she tried just that, half-heartedly enough to survive. But rather than embracing and restoring their damaged daughter, James and Alice McKellan, still raw and embittered, berated Caroline for her selfish affront to her parents and to the memory of their beloved son.

Derailed by these events, Caroline floundered. A happy, beautiful child grew into a confused and troubled teen, searching for her place in an unsettling world. Stunningly attractive and ferociously independent, she brandished her beauty like a machete, flailing at allies and suitors alike as she stumbled headlong through a terrifying adolescence.

"I'm deadly serious," she said defiantly, challenging the artist's resistance. "I *know* you want to paint me, you said so at dinner!" She deposited herself onto the timeworn seat of an old Windsor chair, her outline silhouetted by the dim northern light filtering through the bay window of the once dilapidated outbuilding that the Elliotts had refitted as a studio.

Caroline was right. Grant Elliott would have liked nothing more than to paint the precocious sixteen-year-old. A tinderbox of beauty, grief, anger, and rebellion, she was captivating and provocative. He'd struggled to wrest his eyes from her two nights earlier, when the McKellans hosted the Elliotts for dinner. It was his first glimpse of Caroline in more than a year, and the changes were startling. She'd grown into a beautiful young woman: tall, lithe, and brash, with piercing blue eyes, porcelain skin, and a luxurious mane of strawberry blond hair. In passing dinner conversation he'd mentioned his interest in painting her, but his hosts were decidedly cool to the notion. He pursued it no further.

But to Caroline, Grant's remark was a summons—an invitation to pursue her covert ambition. After all, she figured, she had nothing left to lose.

Grant thought of his wife. Becky Elliott was wary of her husband's attraction—and of Caroline's allure. Her apprehension was justified. Three years earlier, he'd developed a similar infatuation—a twenty-year-old he'd spotted in town and persuaded to pose for him. When rumors of their affair had begun to circulate, Becky confronted him. He caved like a house of cards. Never again, he swore.

"Yes, I did ask your parents," Grant acknowledged, "but they refused to even consider it." Caroline could scarcely have thought otherwise. The accident had transformed her casually churchgoing parents into iron-willed, God-fearing zealots. An attractive daughter was just another cross they were destined to bear. While they respected Grant's accomplishments and cherished his friendship, they'd hardly trust him with their only remaining child. They'd heard the rumors, too.

"I don't care what they said," Caroline hissed.

Grant sighed, shaking his head as he pulled up a chair. They glared at each other, neither relenting. Her determination unnerved him. Against his better judgment, he pondered the possibilities. He'd been in a rut for longer than he cared to admit. He'd grown bored with his bloated portfolio of craggy Longmire faces, homogeneous landscapes, and insipid still lifes. In truth, he hadn't been truly inspired since his ill-fated encounter with Anita Bennett, the muse whose promising run had been sabotaged by his own libido. But where Anita had been twenty, Caroline was four years younger, and her parents were longtime friends and neighbors.

"Look, Caroline," he said, opting for candor. "I'd love to have you pose for me, but my wife—"

"I heard what happened with that other woman," she boldly interrupted, "and I don't care. I'm not here to seduce you; I want to *inspire* you." A tentative smile graced her lips. "We can meet in secret," she said, her voice ratcheting down to a conspiratorial whisper. "There's no need to tell anyone. Just give me a chance," she pleaded, her hands clasped in a prayerful gesture. "If it doesn't work out, I'll never ask you again. I swear."

Caroline's irresistible force had collided with Grant's immovable object and sent it reeling. He knew what he *should* do: disabuse Caroline of her fanciful notion and escort her from his studio with polite regrets.

The old Windsor creaked as the artist rocked back in his chair. Caroline sensed he was wavering. Her spirits rose accordingly.

"Okay, look," he said, even as he chided himself for retreating. "You're here. Let's make the best of it. Pose for me. One quick sketch. And then I'll think about it."

"Yes!" she said triumphantly, pumping her fist into the air. Her face lit up like a Shenandoah sunrise.

"I said I'd *think* about it," Grant cautioned, raising a hand to temper her elation. "I'll discuss it with Becky. But," he reiterated, "we'll still need your parents' approval."

While his caveat dampened her momentary euphoria, Caroline saw little advantage in challenging it. She'd fight that battle another day.

"Okay, then, let's move you over there," he said, directing her to a spot where the light from the window would cast her face in partial shadow. He positioned her in the Windsor, tilting her head gently upward and to her right. "Like this," Grant said, placing one hand upon her cheek and the other on her chin, rotating her head ever so slightly. He stepped back repeatedly to evaluate her pose, making subtle adjustments. Caroline eagerly complied with his instructions.

Grant placed a matching Windsor about five feet from where Caroline sat. He grabbed a large sketchpad from his worktable and selected a pencil from a collection in a jar on the windowsill. "Stay as still as you can," he instructed her as he sat down and began to draw.

Caroline's heart raced as he worked. While her excitement rendered it difficult to keep still, she gamely forced herself to maintain her pose.

Grant drew for nearly half an hour. The only sounds that Caroline heard were the scratching of pencil on paper and the rhythmic ticking of an old grandfather clock in the corner of the studio. Though her gaze was directed to his left, her peripheral vision perceived the rapid motion of his eyes and the confident movements of his right hand as he sketched. Caroline's eyes brimmed with anticipation. Finally, as the afternoon light began to desert him, Grant declared the drawing complete.

"May I see?"

She stood up and approached him, peeking over for a glimpse at the sketch. Though Grant's expression was noncommittal, Caroline couldn't camouflage her delight. Her smile was contagious.

"Come back in a week and we'll talk again," he said. "No promises. Understand?"

Caroline nodded. "See you next week," she said buoyantly as she skipped toward the door and let herself out.

Grant sat down to contemplate the drawing. It was exquisite. *She* was exquisite. The possibilities were endless. Most importantly, he was *inspired* to a degree he no longer thought possible. Grant knew he had to paint her, whatever the consequences.

Chapter Three

For two days, Grant obsessed over his drawing of Caroline, summoning the courage to discuss it with Becky. After the debacle with Anita Bennett, how could he not? She'd either reject him outright, a look of disgust on her face, or agree, with the utmost reluctance, conditional upon the McKellans' consent. Finally resolved to address the matter, he braced for her reaction.

Grant brought the sketch up from the studio before dinner. He chose the most propitious moment, their pre-dinner ritual: her glass of Chardonnay and his belt of scotch. The alcohol, he hoped, would facilitate discussion and temper his wife's reaction. With some trepidation, he related the details of Caroline's visit. "She was adamant," he recalled. "Wouldn't take no for an answer."

Becky shook her head. "It's no wonder, the way you stared at her at dinner last week."

"Come on, Becky," he whined. "You could see it as plainly as I could. Caroline's changed; she's grown up. She's not only beautiful, she's a veritable *force*." When his wife failed to respond, he unveiled the drawing, sliding it across the kitchen counter. "I didn't have the heart to just send her away, so I had her pose for this."

Becky studied the sketch deliberately, the same way she approached every detail of Grant's artistic life. She'd been a twenty-two-year-old grad student, and Grant an emerging artist, when they'd met in New York City shortly after the War. She'd posed for him then, on a whim, and knew first-hand what could follow from that. They married a year later. With short, neatly trimmed brown hair; sharp, intelligent eyes; a delicate chin; and an engaging smile, she was still attractive at forty-three. And like Caroline, Becky, too, was a force: she scrupulously managed every aspect of her husband's career, from the recording of every artwork to dealings with commercial galleries, museums, and art professionals. She'd earned a reputation in the art world as a shrewd businesswoman, a savvy promoter, and a fierce protector of her husband's artistic legacy.

"Yes, Grant, it's good, very good," she conceded, sipping her wine through a scowl. "But she's . . . what, *sixteen*?" She looked up from the drawing, fixing her eyes on his. "Is she going to become your infatuation *du jour*? She's jailbait, Grant, for God's sake!" Her tone made him cringe. "Do the McKellans know about this?"

"No," he admitted, draining his scotch in a single gulp.

She placed her wine glass firmly on the counter. "Well, no matter how I feel about this, there's no way she can model without their consent." She was resolute. "Let it go," she cautioned him, eyebrows raised.

Grant bit his lip. Even if Becky could be persuaded to cooperate—and he harbored little optimism in that regard— he was certain the McKellans would object. Unless Caroline could miraculously persuade her parents, he could proceed only by deceiving both his wife and their neighbors.

Despite Becky's admonition, Grant couldn't let it go. To the contrary, his obsession with painting Caroline grew more intense with each passing day. His compulsion to paint her was as steadfast as her determination to pose for him. Though he knew he should rebuff her, he nevertheless indulged his imagination, pondering duplicitous strategies to accommodate their mutual desires as he thrashed through a succession of sleepless nights.

A week after Caroline's visit, Grant met in his studio with Brandon Blake, a promising young artist who'd become his friend and protégé. A graduate of the Pennsylvania Academy of the Fine Arts in Philadelphia, Blake had risen quickly through the ranks of contemporary realist painters. He'd relocated to Longmire the previous year, exchanging a cramped Philadelphia loft for a spacious studio in a converted old barn he'd rented just a half-mile away. Powerfully built, with a mop of red hair and an ample beard to match, he had the size and strength to handle the physical challenges presented by his monumental paintings.

Later that morning, after counseling the young artist about his latest undertaking, Grant broached the subject that had consumed him for the past week.

"I've got a hypothetical to pose to you," he began, "but I'm afraid it's a bit..." Grant fumbled for the right adjective. He settled for "irregular."

Blake eyed him quizzically, stroking his beard. "You've got my attention."

"Imagine an older, established artist, in a bit of a rut, encountering an irresistible young woman who insists on posing for him."

"Go on..."

"She's feisty, mysterious, incredibly beautiful. Eyes as blue and deep as the Caribbean, strawberry blond hair that shimmers—"

Brandon raised his hand to stem the torrent of accolades. "I get the picture. You want to paint her. What's the rub?"

"She's sixteen, she lives next door, her old-school parents will never consent, and Becky's not too keen on the idea, for reasons you can probably imagine."

"I see." Brandon puckered his lips, suppressing a smile.

As Grant began to elaborate, he was interrupted by a pounding at the door. From the force of the blows, he presumed it was Caroline. "Speak of the devil," he muttered.

Grant opened the door, smiling as he beckoned his young neighbor inside. She strode in confidently, clad in tight-fitting bell-bottom jeans and a red mohair sweater, her hair gathered in a perky ponytail. Brandon's jaw slackened. "Caroline McKellan, meet my friend and fellow artist, Brandon Blake." Flashing a toothy grin, Caroline grasped Brandon's outstretched hand and shook it firmly.

"Didn't mean to interrupt, Mr. Elliott, but you said to come back in a week."

"I did indeed," he acknowledged.

"Uh . . . listen," Brandon murmured. "Maybe I should leave you two alone . . ."

"No, no," Grant replied. "This concerns you, too." The young artist's eyes registered his bewilderment.

Grant asked Caroline if she'd consulted her parents. "No need," she said, shaking her head dismissively. "I know *exactly* what they'd say."

"So," Grant said, without conviction, "I don't see—"

"Like I said," she protested, "they don't need to know." She was as persistent as she'd been a week earlier.

Grant's lips tightened. "Wait outside a few minutes, Caroline, would you?" She nodded. As she stepped out of the studio, Grant approached Brandon.

"I know this is crazy," he conceded, "but I've gotta do this."

He exhaled deeply. "In a way where no one's the wiser until the time's right."

Brandon shook his head in disbelief. "How can you even *think* about it if her parents object? Didn't you say she's *sixteen*? Wait a couple of years, Grant, for Chrissake!"

"I can't, Brandon. My work's becoming monotonous. I can pump out more tedious landscapes and still lifes or I can paint her. In fact," he said, breathlessly, "I can do both simultaneously if I have to."

"What about Becky?"

"She doesn't have to know."

"How won't she know?" he asked incredulously. "She's sitting in your house but fifty yards from here!"

"That's where you come in," Grant said. There was an ominous gleam in his eye.

Brandon shifted uncomfortably. "What's *that* supposed to mean?"

"You've got a big studio. Let me borrow just a corner once a week. We won't bother you—you can do your thing and I'll do mine. And," Grant added, with a sly grin, "you can act as chaperone . . . so I won't be tempted to commit a felony."

"You can't be serious!"

Grant nodded, albeit sheepishly. "And you've got more than enough space to store the paintings." He shot the young artist an imploring look. "Whaddya say?"

Brandon found himself in an untenable position. Over the past three years, Grant Elliott, one of the country's most revered and accomplished artists, had selflessly advised and mentored him, never accepting a dime for his counsel. He'd elevated Brandon's art and career, merely for the pleasure of giving back to the community of artists that had once counseled him. As uncomfortable as he felt, how could he deny

Grant the only favor he'd ever asked of him? And, having met the young woman, he understood—perhaps as only a fellow artist could—the irrational compulsion that might spur such a perilous undertaking.

Brandon rolled his eyes. "All right," he shrugged, "I don't like it, but I'll do it."

Chapter Four

In what would soon become a weekly routine, Caroline arrived at Brandon's studio for her first formal modeling session on the following Thursday afternoon. She came directly from school, walking nearly a mile, a bulging knapsack strapped to her back. Art club, she told her parents. In a convoluted way, it was the truth.

From Brandon's perspective, Thursday afternoons were ideal. He'd set aside that time for a studio art course he taught at a local community college. He'd rather not be present anyway, he told Grant: it made him feel culpable, an accessory to deception. "And I'll be damned if I'm going to play chaperone," he swore.

For their initial session, Grant had invited Caroline to wear something special to her. She'd stuffed it in her knapsack, extracting it as they prepared to begin.

"Why that?" Grant asked, watching her slither into an old, gray sweater that was several sizes too large, stained, and peppered with holes.

"It was my brother's," she said matter-of-factly.

Grant was measured in his response. "Would you like to talk about him?" he offered. She shook her head.

Caroline sat on a simple, wooden chair across from the portable worktable Grant had commandeered from a corner of the massive barn that served as Brandon's studio. The single room was framed in bare wood, with heavy overhead beams propping up a gabled roof. A cast iron wood stove provided comforting warmth. A loft, filled with the disused relics of a once prosperous farming operation, rose above three sides of the barn. In the rear, Brandon had erected bins for the storage of artwork. Around them stood an array of gigantic canvases in various states of completion. Unlike Grant's more intimate works, Brandon's paintings were bustling with figures, some clothed, but many not. Not the ideal setting for a sixteen-year-old, but it would have to suffice.

"Make yourself comfortable," Grant said, arranging pencils on the table beside his sketchpad. She settled in slowly, tugging repeatedly at her sweater, hiding, as best she could, the rolls of excess material. Though she faced him directly, her gaze seemed distant. Long, thick tresses of reddish blond hair flowed past her shoulders, falling upon her breasts delicately, like a curtain of silk. Her lips were pressed firmly together, her eyes bright and unadorned. She folded her arms snugly across her chest, as if to embrace that ratty, gray sweater. The nervous anticipation she'd manifested during her trial sitting two weeks earlier was no longer in evidence.

There was little conversation between the artist and his fledgling model. In her facial expression and body language, Grant intuited Caroline's grief. She'd escaped into a world deep within herself, her thoughts steeped in melancholy and loss. Words were superfluous. Her ability to telegraph her emotions, and his capacity to decode them, astounded him. Engrossed, Grant sketched furiously, almost unconsciously, rendering her likeness in a bust-length format on the oversized sketchpad. He captured every nuance of her expression and posture, recorded the texture, stains, even the holes, in her sweater. Grant took note of the rustic context of the bare section of barn wall that rose up behind her, scribbling detailed color notes beyond the outlines of the figure he'd drawn on the page.

When his sketch was nearly done, Grant peered one last time into the depths of Caroline's eyes. He noticed them moistening. As he observed, a lone teardrop descended from her left eye. Moments later, a companion tear wove a parallel path down her right cheek. She remained still, making no effort to conceal her silent weeping. Mesmerized, Grant revised the sketch to incorporate what he'd witnessed. He felt her loss almost as if it were his own, with an intensity that surprised him. In over forty years of drawing portraits, he couldn't recall such a transference of emotion.

"That's enough for today," he told her at last, his voice almost quaking. "You did a marvelous job, Caroline. Thank you."

She sighed, the tension in her arms and shoulders slackening as if she'd been liberated from a trance. She smiled weakly as she rose from her chair. Carefully, almost reverently, she removed her brother's sweater and replaced it in her knapsack.

Grant reached into his wallet, withdrawing a twenty-dollar bill. He smiled as he handed it to her.

"What's this?"

"Your modeling fee."

Caroline blushed. "I didn't expect to be paid, Mr. Elliott." She shrugged. "That's not why I'm here."

"Standard fee for rookie muses," he laughed. "You earned it."

She smiled grudgingly. "Thanks, then," she said, slipping the bill into her knapsack. "Next Thursday? Same time and place?"

Grant nodded, watching as she collected her belongings and left Brandon's studio. He was astonished by her indefatigability. Where Grant was emotionally spent, Caroline displayed minimal aftereffects from the strain of holding both pose and expression for so long. Her command over her emotions amazed him.

Grant poured himself a cup of coffee from the pot Brandon had left warming atop the wood stove. As he sipped, he contemplated the drawing he'd just completed. He studied the background, made minor adjustments, scrawled a few final notes. With a ruler, he drew a grid over the sketch to facilitate its transfer to the thirty-by-twenty-five-inch canvas he'd prepared and lined in corresponding fashion using a piece of sharpened charcoal.

Typically, Grant would do additional preparatory studies and let his thoughts percolate before commencing work on a significant painting. But this time, he couldn't wait to begin. With the charcoal, he carefully transferred the outline of the drawing from the sketch to the canvas, using the grids he'd drawn as a guide. He then readied his palette, using tempera paints he'd mixed himself from a recipe of powdered pigments, distilled water, and egg yolk. It was his signature medium, with roots in the Renaissance. Drying rapidly, it allowed for the delicacy of the built-up brushstrokes for which Grant had become known and admired.

And so began the laborious process of painting the work he'd call *Grief.*

Chapter Five

Jerry peeled six hundreds off his modest roll of cash and handed them to Gus. He'd need to rent a U-Haul to empty the contents of the storage locker, but his first order of business was to satisfy his burning curiosity.

Gus unlocked the unit for him and noisily lifted the overhead door. "Knock yourself out," he said.

Brandishing his flashlight, Jerry wormed his way into the back corner of the locker. He slid the file cabinet forward as far as he could, allowing easier access to the canvases. Shunting a few encroaching boxes to the side, he grabbed the outermost painting by its wooden stretchers. The inscription on the back of the canvas read "Cornelia." The number "1" appeared below it as well as the title, *Grief*. The artwork, which was about two feet by two-and-a-half feet, was unframed, and therefore easy to extricate from the stack and carry from the dusty locker into the sunlight.

Jerry emitted an audible gasp when he flipped the canvas to reveal the painted surface. He found himself face-to-face with a bust length portrait of a fabulously attractive young woman: a waif, he surmised, noting the holes in the gray sweater she wore. Her silky, reddish-blond hair cascaded past her shoulders, falling gently upon her breasts. Her arms were folded tightly across her chest. The detail was extraordinary: every stitch of the sweater was visible—even the holes were rendered meticulously. Every strand of her hair was drawn with precision. Her eyes were moist. He even detected a faint trail of tears on each of her cheeks. Her sadness was palpable. It certainly explained the title.

Jerry propped the painting carefully against the building, crouching down, with considerable difficulty, to examine it more closely. There was something about the surface. It didn't look like oil, nor did it have the glossiness he typically associated with acrylics. He'd seen only a few tempera paintings—or at least paintings that he knew were painted in that egg-based medium—and couldn't rule that out as a possibility. Whatever the medium, the execution was absolutely first-rate.

He scanned the four corners of the painting for a signature or monogram. Nothing. He flipped it over again to the back, scouring the surface of the stretcher for some kind of clue. Again, nothing. Who painted something of this quality without signing it? And why?

Judging from the hairstyle of the subject, the color of the wood of the stretcher (only slightly oxidized), the appearance of the rear of the canvas (relatively bright, with just a thin layer of dust and dirt), he figured the picture couldn't be more than forty or fifty years old.

If he didn't know better, he'd have guessed the painting was by Andrew Wyeth or Grant Elliott, but he knew the chances of that were more remote than his shot at winning the Florida Lotto. They did have a host of imitators, and this one, he thought, was among the more talented. But even if he didn't know who'd painted this sad young lady, he was confident he'd be able to recoup his six-hundred-dollar investment with this work alone. The rest would be gravy.

Jerry stood up and smiled. He was pleased with himself and eager to determine if the rest of his haul was of comparable quality. Surely there'd be a signature, date, or some other clue on one of the other paintings to help him make sense of what he'd acquired.

He took a quick inventory of the other items in the storage unit. The few pieces of well-worn office furniture were of little or no value—hardly antiques—and not worth the hassle of moving and selling them. And having sampled the contents of a few of the dozen or so cardboard boxes—musty old files— he deemed them of no import to anyone other than the poor sap who'd rented the unit. And since he was dead, they wouldn't matter to that poor sap anymore either. Certainly Gus, or one of the hulking young helpers he employed, could be persuaded to help him remove this dross to the on-site dumpster in exchange for a crisp twenty-dollar bill.

But as Jerry contemplated loading the canvases into his SUV and chucking the rest into the dumpster, it occurred to him that somewhere in that jungle of paper might be a clue unlocking the mysteries behind his newly-acquired collection of art. So, with the help of Gus's muscle—and for substantially more than the twenty-dollar bill he'd anticipated—Jerry dumped the old furniture and stacked the paintings and cartons into a rented U-Haul and moved the whole kit-and-caboodle into his already bulging garage.

Chapter Six

Modeling could be draining and dull, but Caroline embraced her new calling with unmitigated enthusiasm. The silence of their earlier sessions had given way to a lively and familiar banter. Slowly, Caroline shed her once impenetrable cloak of defiance and began to reveal herself.

She talked about her late brother, Trent, her "best friend," who'd encouraged his younger sister to imagine a different life even as he'd languished under the weight of his destiny on the family farm. "He felt trapped," she told Grant. "He considered joining the Army, but with Vietnam," she lamented, "he was doomed either way."

She expressed her disgust for the war, a particularly contentious subject among the rural populace of northern Virginia. She spoke of her brother's best friend, who'd perished the previous year in the Battle of Khe Sanh. "What does that God-forsaken country have to do with us?" she asked Grant, a once staunch supporter of the conflict whose doubts were steadily multiplying. The intensity of her anger surprised him. "We fought our own damn Civil War," she fumed, "why fight theirs?"

Grant savored the unbridled passion that Caroline injected into their weekly routine. Without realizing it, he'd become her confidante, a *de facto* parent to whom she could express her hopes, fears, triumphs, and insecurities. Her relationship with her own parents had grown increasingly strained. Still enveloped in their grief, they'd remained distant, offering their daughter neither solace nor succor. Emotionally bruised, but intelligent and thoughtful, Caroline thirsted for more than her parents could offer, and Grant was there to provide it. When she asked his advice, he offered it; when she unburdened herself, he listened. With no children of his own, Grant relished the role.

In the spring, when the weather grew milder, Grant sketched Caroline outdoors. On a balmy Thursday afternoon in May, he followed her to a stand of lush white peonies that rose from a bed beside Brandon's barn. Toting his sketchpad and pencil, he watched as she reached to cup a delicate flower in her right hand, bending down to inhale its fragrance, her eyes squeezing shut with pleasure.

"Hold that pose!" Grant blurted out, startling her. She drew back reflexively. "Can you do that again?" He was asking a lot— the stance was awkward, bending at the waist, her face pressed up against the heart of the flower, its stem gently caressed between the index and middle fingers of her right hand, her palm tilting upward. The pose exposed her right wrist, which bore the scars of her failed attempt on her life.

Grant drew close to her, crouching down to catch her face in full profile. He sketched quickly, sensitive to the difficulty of her pose. Caroline cooperated fully, as she always did, pausing every now and then to stretch, cheating only occasionally to steal a glimpse at the image gradually emerging from his sketchpad.

"You're drawing my scar, aren't you?" she asked him in a muted voice. It was an observation more than an objection.

"It's a part of who you are," Grant replied, his focus shifting between his sketch and his model.

Caroline pursed her lips, inhaled deeply, and nodded almost imperceptibly. "I suppose so," she said.

Grant had never raised the issue of her suicide attempt. To do so, he feared, would be unduly intrusive. But as it was she who'd broached the subject, he chose to pursue it. "What compelled you," he asked, lifting his gaze from his drawing, "to . . ." He let the question trail off, hesitant to characterize the act.

Caroline straightened up, relaxing, training her eyes on his. "I was thirteen," she said somberly. "Trent had been gone almost two years." She took another deep breath. "I felt," she said haltingly, "like I didn't matter anymore . . . like he'd taken part of me with him when he left us. And no one noticed that *I* was still living." She paused, her eyes moistening. "I *hated* the farm," she said bitterly. "I felt like there was nothing left for me there." Grant listened silently, absorbing her heartbreak and pain. "I'm not sure if I really meant to do it," she admitted, her voice reduced to a whisper. "Maybe I just wanted to make them realize I was *there*." Regret filled her eyes. "But it just made them angrier." Lowering his sketchpad to the ground, Grant stepped forward, reaching out to embrace her. She plunged into his arms, tears flowing freely.

It was the first time Caroline had expressed her true feelings about the incident to anyone. In her desperate plea for comfort and understanding, she'd merely exacerbated her parents' indomitable grief. Tone-deaf to her agony and torment, they'd spurned the message she'd so perilously sought to convey. Caroline's catharsis was liberating. She released her grip, brushing the tears from her cheeks. Their eyes met again, exchanging gratitude for empathy. She stepped back, returning her attention to the peony, bending down to resume her pose. "Back to work," she said, a smile returning to her face. Grant nodded, bemused, once again, by her uncanny ability to shift emotional gears.

Grant completed several sketches in the garden that afternoon. Later, he'd synthesize the drawings into a detailed study for his painting. He rarely painted during his sessions with Caroline—there was plenty of time for that during the rest of the week. Becky knew better than to intrude on Grant in his own studio, so he had no compunction about working on his Caroline series there. He usually worked on several projects concurrently, so there was no drop-off in production to trigger his wife's suspicions.

In the brief eight months of their collaboration, Caroline had evolved into the most influential muse of Grant Elliott's long and storied career. The pictures she'd inspired were the most sensitive and emotional works he'd ever produced. More importantly, he was motivated again. The process of painting had become a voyage of revelation instead of a chore. His renewed enthusiasm informed his other work as well. Both Becky and Brandon had said as much, though only Brandon knew the reason why.

Yet as much as Grant reveled in painting his muse, he was fast approaching an impasse. He knew that his series would never fully develop until he was free to exploit the haunting power of Caroline's graceful body. For months, he'd avoided confronting the issue, content with painting her clothed in the manner she felt most comfortable, her quirky wardrobe a reflection of her engaging personality. But there was so much more to explore. He chafed at his indecision, his hesitation to advance their collaboration to the next level. In painting her at all, they'd both defied strictures: marital, parental, and societal. Caroline was seventeen now, finishing her junior year in high school. His common sense told him it was still too early, that he should hold fast, at least for another year. But common sense wasn't always Grant's forte.

Chapter Seven

School was out. It was obvious from her appearance when she waltzed into Brandon's studio on the third Thursday in June. Caroline typically wore her school attire, but today arrived in a revealing halter-top and a highly abbreviated pair of cut-offs.

"Not the look I was anticipating," Grant snickered, watching her fling her pocketbook onto a chair.

"School's out, old man," she giggled. "Besides, I figured it was about time I posed in the nude."

She'd lobbed a grenade. Should he cower in his foxhole or indulge her—and himself? Despite all of his ruminations, Grant remained ambivalent.

His vacillation amused her. "Don't tell me you haven't thought about it," she said. "Or aren't you *man* enough to handle it!" She was laughing now, teasing him. "Besides, what self-respecting muse is too tight-assed to go bare-assed?"

Grant wanted desperately to accommodate her. And it helped that she'd initiated the debate. Yet for all her enthusiasm and precociousness, she was still seventeen.

"Caroline . . . I just don't—"

His dismissal was barely out of his mouth when she slipped off her top and unzipped her shorts.

"Caroline!"

After unhooking and discarding her bra, she wriggled out

of her panties, playfully rotating them around her index finger. She hummed a classic striptease ditty while pirouetting for Grant's entertainment. "C'mon, Grant, get with the program!" she cackled.

Caroline rarely had difficulty in making Grant smile. And if her audacity and humor weakened his resolve, her figure sealed the deal. Hers was a woman's body, but with lingering traces of receding adolescence. Her curves were sensuous, more subtle than voluptuous. Her skin was creamy and supple, her breasts round and firm—as if turned on a potter's lathe. A small birthmark, in the shape of a heart, graced her upper back, just beneath her right shoulder. When she moved toward the window, a stream of sunlight revealed a tinge of red in the small patch of hair that rose from between her legs.

Caroline was justifiably proud of her body. She moved with the grace and confidence of a woman acutely attuned to the power of her beauty. Fully unclothed before him, she eagerly awaited his reaction. "Say something!" she implored him, a coy smile plastered across her face.

"I'm sorry," he said. "I'm speechless." She took it as a compliment, her smile broadening.

"Okay, then, let's get on with it!"

Grant gathered himself, abandoned any further pretense of resistance, and turned his attention to the formulation of her pose. Brandon had a cot in the studio, which Grant repositioned beneath a north-facing window. A rustic armoire yielded a pair of fresh sheets, a pillow, and pillowcase.

"Why don't you lie on your left side," he suggested, "facing me."

Caroline pounced giddily onto the cot, above the sheet with which Grant had hastily covered it. She rolled onto her left hip as he'd directed.

"Drape your right arm over your head," he said. She complied. Grant reached over carefully, extending her arm slightly. "Grip the back of the pillow with your right hand," he said. "That should make it easier to hold your position."

"Where do I put my left arm?"

"Lay it at the edge of the pillow, reaching out toward me."

Grant placed his hands upon her cheeks, adjusting the position of her head, then arranged her hair so that it coursed across her neck, coming to rest at the swell of her breast. He draped the second sheet over her, pulling it up to her hips, leaving a hint of exposed pubic hair.

"Close your eyes," he directed, "and relax."

"We good?" she asked.

"You're perfect."

Chapter Eight

Fort Myers, Florida
April, 2010

Jerry sat in a beach chair in his garage, surrounded by artwork and boxes, clad in an old pair of Bermuda shorts and a Red Sox tee shirt. His SUV was relegated to the driveway—there was no room left in the garage. The latter had been cramped to begin with, but Gus's crew had covered nearly every remaining square inch with the cartons removed from the storage locker. He sighed deeply, his face dripping with sweat.

It'd been a long and frustrating week. He'd begun with a careful inspection of the artworks. There were a dozen canvases as well as a large leather portfolio he hadn't previously noticed. It had been wedged in the back corner of the storage unit, its presence obscured by the paintings. Inside it were sixty-two works on paper: mostly pencil sketches, though the collection included several highly finished watercolors. All of the work was gorgeously executed, and all quite clearly by the same talented hand. Whether set indoors or out, the backgrounds were uniformly rural. But what had most intrigued Jerry was that every work featured the same young model he'd discovered on the first canvas he'd liberated from the locker. The works on paper, as best he could tell, were mostly studies for the full-blown paintings.

Jerry knew he'd made an important discovery. But his search for the artist's identity was exasperating. Not a single painting, drawing, or watercolor contained even the hint of a signature. The drawings and watercolors, in fact, bore no inscriptions at all. Like *Grief,* the painting he'd inspected outside the storage locker, each of the canvases bore a number ranging from one to twelve, a title, and above those lean snippets of information, the name *Cornelia.* No dates, no site locations, no other clues to jumpstart his research.

Thus far, Jerry had told no one about what he'd dubbed The Cornelia Paintings. Part of him was afraid to, worried it was too good to be true, that someone would emerge from the woodwork to challenge his claim to the art. None of his fellow dealers at Barnacle Bill's would have the knowledge or sophistication to fully appreciate his discovery. In any event, the more people who knew, the more threatened he'd feel.

Frustrated by his inability to unravel the riddle through physical inspection alone, he'd spent the better part of the week poring through the boxes that littered the floor of his garage, desperately searching for clues. For the most part, they contained legal files from as early as 1998 to as late as 2006. Most of the correspondence bore the letterhead of Martin S. Becker, Jr., Attorney-at-Law, with offices at varying addresses in Fort Myers. Jerry inspected the documents in the first several boxes more deliberately than the others, ultimately concluding that immersion in a decade's worth of legal minutia was useless at worst—and mind-numbing at best. He was again tempted to chuck the lot of it, freeing his garage for the storage of his Blazer, but again resisted, fearful that answers might still be lurking in the unplumbed depths of one of those musty cardboard cartons.

The aluminum frame of the beach chair groaned under Jerry's ponderous weight. Wading through files was tedious duty and he'd little to show for his effort. He'd earned a break. Rising from his chair, he ambled to the battered old mini-fridge in the corner of the garage. He extracted a cold can of Bud, slammed the refrigerator shut, and returned to his seat.

Yanking off the pop-top, he reviewed what he'd discovered thus far: he'd stumbled upon a dozen excellent paintings, possibly in tempera, along with a portfolio of related studies, by a single, highly accomplished artist, all portraying a stunningly beautiful young woman. They'd been executed, in all likelihood, in a rural location over a relatively compressed time period, probably during the third quarter of the twentieth century. Finally, he'd surmised that the art was most recently in the possession of attorney Martin S. Becker, Jr., of Fort Myers, Florida, now deceased.

Jerry took a long gulp of his beer, brushing an errant stream of liquid from his chin. A sigh of satisfaction emerged from his lips. He contemplated his next step, deciding to begin his investigation with the only clear lead he had, the name Martin S. Becker, Jr. Wrenching himself from the beach chair, he abandoned the jumble of cartons and returned to his condo to telephone Gus.

"What can you tell me about the guy who rented that storage locker?"

"Stuff's supposed to be confidential, buddy," Gus replied in his habitually irksome manner.

"You told me the guy was dead, so he's not likely to complain now, is he, Gus?"

"Always pushing the envelope, aren't you, Jerry?"

"Yeah, I am," Jerry snapped back, peeved. "Yes or no: was his name Martin Becker, Jr.?"

"Pretty good guess is all I'll say." He'd said enough.

"Anything you can tell me about him?"

"Nothin' at all—'cept, like I told you, he's dead."

"Thanks a lot, Gus."

The following morning, Jerry drove to the Justice Center of Lee County, Florida, where he asked to see the probate file for the late Martin S. Becker, Jr.

"Fill out these forms," said the clerk in a pronounced Southern drawl, "and c'mon back in a week."

Jerry sighed, filled out the forms, and cooled his heels for the next week, combing through library art books and internet images for whatever visual evidence he might stumble upon that might lead to the identification of the creator of the Cornelia Paintings.

Chapter Nine

Longmire, Virginia
June, 1969

The worktable lamp was still burning when Brandon
returned to his studio later that evening. As he walked
over to extinguish it, he noticed the sketch illuminated beneath
it. It was Grant's latest drawing of Caroline—but this one was
different.

Brandon sat down and studied the drawing. He was loath
to admit it, having resisted his mentor's decision to embark on
his covert series with Caroline, but he'd monitored Grant's
progress with interest. The paintings, he judged, were among
the finest works of the artist's career. But *this* was
unexpected—it signaled a major shift in direction. Grant had
transcended the boundaries implicit in the earlier paintings of
his series, works that were emotionally evocative, albeit
chaste. Now, for the first time, he'd captured the raw energy
and powerful sensuality of the young female form, at the
juncture between adolescence and maturity. Though merely a
sketch, it bowled him over. Any lingering concerns about
impropriety were dwarfed by his admiration for Grant's
watershed accomplishment.

What most struck the younger artist wasn't Caroline's
nudity. It was her commanding aura. He'd recognized her
breathtaking beauty on the day he first met her nine months
earlier in Grant's studio. But she possessed something more:
that rare, indefinable charisma that Grant had exploited so

masterfully in each of his works to date.

Poring over the drawing, he had an epiphany. He was then in the planning stages of his most ambitious work to date, a mammoth, twelve-by-twenty-foot canvas tentatively entitled *End of Time*. As he conceived it, the work would stand as an expression of the hopes and fears of his generation, a generation embroiled in war and discontent, in which nuclear apocalypse loomed as a horrific possibility. Brandon envisioned a frieze of nine figures struggling for survival, poised against a landscape of nuclear devastation. He'd persuaded several of the young college students from his studio art class to model for him, but lacked the right female model to pose for his dramatic central figure. Caroline, he realized, was the solution to his dilemma, the ideal model for this dominating presence, his symbol of defiance and regeneration.

Brandon visited Grant's studio early the next morning. He found his mentor hard at work on another of his classic Shenandoah Valley landscapes.

"Keeps food on the table," Grant said with a hint of embarrassment. He raised an empty coffee mug. "Just about to have another cup. Can I get you one?" Brandon nodded. Grant poured his friend a cup and refilled his own. He pulled up a chair, beckoning Brandon to join him.

"I saw your latest sketch of Caroline last night," Brandon said.

Grant chuckled. "Seems we've ventured into new territory." He lifted the mug to his lips and drank. "It was *her* idea," he quickly explained. "She stripped down to nothing before I could stop her."

Brandon flashed a wry smile. "Bet you were devastated." He sipped his coffee.

Grant grinned, eager to change the subject. "So what brings you out here so early?"

"As a matter of fact, it's your muse," Brandon said. "It struck me last night that Caroline would be perfect for the lead figure in *End of Time.*"

Grant put down his mug. There were implications to Brandon's observation. Muses weren't a dime a dozen. They were the product of painstakingly cultivated personal relationships based on mutual understanding, trust, and affection. Was his affection for Caroline so strong as to breed jealousy?

"Too young, don't you think?" It was the first excuse that came to his mind.

"Not at all," Brandon replied. "She's supposed to represent humanity's hope for the future. Youth and resiliency is what I'm after."

Grant rubbed his palms together. Brandon was seeking Grant's blessing. Why did it bother him so? What right did he have to be possessive of Caroline?

"You'd paint her without parental consent?" The irony of Grant's question was obvious the moment it emerged from his lips.

"You've blazed that trail already," Brandon laughed. "Besides, I'm already an accessory to your crime."

"What if her parents see the picture?"

"Unlikely. It's going directly to my dealer in New York."

Grant's quandary was akin to the one that Brandon had faced last fall, when the younger artist agreed, out of debt and loyalty, to an arrangement he couldn't countenance. Grant knew that it was he, this time, with the debt to pay. Brandon had permitted the use of his studio to facilitate Grant's deception. How could he deny him the use of his model?

Besides, he'd exhausted his supply of excuses.

"She'd be great for the part," Grant declared, suppressing his reservations. "You can ask her yourself when she comes by next Thursday."

And he did.

"Absolutely!" Caroline squealed, thrilled at the prospect of anchoring a major work by Brandon Blake, her visage, nearly eight feet tall, looming over the heart of the boldest work of the rising young artist's career.

Grant concealed his disappointment. To allay his sense of exclusion, he asked if he might also sketch Caroline while she modeled for Brandon. "It'll go into storage, like the others," he assured his protégé. "I wouldn't want you to feel like I'm trying to upstage you."

Brandon's ego was less threatened than Grant's. "Of course," he said.

They decided to dedicate Caroline's next session exclusively to Brandon's project.

Chapter Ten

Brandon Blake awoke at six in the morning with a metaphorical elephant on his chest. A tingling sensation shot through his left arm; his breathing was shallow and labored. He dialed 911. And waited. The next dozen minutes were the longest of his life.

Brandon was fifty-six, at the pinnacle of his career. The Pennsylvania Academy of the Fine Arts had just honored him with a lifetime retrospective. His mind raced as the paramedics fed him into the maw of the ambulance.

Treetops skittered by through the vehicle's back window while the siren blared. Lying on his back, an IV bulging uncomfortably from his right hand, he pondered his life.

Forty-two canvases hung in the upstairs galleries at the Academy. The reviews were heartening. "After years in the shadow of his mentor, Grant Elliott, Brandon Blake has unequivocally come into his own," one critic wrote. If that were the measure of his life, he'd depart it with few regrets.

He thought about the keynote painting in the Academy exhibition. *End of Time*, painted in the summer of 1969, was his masterpiece. It was a monumental work, a frieze of colossal figures scattered across a post-apocalyptic landscape. Crowds lingered before it in awe. Who, they wondered, was that evocative central figure, a breathtaking female wrapped in a toga, with an expression that words were inadequate to describe?

Brandon had steadfastly refused to identify her: to reveal her would dishonor the commitment he'd made to his dear friend Grant Elliott a quarter century earlier. Her image had been reproduced in art journals and coffee table books repeatedly during the intervening years. He wondered if she'd ever known.

Strange that he should think of Caroline now—while his life hung in the balance. He hadn't known her well—certainly not as Grant had. Though she posed for him but once, his memory of that session was as vivid as if it had occurred yesterday. Her beauty, grace, and determination had translated seamlessly onto canvas. Her dominating presence was the linchpin of *End of Time*, the ingredient that lifted the composition to the iconic status it now enjoyed. Her departure in the spring of 1970 had been sudden, its impact on Grant profound. What had become of her, he often wondered—and the child?

Brandon Blake survived his heart attack, but the damage was significant. Lying in his hospital bed, hooked to an array of machines, he was buoyed by the welcome appearance of his old friend. Frail at eighty-four, his body ravaged by arthritis, Grant Elliott was but a shadow of his former self. His health had been fragile over the last several years and painting had become an ordeal. But his wit remained sharp and his eye observant.

"You look like shit," Grant said as he shuffled into the ICU.

"So do you," Brandon shot back. Grant smiled.

Though their friendship had endured for nearly three decades, they'd seen less of each other in recent years, due to Grant's failing health. Brandon was humbled when the older artist made the heroic effort to attend the opening of Brandon's retrospective in Philadelphia. The brief, heartfelt tribute Grant had delivered on that occasion was a memory Brandon would cherish as long as he lived. He wondered now how long that might be.

"I counted on you to survive me," Grant quipped. "That speech wasn't meant as your eulogy."

"I'm not done yet," Brandon laughed, "but keep a copy handy, just in case."

Amid the beeping and chiming of instruments and the chattering of hospital staff, the two old friends reminisced.

"You know, I've been thinking lately about Caroline," Brandon said soberly.

"I've never stopped," Grant replied.

"We need to do something about the paintings."

Grant nodded. "I know."

"I think we should draw up something formal," Brandon proposed, "to clarify what happens if I'm no longer around to preserve them . . . or to distribute them when the time comes."

Their understanding had been anything but formal. Premised on the supposition that Brandon would outlive both Grant and Becky, it reflected the unqualified trust and respect of the older artist for his protégé. Brandon was to hold the Caroline paintings until both of the Elliotts were gone. At an appropriate time thereafter, Brandon would reveal the works to the art world in a manner he calculated would best preserve the honor and legacy of the Elliott family. Though artists and not lawyers, they understood that the artworks would be part of Grant's estate, which would have passed to Becky upon his death, and through her estate thereafter, whether or not she'd known of their existence. But, as Grant was about to acknowledge, he had another plan.

"I want them to go to Caroline," Grant said, "assuming we can find her."

On a cold day in March, several weeks after Brandon's release from the hospital, the two artists met at the Longmire office of the law firm of Becker & Becker. Their appointment was with Martin S. Becker, Jr., the son and successor to the law practice of Grant and Becky's longtime personal attorney Martin, Sr., who'd recently passed away. Although the Elliotts had no experience with the younger lawyer, they'd trusted and relied upon his father for forty years. Martin, Sr. had crafted their estate plan and counseled Becky on matters relating to her management of Grant's career. Though he'd certainly have preferred the advice of the late Martin, Sr., Grant had no one else to turn to, and neither the energy nor desire to seek new and unfamiliar counsel at this late stage in his life.

A tall, well-built man in his early thirties, Marty Becker was anxious to make a favorable impression. He wore a conservative gray suit, a regimental striped tie, and a broad smile as he greeted his visitors with vigorous handshakes. Casually dressed in clashing plaid shirts and blue jeans, Grant and Brandon took their seats on the opposite side of Marty's desk. After introducing Brandon, Grant got right to the point.

"We've come to discuss a sensitive matter," he began. Marty nodded obsequiously. "We'd like your help in documenting an arrangement for the disposition of a series of artworks." Grant went on to explain the informal understanding in force between the artists over the last twenty-four years.

"The collection includes a dozen paintings and perhaps fifty or sixty preparatory drawings and watercolors," Brandon added.

"Mm-hmm." Marty stroked his chin with his left thumb and index finger. "You mentioned this was sensitive," he said. "May I ask why?"

Grant hesitated, biting his lip. He glanced at Brandon, who shook his head almost imperceptibly. "It's enough for you to know that the very existence of these works must remain secret until both Mrs. Elliott and I are gone," Grant asserted. He leaned forward, fixing his eyes on those of his attorney. "It is *absolutely essential* that Becky know nothing about this. Only the three of us in this room can know. Do I make myself clear?"

"Of course," Marty said, nodding in acknowledgment. While he could speculate on what Grant's reasons might be, he was clever enough not to inquire further. "You can rely on my discretion," he assured them with a tight smile.

Marty's secretary interrupted the proceedings, bearing a tray laden with three mugs of coffee. Grant paused while she distributed the beverages.

"Thank you, Gladys," Marty said curtly, waving her out of his office as if shooing a fly.

"I'd like Brandon to remain in possession of the works as long as he lives," Grant continued following her departure, "but if he's impertinent enough to check out before Becky and I do, there needs to be a way to achieve our objectives in his absence."

Marty leaned back in his chair. "So, what happens to the paintings when you and Mrs. Elliott are no longer with us?"

Grant avoided a direct answer. "If it's permissible, I'd like to provide specific instructions in a sealed envelope to be held with whatever documents you prepare. I'll deliver it to you when the documents are ready for signature," he said, interrupting his directions for a sip of coffee. "And it shouldn't be opened until Becky and I are gone."

Marty nodded submissively. It was an unconventional approach to the distribution of assets, but Grant was the client and it wasn't Marty's place to question his judgment or motives. Simple cooperation would maximize the likelihood of retaining the Elliotts' business.

"Won't be a problem, Mr. Elliott," Marty assured his client.

"We'll set up a simple trust to own the art," he said, pausing to sample his beverage. "Brandon can be the trustee, and I can be the successor trustee if anything should happen to Brandon, God forbid, before you and your wife pass away. And the paintings and drawings can remain where they are." The attorney then rattled off a bevy of details to which neither of the artists paid much attention.

Grant and Brandon were satisfied. Brandon agreed to disclose to Marty the location of the art in Brandon's studio storage bins, and to provide a key to allow him access to his studio if it became necessary for the attorney to retrieve the paintings in the event of Brandon's death. Grant undertook to furnish the sealed letter identifying the beneficiary or beneficiaries of his largesse.

"How shall I refer to this group of artworks?" Marty inquired.

"I've marked the backs of the paintings with the name *Cornelia*," said Brandon. "Call 'em the Cornelia Paintings, if you like."

Grant looked at him curiously, but withheld his question until they'd left Marty's office.

"Why Cornelia?" Grant asked as they exited the building, stepping into the chill March air.

"It's an anagram for Caroline," Brandon answered with a grin. "Preserves the secrecy and adds to the mystery."

"Clever," Grant laughed, patting his old friend on the back.

Chapter Eleven

Longmire, Virginia
July, 1969

"What the hell am I supposed to do with *that*?" Caroline giggled. It was a logical question, perhaps, when handed a torn and soiled white sheet to wear. "Don't you do laundry?" She held the tattered sheet before her in disbelief. "Am I supposed to be a ghost? A member of the KKK?"

The two artists broke out in laughter.

In Brandon's vision, the central figure of his masterwork would be clad in a ragged white toga. The toga was meant to suggest power; the color white to represent purity. The gashes and stains were intended as a reflection of the destruction of the society to which the symbols related. The allegorical allusions escaped Caroline.

"It's meant to be symbolic," Brandon said, explaining his references and their intended meanings to the befuddled teenager.

"Damn!" Her expression was one of mild amusement. "How the heck do I wear this thing?"

Grant smiled as she stripped to her undergarments and fumbled with the sheet. "Let me help you," Brandon offered, laughing. "But, if it's okay with you, you'll have to lose the bra."

"Oh," she said, casually unbuckling her bra and flinging it onto the cot where she'd strewn the rest of her clothing. Caroline bared her breasts without an ounce of self-consciousness.

Brandon spent the next twenty minutes, with the reluctant assistance of Grant, draping and re-draping the tattered garment around Caroline's torso, provocatively exposing her left leg and right breast. A glut of straight pins secured the toga in place.

"Ouch!" she yelped when Brandon accidentally impaled her. "Ever hear of safety pins?"

"Good idea," Brandon smiled, "in retrospect." Caroline flashed him a mock sneer.

"If this painting gig doesn't work out," Grant ribbed his protégé, "you can take up tailoring." He watched as Brandon adjusted the toga to reveal the desired quantum of flesh. "Give her a crown and a torch and she's a lewd Lady Liberty," he joked, to which Caroline playfully responded by raising her right arm in imitation of the statue's classic pose.

When Brandon was satisfied with his sartorial handiwork, he directed Caroline to a makeshift podium. She shuffled over with considerable difficulty, constrained by the imminent threat of perforation from the profusion of pins. He helped her onto the podium, positioning her in a striding posture, as if moving diagonally to her right, her left leg forward, a heavily budded green branch clenched in her right hand (indicative, he claimed, of both the destruction of nature and its imminent rebirth).

"Obviously," she said, laughing.

Although the pose was awkward and the costume constraining, Caroline reveled in her assignment, smiling and joking through three challenging hours of modeling with a minimum of breaks.

While Brandon sketched her in oils, rendering her much as he saw her, Grant drew her in charcoal from a different angle, ignoring the stains and ruptures in the toga, imagining her instead as a latter-day Lady Liberty. In the days that followed, he would expand his sketch into a full-length work in tempera. The toga instilled a sense of romance and timelessness, Grant fancied, reminiscent of the classic portraits of women in flowing gowns from the late 19th and early 20th centuries. Brandon used his oil study to complete the most important figure in *End of Time*, a work that would become the hallmark of his burgeoning career.

Chapter Twelve

Fort Myers, Florida
September, 2005

Almost a dozen years had passed since Marty Becker's first meeting with Grant Elliott and Brandon Blake. Much had changed since then—and not for the better.

It's not easy to fill the shoes of your father. Not if your father was Martin Becker, Sr. The elder Becker had been a war hero, rising to the rank of major by age twenty-five. He attended law school at the University of Virginia on the G.I. Bill, founding his eponymous law firm in 1949. Starting from scratch, he parlayed his intelligence, hard work, and personal charm into a thriving law practice while serving his community as mayor for sixteen years. Martin Becker, Sr. was a man you could look up to and trust.

Not so, Marty, Jr., who was nothing at all like his father. Sure, they shared the name, the towering height, the chiseled good looks, and the athletic bearing. But Marty was never blessed with his father's talent, intellect, drive, or integrity.

The elder Becker was fully cognizant of his son's shortcomings. As blood is thicker than water, he gave him every chance to succeed. He'd admitted Marty to his law practice in 1990, rechristening it Becker & Becker. He'd mentored him, promoted him, introduced him to his clients. And his efforts might have borne fruit, if time hadn't run out. Marty's father died unexpectedly in 1992, leaving his thirty-one-year-old son in charge of a booming law practice, but sorely lacking in the tools required to manage the challenging transition.

What Martin Becker, Sr. had taken forty-three years to build, Marty, Jr., frittered away in five. Unable to meet the high standards set by his illustrious father, Becker & Becker hemorrhaged clients. By 1997, the practice was moribund, his marriage had soured, and he'd turned to the bottle to mitigate the pain. A year later, a broken alcoholic, he closed up shop and fled to Florida, evading disgruntled clients and creditors, hoping to start over, in a context of lower expectations, in the city of Fort Myers.

Marty lounged in a cluttered office within the suite he shared with a bail bondsman and a tax preparation accountant on the third floor of a nondescript building in a decaying corner of downtown Fort Myers. It was his third location in seven years, the only one from which he hadn't been evicted. He poured himself three fingers of bourbon from the half-empty bottle in his bottom desk drawer. His practice subsisted—if you could call it that—on $100 wills, probate matters, and whatever else he could scare up from mortuaries, old folks' homes, and the lowest tier of the city's business community. Like most days, there was little on his agenda for the morning.

Marty leaned back in his chair, stretched out his legs, and deposited his size-twelve-and-a-half feet on top of his desk. He took a gulp of bourbon, licking his lips in approval. He unfurled the local paper, turning first to the death notices, circling those he deemed promising. At the top of the page, beside the notices, his eye caught a familiar name. He bolted upright, spilling what little remained of his bourbon. "Becky Elliott, Wife of Famous Artist, Dead at 80" read the headline of the obituary.

Rebecca Turner Elliott, wife of the late artist Grant Elliott, died peacefully yesterday in Longmire, Virginia, at age 80. A twenty-two-year-old art student in New York City when she met her husband in 1947, they were married in 1949. Mrs. Elliott was a familiar figure in art circles, managing her husband's career until his death ten years ago. In 1998, she published The Art of Grant Elliott, a massive volume universally recognized as the definitive catalogue raisonné of his oeuvre. Funeral arrangements are private.

"Finally!" Marty chirped. They were all dead now: Grant Elliott in 1995, Brandon Blake in '97 and now Becky. He'd feared she'd never expire, her pesky survival forever obstructing the implementation of his dubious plan.

He discarded the newspaper, swiveling his chair around to access his battered, gray file cabinet. He opened the bottom drawer and reached for the unmarked red folder at the rear. Opening the folder, he withdrew a large manila envelope containing a document captioned "Trust Indenture." He'd read it a hundred times before, but its sudden relevance persuaded him to refresh his memory.

The trust was straightforward. It provided that a certain collection of artwork, meticulously identified and itemized on an attached schedule, was to be held in trust until the death of both of Grant and Becky Elliott. It would pass at such time to the persons or institutions specified in a letter of direction referencing the trust and signed by Grant Elliott. When Brandon Blake, the initial trustee, died from his second heart attack in 1997, Marty had automatically succeeded him as trustee.

The second item in the file was a white business envelope

marked "Letter of Direction." It contained a pair of two-page documents. One, the letter Grant Elliott had scribbled out with Marty's assistance in 1995, updated and replaced the letter of direction he'd initially prepared a year earlier when the trust documents were executed. Marty meant to destroy the substitute letter—his plan made it irrelevant—but hadn't quite gotten around to it. He was particularly proud of the second document, a bill of sale he'd concocted supplanting the letter of direction and purporting to convey the "Cornelia Paintings" to him. It was his "Get-Out-of-Jail-Free" card, 'insurance' he could trot out, if necessary, to counter any accusations of impropriety.

When the time came, Marty figured, he'd sell the portfolio gradually, in bits and pieces, reserving the proceeds for himself. No one alive would be likely to challenge his actions.

Marty had little reason to worry that the secrecy surrounding the Cornelia Paintings had been breached; he'd kept his mouth shut and presumed that Grant and Blake had done the same. Had Becky Elliott learned of the existence of the trust or the paintings, he'd have heard by now. So as far as Marty knew, he was the only one left with knowledge of the existence of the artworks, except perhaps for this woman Cornelia, whoever she might be.

Within days of Brandon Blake's death eight years earlier, Marty had entered his studio with the key Blake had left him. Locating the artworks within an array of bins at the rear of the barn, he'd checked them off, one-by-one, against the detailed list attached to the trust indenture. He'd have helped himself to several of Blake's pieces as well, but their size was prohibitive. Besides, if anyone armed with an inventory of Blake's works discovered anything missing, eyebrows would be raised. Marty had a lucrative plan in place already; there was no need to be greedy.

Marty had stashed the Cornelia artworks in a spare closet in the apartment he'd rented after his wife had left him, then transported them to Florida when he'd fled Virginia in 1998. He rented a small, air-conditioned storage locker at KeepSafe Storage Company, an obscure, mom-and-pop storage facility on the east side of Fort Myers. Neatly stacked and out of sight at KeepSafe, they were rarely out of mind.

While awaiting Becky Elliott's demise, Marty had been doing his homework. From his probate practice, he knew that the best way to dispose of pretty much anything anonymously was to consign it to auction. The Cornelia Paintings were unsigned, but a copy of the Trust Indenture and the attached inventory should satisfy even the most fastidious auctioneer that the artwork was created by Grant Elliott, that it was the legitimate property of the trust, and that he, as named successor trustee, had ample authority to consign and sell it. How he applied the proceeds were no one's business but his own.

Marty's scheme seemed virtually foolproof. And although he could certainly benefit from an infusion of cash, he'd promised himself to delay implementation of his plan for six months after Becky Elliott's death—long enough, he reckoned, to allow for the emergence of any unanticipated claimant for the Cornelia Paintings. If no one stepped forward by then, he'd be on his way to an early and unusually comfortable retirement.

Chapter Thirteen

Longmire, Virginia
August, 1969

Caroline stood in a corner of Brandon's studio, stark naked but for a pair of sandals. She'd posed for Grant all morning, but the results dissatisfied him. He'd drawn her from behind, standing in the open doorway, contemplating the meadows beyond; reclining on the cot in poses inspired by the masterpieces of Manet and Modigliani; standing by the window, gazing at the verdant hills. But his sketches seemed wooden, uninspired. He suggested they take a break while he reviewed the morning's output.

Caroline slipped a Beatles tape into the cassette player. When she'd chafed at Grant's penchant for Beethoven—which she ridiculed as "old fart music"—he'd relented, indulging her by playing the music she chose. While the roar of *Back in the U.S.S.R.* failed to engage him, at least it smothered the clang and whir of the portable fans that strained to combat the stifling late summer heat.

"You can put on your robe now," he told her. "I may be a while."

"Too hot," she responded, electing to remain unclothed.

Caroline retrieved a copy of Kurt Vonnegut's most recent novel, *Slaughterhouse-Five*, from her backpack. Still standing, she cradled the book in her right hand as she found her place. Running the fingers of her left hand unconsciously through the silky waves of her strawberry blond hair, she began to read.

As Grant glanced up from his jumble of sketches, he did a double take. Unconsciously, Caroline had assumed the perfect pose, the one that had eluded them all morning. Without her knowledge, he grabbed his pencil and began to draw.

"What're you doing?" she muttered a few minutes later, noticing his feverish activity, his eyes riveted on her.

"Don't stop! Keep on reading. We're on a roll!" he crowed.

Caroline grinned. "Well, you better work fast, 'cause I've got only a few pages left."

As he sketched, he asked about the novel that she found so absorbing.

"It's weird, but cool," she cooed. "It's about this poor guy named Billy Pilgrim who gets 'unstuck' in time. He's a prisoner of war in Dresden when the Allies blow it to bits. He lives through a plane crash. Gets kidnapped by aliens. But mostly," she said thoughtfully, "it's about the horror and stupidity of war."

Their conversation about the travails of Billy Pilgrim expanded to a host of additional topics. They talked of Vietnam, Neil Armstrong's walk on the moon, and the half million people who'd converged on a tiny hamlet in upstate New York for a music festival that would define her generation. She opined on bell-bottoms, love beads, peasant skirts—even the so-called sexual revolution.

"Ever fallen in love with one of your models?" she asked him.

Her question caught him off guard. "Becky posed for me back in '47. So the answer, apparently, is yes."

"What about that girl in town, the one that got you in trouble with your wife?"

"A mistake I'd rather not discuss."

Undaunted, Caroline pressed on. "Did she seduce you . . . or did you seduce her?"

He shook his head. "Things happen, Caroline."

"Was she prettier than me?" she asked with a smirk.

"No."

"So, why—"

"Drop it, Caroline."

She did, but her interest in the subject unnerved him. Grant had become increasingly aware of her growing fondness for him. In contrast to her parents, he was available and receptive to her. He listened, empathized, and counseled. As their relationship evolved, she peppered him with ever more personal questions.

At first, he'd dismissed her frequent displays of affection as a sort of surrogate-fatherly devotion. He'd felt it in her easy banter, the warmth and frequency of her hugs, the playful kisses she'd bestowed upon his cheek. But lately, he'd detected something more problematic: suggestive humor, the provocative ways she displayed her body, her response to his touch as he adjusted her pose. On one occasion, celebrating the conclusion of a longer-than-anticipated session, she leapt into his arms, still naked, and hugged him tightly. He felt the warmth of her skin, the goose bumps resulting from his touch. She reveled in her nudity, teasing him flirtatiously, boldly daring him to follow suit.

"It's hotter than hell in here," she chuckled one afternoon, "why not *paint* in the nude?"

While he laughed off her suggestion, he knew she was testing his limits. He'd painted many naked women in his time, but none had thrilled him as Caroline did. He tried to hide it, wrestling his base instincts like a recovering alcoholic battling the bottle. Still, he restrained himself. Until one day he couldn't.

Chapter Fourteen

Fort Myers, Florida
March, 2006

The rain began mid-afternoon on Friday. Flood warnings had been issued. Marty peered out his kitchen window at the sheets of rain while thunder rumbled overhead. Opening a cabinet, he reached for his bourbon. He twisted off the cap, filled his glass, and strode into the living room, seeking refuge in his favorite recliner. Soon, he was daydreaming, imagining how he'd transform his life with the windfall from the sale of the paintings.

In February, five months after Becky Elliott's death, he'd begun to get itchy. He'd grown weary of chasing down clients in retirement homes, bored with the pencil-pushing tedium of his moribund legal practice. While hardly flush with cash, he'd enough to get by until his ship came in. Why go through the motions when he'd soon be a wealthy man?

So Marty retired. He was barely working as it was, so why not make it official? He cancelled the lease on his office and moved its contents to KeepSafe Storage. He'd already paid for the space, and it was less trouble to move everything lock, stock, and barrel than to waste time sorting through the cartons of crap lining the perimeter of his office.

Earlier that week, just shy of the six-month anniversary of Becky Elliott's death, Marty finally set his plan in motion. He spoke with some old hag at Sotheby's in New York, a self-proclaimed "expert" in American art, about auctioning his mother lode of Elliotts. She perked up at his mention of the renowned artist, fairly drooling over the potential of a seven-figure commission. "By all means, bring them in!" she urged. As a prospective consignor, Marty insisted on total anonymity. "No problem," she assured him, "discretion is our business!"

In response to her cascade of questions, Marty just snickered. "Discretion is my business, too," he snapped back. An appointment was set for Tuesday.

Marty planned to stop by KeepSafe on Saturday, select two representative paintings from the storage locker, and retrieve the red file containing the trust instrument as proof of the authenticity of the artworks, his status as trustee, and his authority to dispose of the paintings. He'd drive the file and paintings to New York over the succeeding two days, arriving in plenty of time for his Tuesday morning meeting.

Marty rechecked Grant Elliott's auction sales records on the internet. A slightly larger work, a painting of a young female nude called *Anita Reclining*, sold for $600,000 in late 2005. Multiply that by a dozen and the result was staggering.

It was still pouring on Saturday morning when Marty awoke around ten. He found himself splayed, face down, on the living room couch, the empty bourbon bottle lying on the floor beside him. He arose unsteadily, wobbling into the kitchen. He opened the cabinet, extracting a fresh fifth of Jim Beam. "Starve a cold, drown a hangover," he grunted. He broke the seal and helped himself to a morning wake-me-up.

While clearing the cobwebs, he dressed; snatched his keys, raincoat, and umbrella; and sprinted into the parking lot, splashing through puddles of water. His shoes soaked, he fiddled with his keys, laboring to unlock his car for the trip to KeepSafe.

Not bothering to fasten his seat belt—"seat belts are for sissies," he was wont to say—Marty backed blithely out of his parking space, then gassed it out of the lot, down the road, and onto the rain-slicked highway. When the storm intensified, he flipped the wipers on high. Still, he could barely see ten feet ahead. But the speed limit on the highway was sixty, and he was no wimp. He stepped on the accelerator and changed lanes abruptly. What he failed to notice was the line of vehicles paused at the red light in front of him. His senses dulled by the bourbon, he pumped the brakes frantically, but a second too late. The car hydroplaned, hurtling forward into the rear end of a tractor-trailer. The impact was horrific, a cacophony of screeching rubber, twisting metal, and broken glass. He flew through the windshield like a missile.

Martin S. Becker, Jr. would fail to show up for his appointment at Sotheby's that Tuesday morning, the same day on which his tersely-worded death notice would appear in the local newspaper. Some two-bit, stiff-chasing attorney would circle the announcement and wrangle himself an appointment as probate attorney for the poor slob's estate. In that lawyer's haste to close out the estate and collect his fee, he'd fail to uncover the storage locker, or the millions of dollars of artwork it contained. *C'est la vie.*

Chapter Fifteen

Five Miles Northwest of Longmire, Virginia
March, 1970

Trucks rumbled by as she trudged along the shoulder of the highway. A knapsack, brimming with schoolbooks days before, now bulged with the clothing she'd whipped from her closet and bureau in her haste to escape. Tucked into the bottom was a change purse containing almost $800 in cash, money squirreled away from her modeling gigs for Grant and, on one particularly memorable occasion, Brandon Blake. Beside it was a hastily folded portrait, the sketch Grant had done of her on that fateful day eighteen months earlier when she'd appeared at his studio pleading to pose for him. He'd presented it to her as a Christmas gift, apologizing for failing to frame it, knowing that to do so would make it harder to conceal from her parents.

Caroline slogged ahead, bundled against the late winter chill in the heaviest coat that she owned, her right thumb extended in pursuit of a ride, her left hand cupped beneath the swelling in her abdomen.

Living at home was no longer feasible. Her parents, blinded by their pernicious brand of religious zealotry, could barely stand to look at her. She'd hidden her pregnancy as long as possible, wearing airy dresses to school and sweat clothes or loose pajamas at home. But the subterfuge crumbled in early December when her mother entered the bathroom with a change of towels as Caroline exited the shower. Her mother's shrieks still reverberated in her memory.

Caroline had dismissed the obvious signs, attributing the queasiness and the interruption of her periods to other causes, afraid to acknowledge what she suspected was true. Her emotions were muddled, often contradictory. At times, she'd prayed for a miscarriage, a natural resolution to a confounding dilemma. At other times, she felt elation, honored to carry a child endowed with the genes of a genius.

The inevitable confrontation with her parents had occurred on a Saturday, shortly after her mother's frightful discovery, minutes after her father's return from errands in town.

"What is the *matter* with you!" he bellowed as she stood in the living room to which she'd been summoned. She braced for the onslaught. "How could you do this to us?" her father demanded.

"To *you*?" Caroline seethed. "I didn't do *anything* to you!"

"You've embarrassed your entire family," he blustered, pounding his fist onto the coffee table. An ashtray tumbled over the edge, spilling its contents onto the carpet. Caroline glanced at her mother, who scrutinized her with a combination of compassion and disgust, and then at her father, his face crimson with rage. She cringed in anticipation of the question that was sure to follow. "Who did this to you?" he hollered.

Caroline stared at him coldly, her lips pursed. She made no effort to respond. Her silence only intensified his rage. "Answer me!" he commanded.

Caroline steadfastly maintained her silence. Her father lunged at her, slapping her violently across the cheek with his left hand. Her mother gasped. Caroline staggered backward, stumbling to the floor. As her mother moved to assist her, her father stared his wife down. "Let her be!" he ordered. And to his daughter: "This isn't over."

Caroline lifted herself from the floor, turned, and defiantly left the room, tears streaming down her cheeks. She slammed her bedroom door behind her and remained there until it was time for school on Monday morning.

It was Caroline's senior year. She'd thrived academically. The satisfaction she'd derived from her clandestine calling as artist's muse had softened her, deflating her anger, fortifying her confidence, and liberating her socially. When she could no longer camouflage her condition, everything changed. It began with snarky rumors, then taunts. Her anger and defiance returned. Her endurance was tested by the cruelty of her peers. Her world came crashing down.

The studio was Caroline's sanctuary. Grant was the first to recognize the change in her body. He'd noticed it in early November, while arranging her in a reclining position on the cot.

"What's this?" he said, his eyes widening as his hand brushed across the incipient swell of her belly. He'd come to know her body as well as Caroline herself.

She'd prepared for this moment. Or at least she thought she had. In her fantasy world, she'd imagined him smiling with paternal gratification, embracing her, proclaiming himself ready and willing to navigate the muddy waters that would complicate their mutual journey into parenthood. Her nightmares, on the other hand, conjured up angry denials, rejection, and banishment from his life. The reality, she presumed, would be somewhere in between.

She studied him carefully. He'd lifted his hand a little too quickly, she felt, as if singed by the touch of her belly. His face contorted as he made the connection to that indiscretion, the unforgivable act of weakness he swore he'd never repeat. "Is it

gh he wasn't sure how.
t now she'd abandoned
um from hurt to guilt to
by painting, but most of
or which she had posed.
is despair. He put down

nd painting impossible.
e to concentrate. On the
nt had already informed

lon said, handing Grant a
u'd want to see it right

essed to him in a feminine
but no return address.
n prodded him.
the letter opener on his
open. He withdrew its
led on paper torn from a
he began to read.

e studio, you're out of
by now, I've flown the
goodbye. I miss you

at home. How can you
espised and ridiculed?

mine?" he asked tentatively, his voice quavering.

Caroline hesitated. She'd been poised to tell him the truth, but her resolve abruptly faltered. Her relationship with Grant Elliott hung in the balance. If she confirmed his responsibility, their further interactions, if any, would be governed by his fears: fear for his marriage, his reputation, even criminal conviction. The fact that he asked her the question—*is it mine?*—struck her as an affront to her character. He'd offer her money—for her silence or the abortion her parents forbade her—and their collaboration would come to a screeching halt. She didn't want his money; she wanted his friendship, respect, and yes, even his love, if that were possible. But in that moment, she knew that it wasn't.

"No," she heard herself mutter. "It's not yours." She had all she could do to keep from bawling, straining to maintain the falsehood she believed would protect him and preserve their relationship.

"How do you know?"

"I had my period after we made love," she lied again.

"Who's the father?" he asked, his heartbeat calming.

"I'd rather not say."

"What will you do?"

"I don't know," she said.

"I'm here for you," he avowed, though she no longer truly believed it.

And then, it was as if nothing had happened. Grant found her condition intriguing, artistically inspiring, and drew her that day, and over the succeeding months, as she swelled with pregnancy, heartbreak, and fear.

Chapter Sixteen

Longmire, Virginia
March, 1970

Becky informed him at lunch. Grant was wolfing down a egg salad sandwich, eagerly anticipating his afternoon session with Caroline at Brandon's studio.

"Alice McKellan dropped by this morning," Becky told him "Said Caroline left for school yesterday and never came home."

Grant nearly choked on his sandwich. "What do you mean never came home?"

"Ran away, it seems. Some clothes were missing, including an old sweater of her brother's that Alice said she cherished."

The color drained from Grant's face. "Did they call the police?"

"The police say there's nothing much they can do. Kids run away all the time, they told her."

"My God!" Grant shuddered. "Shouldn't we all be out looking for her? She's pregnant, for God's sake!"

Becky was surprised by the intensity of her husband's reaction. But even more so regarding Caroline's pregnancy—and Grant's awareness of her condition. "What? Since when?"

Grant realized he'd spoken without thinking. He needed a plausible cover for his potentially explosive gaffe. "I, uh, heard about it sometime last month," he sputtered. "Brandon mentioned it."

"Brandon? How the hell would he know?" Becky wrinkled her forehead as she peered at Grant.

wait. He felt he'd let her down, t
She'd confided in him, trusted hin
him. His emotions spanned the sp
desolation. He tried to distract hin
his canvases were works in progr
Studying her image just heightene
his brush and returned home.

Over the next several days, Grant
He moped about in his studio, un
fourth day, Brandon paid a visit. (
him of Caroline's disappearance.

"This arrived this morning," Br
small, white envelope. "Thought
away."

Grant stared at the envelope. Ad
hand, it bore an Indianapolis postma

"Gonna open it or what?" Brand

Biting his lip, Grant reached f
worktable and slit the envelop
contents: a three-page letter scri
spiral-bound notebook. Unfolding

Hey Old Man,

If you're waiting for me at
luck. As you've probably hear
coop. I'm sorry I couldn't s
already.

I could no longer bear livin
live where you're constantly

Where the mere sight of your bloated tummy is an embarrassment to the ones who are supposed to support and protect you? Our arguments were endless. The last was the worst. They demanded I surrender the baby for adoption. I refused. We fought for days. I need a better environment for my child—someplace we can grow together, without judgment. There was no real choice but to leave. I hope you'll understand.

There's something else I need to tell you. I hope you're sitting down.

Grant sighed heavily. He took her advice: he pulled up a Windsor and sat down. He had a notion about what might come next, though he tried valiantly to dismiss it. Brandon saw the alarm building in the older man's eyes as Grant slipped the first sheet beneath the others and perused the second page of Caroline's letter.

You asked me if the baby was yours. I could see the fear in your eyes when you spoke. An honest answer threatened your marriage, your career and our relationship. I couldn't risk that, Grant, so I lied to you. But the baby is OURS, Old Man, ours together, and I'm PROUD of that and always will be. Our child is going to be special. I can feel it. How could I abandon such a precious gift?

I've told no one that you're the father. I hope you'll keep our secret—it'll be easier now that I'm gone. All hell would break loose if the truth came out. Just think what it would do to your wife and my parents!

Trust me—I'm going to be fine. I can fend for myself. I saved my modeling money, so I'm not without means. I'm ready for my freedom and stubborn enough to see it through.

I LOVED being your muse. I was damn good at it, too, don't you think? I hope that one day people will see your beautiful paintings, but if not, I'll understand. Whatever happens, I'll always cherish the time we spent together. Think of me when you need inspiration. Perhaps we'll meet again. In the meantime, know that I love you.

Peace and Love,
Caroline

Grant exhaled deeply. He leaned back and closed his eyes. When they reopened, tears had begun to form. He handed the letter to Brandon with a nod, encouraging him to read it. The young artist gasped, his jaw slackening, when he reached the momentous fourth paragraph. He grabbed the other Windsor and plunked himself down.

"I had no idea," Brandon said, his eyes widening.

"I did, but she'd told me otherwise," Grant acknowledged. He shook his head slowly. "I'm gonna be a father, at sixty."

Brandon suppressed a smile. "Not sure whether to offer condolences or congratulations." He reached out to touch Grant's arm. "No judgment from me," he assured his friend, "but this is one heck of a clusterfuck. What're you gonna do?"

"What *can* I do?" Grant sighed. "There's no return address and who knows if she's still in Indianapolis?" He wiped the tears from his eyes. "I've got to hand it to her, she's wise beyond her years . . . and gutsy as hell."

"She's clever," Brandon observed. "She'll land on her feet."

"I pray to God that she does."

Chapter Seventeen

Fort Myers, Florida
May, 2010

Two weeks after filing his records request with the probate court, Jerry returned to inspect the files he'd requested. The clerk, a woman in her forties with the mien of a librarian, set off to retrieve the materials. After vanishing for ten minutes, she returned to the counter with a slim file.

"That's all there is?"

"Yup, that's everything. You can review the file over there," she said, directing him to a cluster of tables and chairs.

Jerry pulled up a chair, sat down, and opened the file. There was virtually nothing inside. The decedent's name and date of death appeared at the top of the first page, along with the designation "Intestate."

Jerry returned to the counter. "What does 'intestate' mean?"

"Died without a will," the woman informed him.

"But he was a probate lawyer! How could he die without a will?"

"The cobbler's children go barefoot," she said with a tight smile.

Shaking his head, Jerry returned to the file. Under the heading "Marital Status at Time of Decease" someone had inscribed "Divorced." Under "Beneficiaries" appeared the notation "none located." On the second page was an abbreviated inventory of Martin Becker, Jr.'s estate. It contained one line, "Miscellaneous household items" ascribing a value of "nominal." Scribbled at the bottom of the page was the notation "Decedent's automobile involved in fatal accident; total loss. Outstanding liens in excess of insurance proceeds."

Jerry returned to the counter one final time with the file. "This means that the guy died without a will, with no assets, and no beneficiaries? Am I interpreting this correctly?"

The clerk opened the file, scanning it quickly. "Yup," she said.

While the probate file provided no clues to the identity of his artist, it offered Jerry comfort on at least two fronts. First, the existence of the Cornelia Paintings had been unknown to the representatives of Becker's estate. Second, with no known beneficiaries, the chances that someone would raise a competing claim to ownership of the artworks were diminishing.

With no new leads to pursue, Jerry decided to assess the value of what he had. After poking around the internet for the requisite expertise, he landed an appointment with Marvin Dawes, head of the American art department at Landrigan's, Florida's premier art auction house. He selected one of his paintings—*Grief*—bundled it with bubble wrap, and stowed it in the rear of his Blazer together with the portfolio of preparatory drawings and watercolors. Armed with photographs of the remaining paintings, Jerry blew across Alligator Alley to Miami for his meeting at Landrigan's.

Clad in a meticulously tailored three-piece suit, Marvin Dawes looked like a Brooks Brothers mannequin. Tall, gaunt, and fiftyish, he sported a precisely trimmed black moustache and tortoise-shell glasses. The contrast with the stocky, balding retiree in shorts and a polo shirt couldn't have been starker.

Dawes greeted Jerry warmly as he entered the conference room.

"Let me help you with that," Dawes said, offering Jerry a hand with the bundled painting. Together, they carefully removed the wrapping. "Hmm," Dawes murmured as the work was revealed, "very nicely painted, indeed."

The expert lifted the unframed work toward the overhead light, shifting his eyes from corner to corner in search of a signature. "Unsigned," he muttered. "Interesting." He flipped the work over, taking mental note of the "Cornelia" inscription as well as the title. Placing it face-up on the conference table, he invited Jerry to tell him what he knew about the painting.

Dawes nodded intermittently as Jerry told his story, chuckling loudly at the revelation of its storage-locker provenance. He unclasped the leather portfolio, sampling its contents, then flipped through the photographs, satisfying himself that the works were all by the same hand.

"I thought maybe Wyeth," Jerry hypothesized. "Or Grant Elliott?"

Dawes emitted another "hmm" before proffering an opinion. "Definitely not Wyeth," he said, releasing a first burst of air from Jerry's bubble. "And while it bears striking similarities to Elliott's work, it's not his M.O. to leave his work unsigned, unframed, or undocumented. His wife never let anything out of his studio without a detailed label and a reference number. Nor can I recall anything by Elliott with this unusually appealing young model."

Jerry tried to camouflage his disappointment. "Couldn't—"

Before he could express his thought, an assistant arrived with a large volume. Dawes thanked her and resumed speaking. "This is Becky Elliott's catalogue raisonné, the definitive catalogue of all of her husband's work. Nothing escaped her purview, except possibly for Grant Elliott's very earliest work, that is, pre-1947, the year they met. But from the looks of the model's clothing, your works appear to date from the sixties or seventies." He opened the book, which was arranged chronologically, to the works produced in the relevant decades. He shook his head as he flipped through the pages.

"None of the photographs matches anything in your collection," Dawes said, "and nowhere in the index is there a reference to the name Cornelia or the title *Grief.*"

"There's one called *Peonies* and another called *Lady Liberty,*" Jerry noted. "Are either of those listed?"

Dawes checked the index and shook his head. "Afraid not," he said. "You're welcome to stay a while and study the volume more carefully if you like, but I doubt you'll find any connections to your paintings."

Crestfallen, Jerry reached for the catalogue, turning pages in desultory fashion, grasping for a ray of hope amidst the disheartening news. He randomly scanned the catalogue photographs, hoping to find a match for the studio backgrounds or outdoor settings appearing in the Cornelia Paintings. As Dawes predicted, he found nothing.

"While I can ascribe this work to 'Circle of Elliott,'" Dawes said in summary, "I can't attribute it to the artist himself. But what you've got is beautifully done and should bring something as a 'Circle of Elliott' painting."

"Something being . . ."

"Perhaps a thousand or two for each of the oils, a couple of hundred for some of the watercolors, a bit less for the drawings."

Jerry frowned.

"We'd be happy to offer the paintings individually, or in small lots, at one of our fall sales; the works on paper could be bundled into larger lots." Dawes was used to disappointing collectors arriving with expectations far exceeding the value of their possessions. He did it respectfully—you never knew if one of those same people might show up some day with a true treasure.

Jerry stroked his chin, pondering his options. He'd make more on the paintings at a Landrigan's auction than on the floor of Barnacle Bill's, and even his consolation-prize numbers would net him a substantial profit. Still, visions of grandeur, however unjustified, die hard, and Jerry wasn't yet ready to throw in the towel.

"No disrespect," Jerry said, "but is there someone out there, an expert on Elliott, perhaps, who I could talk to ... uh ... to exhaust all possible avenues of inquiry?" Jerry had already ascertained that Becky Elliott was no longer living, so he knew there was no recourse available through her.

"Max Winter is a semi-retired art professor at Harvard who's written a number of articles on Elliott, as well as his circle of followers. You could certainly talk with him. I think he'd be intrigued with your paintings, but I seriously doubt he'll conclude any differently. If you like, I can make an introduction by email and you can follow it up yourself."

A glimmer of hope. "That's kind of you. I'll take you up on that."

"Of course," Dawes said, reaching out to shake Jerry's hand. "Thanks so much for coming in."

Jerry rewrapped the painting, secured the portfolio, collected his photos, and considered the prospect of a junket to Boston. Having grown up in neighboring Medford (which he, like the rest of the locals, pronounced "Med-fuhd"), he hadn't been back in three years, since Blanche's funeral. A trip there might do him good—especially if it included a visit to Fenway Park.

Chapter Eighteen

Indianapolis, Indiana
and Points East
March, 1970

He spotted her on the side of the highway, just west of Longmire. An angelically beautiful young woman, her thumb extended for a ride. A trucker's wet dream.

Blasting his horn, he pulled his rig to the side of the road ahead of her. He glanced at the passenger side mirror, watching her approach. What her awkward gait hinted, her belly confirmed. "Wait right there!" he called to her, hopping from the cab. "Lemme give ya a hand!" Caroline flashed an appreciative smile as he liberated the heavy knapsack from her shoulders, opened the passenger side door, and helped her climb into the cab.

"Gol dang, young lady," he drawled, returning to his perch behind the wheel, "don't seem's tho' someone in your condition should be out there hitchin' a ride."

"Couldn't afford a limo," Caroline quipped.

He smiled. "Wilmer's my name," he said, "but they call me Weasel." Small and wiry, he wasn't the stereotypical long-haul trucker. Forty or so, with a sharp beak of a nose, protruding upper front teeth, and greasy, slicked-back hair, he seemed more suited to the back of a racehorse than the cockpit of an eighteen-wheeler.

"Name's Caroline, and they call me Caroline," she said. They smiled in unison.

"Where ya headin'?"

"Wherever you're going."

Weasel checked his mirror, flicked on his left turn signal, tugged at the gearshift, and rejoined the highway.

"Perty young for a mama-to-be," he said as he regained cruising speed.

"Not everything goes according to plan," Caroline replied. He nodded, acknowledging the truth of her observation.

"Where's papa?"

"I'll be raising him—or her—on my own."

"Dang. Sorry to hear that." Weasel paused a moment while he changed lanes. "You hungry? Got a coupla sandwiches and a thermos in that bag behind you. Go ahead, help yourself."

Caroline was starving. She'd walked farther than she'd anticipated, and between the pack on her back and the lump in her belly, she was exhausted. She reached back, unzipped the bag, and extracted a sandwich.

"Stoppin' in Indy tonight. Ya can tag along far as ya like. Get so's you need a pee break, ya just pipe up."

"Thanks, Weasel, I appreciate it."

Caroline devoured the sandwich, washing it down with a swig of lukewarm coffee from Weasel's thermos. Her hunger sated, she quickly fell asleep. Weasel stole an occasional glance at his passenger. On any other day, he might have fantasized about such a beautiful creature, but watching her sleep so peacefully, one hand on her cheek and the other on her abdomen, he felt a curious compulsion to protect her.

They reached Indianapolis eight hours later. Weasel maneuvered his rig into a truck stop, inviting Caroline to join him for dinner at the aptly named Truck Stop Café. Grateful for the company, she agreed, insisting upon paying the bill.

"Well, if that ain't a first," he chuckled, thanking her. Weasel planned to spend the night on the cot in the cab of his truck, but offered to sleep up front if Caroline cared to stretch out in back. He'd been chivalrous to a fault, but Caroline thought better of pressing her luck. With the money in her knapsack, she could splurge for a night at the motel next door.

As cleverly denominated as the adjoining café, the Truck Stop Motel was as fancy as the name implied. The radiator clanged and the television hissed, but the bed sported clean sheets and the armchair was comfortable, if threadbare.

Caroline reached into her pack for the spiral-bound notebook she'd wedged in as an afterthought. She'd forgotten a pen, but the good folks at the Truck Stop Motel had anticipated her lapse. She scooped up the ballpoint, clicking it repeatedly as she contemplated the letter she would write to Grant.

Caroline regretted not saying goodbye, but she knew it would have put Grant in an awkward position—either aiding and abetting her escape or raising roadblocks against it. She'd made up her mind to leave; there was nothing to be gained in complicating it. And besides, it was easier to write what she had to say than to express it face-to-face. She'd tried that once and failed. But why tell him at all? As she figured it, there were two reasons. The first was simple: she always thought he should know, and it made more sense to tell him *after* her escape; Grant would be less inclined to do something precipitous with potentially disastrous consequences. The second reason was a matter of self-preservation. His knowledge offered her the security of a lifeline—an alternative to her parents—if her quest to remake her life failed miserably, leaving her financially desperate. She didn't plan on using that lifeline, but she needed an option if all else failed.

Caroline penned at least a half-dozen drafts, filling her wastebasket with an avalanche of crumpled discards. At first, her words seemed tentative, her tone too uncertain. No, she calculated, that wouldn't do. She refused to betray her anxiety. She had to be upbeat. She was no longer a child—her departure from home was her declaration of emancipation—and she didn't want to sound like one. In the end, her words exuded confidence, in herself and her future.

Trouble was, she had no idea where she was going or what she would do, either tomorrow or for the rest of her life.

Chapter Nineteen

Cambridge, Massachusetts
June, 2010

Max Winter sat before his computer in his gloomy office in the basement of the old fine arts administration building on the edge of the sprawling Harvard University campus. As a part-time professor emeritus, he was lucky to have a window. Unfortunately, it opened onto an airshaft, offering neither light nor fresh air. His office was cramped, his bookshelves overflowing. His desktop was nearly as disheveled as he was, splattered with open texts, random papers, notepads, and yellow Post-It Notes plastered with nearly inscrutable scribblings. A ragged old Red Sox cap hung from a hook on the wall beside his bookcase, on the top of which stood a vintage Nomar Garciaparra baseball bobblehead. Indeed, there was ample reason for his banishment to the basement.

In his prime, Max had been a force to be reckoned with, a brilliant art historian with a unique vision, a facility for the written word, and a photographic memory for works of art. What he lacked was presence, deference to the art world muckety-mucks, and, as the state of his office attested, tidiness. Small of stature, with close-set hazel eyes surmounted by bushy gray eyebrows, he sprouted a prominent nose and an unkempt mop of frizzy gray hair. His arms were thin and hairy, like pipe cleaners. Though sixty-nine years old, he had the drive of a man twenty years younger.

His quirks notwithstanding, his opinion was still highly regarded in his field of expertise, mid-twentieth century American art.

Max plowed through his email inbox, deleting loan solicitations (he rarely spent money), home warranty offers (he'd never owned a home), auto insurance deals (he'd never obtained a license), and sexual performance enhancers (his performances were few and far between), until he found the email he'd been looking for. Marvin Dawes, the American art guru at Landrigan's in Miami, had texted him the previous evening, advising him to expect an email from a Florida retiree named Jerry Deaver. According to Dawes, Deaver had stumbled upon a cache of paintings with similarities to the work of Grant Elliott, though neither signed nor documented. "I thought them sufficiently intriguing to warrant your interest," Dawes had written.

Max read the first several sentences of Jerry's email, but his impatience drove him directly to the attachments. He clicked on the first of a dozen JPEGs. His eyes lit up. A strikingly beautiful young woman in a tattered gray sweater stared out from the screen, lips pressed firmly together, arms wrapped tightly around her chest, tresses of strawberry blond hair drifting over her shoulders and onto her breasts, nascent tears bubbling up in her stunning blue eyes. A powerful and sensitive portrait, very much in the manner of Grant Elliott, Max thought. Eagerly, he clicked on the second attachment. The same captivating model, this time outdoors in a flower garden along the edge of what appeared to be a barn, reaching down gracefully to inhale the fragrance of the flower she cradled delicately in her right hand. Studying the photograph more carefully, he noticed something unusual: a prominent scar running horizontally across her right wrist. A curious inclusion, Max thought: a symbol, like the flower, of the subject's vulnerability. He glanced briefly at the other photo attachments. The same alluring model appeared again and again, sometimes clothed, sometimes not. And to his surprise, at least two of the paintings depicted her in a state of pregnancy.

Returning to the text of the email, Max digested the owner's accompanying observations: the "Cornelia" inscriptions and titles, the absence of signatures, the lack of frames, the supporting collection of studies relating directly to the dozen paintings. Most puzzling to Max was the ignoble provenance of the artworks. How does a recently retired and now deceased Florida lawyer of modest means come into possession of a cache of artworks of such quality, and why does he relegate them to the back of a storage locker?

The story aroused Max's suspicions. Were the works stolen? If so, by whom—this Martin Becker character or Jerry Deaver himself? And from whom? Or might this be the work of a particularly talented forger, one who's concocted a mysterious provenance to seduce wealthy collectors and inhibit additional inquiry?

Max opened his internet browser. He began by googling Martin S. Becker, finding several individuals listed in a variety of locations, one of whom was a Fort Myers, Florida, attorney for whom he also found a 2006 death notice. And there was no dearth of Jerry Deavers. For the one listed as a resident of Fort Myers, Max found nothing more than a phone number and an age bracket (70+) consistent with his expectations.

Max returned to the last paragraph of the email in which Mr. Deaver requested—more accurately, begged—for a personal consultation regarding the artworks. Claiming to be a former Bostonian with no pressing obligations, the impatient retiree offered to drive up from Florida at a moment's notice, armed with several of the canvases and a pair of grandstand tickets for a Red Sox game at Fenway Park.

Max grinned, hit the *Reply* button, and composed his response.

Chapter Twenty

Caroline checked out of the Truck Stop Motel early the next morning. She purchased a six-cent stamp at the front desk, affixed it to her letter to Grant, and deposited the envelope in the mail chute in the lobby. Outside, she glanced across the parking lot in search of Weasel's rig. Long gone, she surmised. To the west, the sky looked threatening. Hauling her knapsack over her shoulder, she crossed over to the Truck Stop Café for a quick bite before resuming her journey.

The café was surprisingly busy for so early an hour. Caroline chose a booth by the window, steering her midriff away from the table as she squeezed herself in. She slid the pack from her shoulder onto the leatherette bench. A middle-aged, platinum-haired waitress approached with a pot of coffee in one hand and a menu in the other. The name "Rose" appeared on the name tag affixed to her clean white uniform above her left breast. Her eyes narrowed when she noticed Caroline's condition.

"Eating for two, I see," Rose said. Caroline nodded without comment. "Coffee?"

"Yes, please."

She filled Caroline's cup. "Traveling alone?"

Again Caroline nodded, turning her head warily toward the window as rain began to splatter against the glass. Within moments it was pouring.

From the presence of the knapsack and her reaction to the weather, Rose deduced that Caroline lacked a source of transportation. "You're not planning to hitchhike in *this*," she said, gesturing toward the window. "In your state?"

"I'll be okay," Caroline replied with a firmness belying her doubts. Hoping to staunch the inquisition, she volunteered her order. "Two eggs, over easy, bacon, a blueberry muffin, and a large glass of orange juice, please."

"Uh . . . okay, sweetie," the waitress muttered, withdrawing from the table, her lips still pinched with concern.

Caroline had given little consideration to practicalities such as weather. She left home determined and confident. But now her mood was turning as gray and muddled as the morning. She shouldn't go out in this, she realized, but neither could she sit here all day.

A young man sat eating alone in the booth behind her. Privy to the brief exchange between Caroline and Rose, he pondered offering his assistance. He finished the last of his pancakes, washing them down with a last slug of coffee. Arising, check in hand, he glanced into Caroline's booth. What he beheld was a Truck Stop Madonna. He was transfixed. He hesitated for only a moment, wary of intruding, but incapable of walking on by.

"Excuse me, miss," he said solicitously. "I don't mean to intrude, but I couldn't help but overhear your conversation with the waitress a few minutes ago." She looked at him blankly, but he continued. "My name's Mike. I'm driving west to Iowa. Got plenty of room in my car. I'd be more than happy to offer you a ride—if you're heading in that direction."

Caroline appraised him quickly. Tall, good-looking, and clean-shaven, with thick, sandy hair and wire-rimmed spectacles, he looked harmless. She'd survived eight hours with a truck driver named Weasel, so why not take a chance with Mike?

"That's kind of you," she said. "But I wouldn't want to hold you up. I haven't eaten yet and—"

"Not a problem, miss, uh . . ."

"Caroline."

"Right, Caroline. I'm in no hurry; happy to wait. Mind if I sit down?"

"No, no," she said, breaking into a warm smile, "please do."

Mike stepped back to his booth, snagging his empty coffee mug. He flagged down Rose. "Could I get a refill?" he asked, waving his cup as he slid into the booth opposite Caroline.

"Where you heading?" he asked her.

"Don't really know," she admitted, fearful that her answer would provoke further inquiry. She was in no mood for an interrogation. Before Mike could say anything more, Rose appeared with Caroline's order and a fresh pot of coffee. As she plunged into her breakfast, Mike allowed her to eat in peace.

Twenty minutes later, Mike and Caroline were on the highway heading west.

Chapter Twenty-One

Fort Myers, Florida
June, 2010

Jerry stuffed his Blazer to the gills in preparation for his first road trip in years. He'd swaddled five of the paintings in bubble wrap, placing them securely into the rear of his SUV along with the leather portfolio of drawings and watercolors. He wore an old pair of Bermuda shorts, a David Ortiz replica jersey, and his sweat-stained Red Sox cap. Blanche would have blanched. He wadded four hundred dollars of cash into his wallet and, most importantly, two tickets to Saturday afternoon's interleague game between the Red Sox and Dodgers at Fenway Park.

Jerry always did his homework. After thirty-two years as an IRS auditor, his fastidiousness was second nature. Before emailing Max Winter, he'd scoured the internet for morsels of information about the background and idiosyncrasies of the Harvard professor. Among his discoveries was a *Boston Globe* interview from 2001 in which Winter proudly described himself as a Red Sox junkie. If he were fanatical before the Sox's first modern World Series victory in 2004, he'd be even more rabid now, Jerry figured. So to grease the skids, he'd decided to invite the professor to join him for a ballgame.

Max's response to Jerry's email was terse: "Pictures interesting, tickets too. Where located?"

"Pictures or tickets?" Jerry responded.

"Tickets!" wrote Max.

Jerry hadn't yet purchased them—he'd do so if and when the professor took the bait. "How about grandstand behind home plate?" he proposed.

"How about box seats a bit closer?" Max countered.

Jerry winced. Box seats would set him back $130 a pop. He hadn't anticipated a negotiation; then again, he'd no right to expect to access the professor's expertise for free. "Okay," he typed before pressing *Send*.

"Throw in a hot dog and you've got a deal!" Max wrote back, upping the ante.

Jerry conceded the hot dog. "Game on!" he wrote, shaking his head.

The ride north was uneventful. With his (hopefully) precious cargo, Jerry stopped only for a night's sleep at a Holiday Inn near Richmond on Thursday, spending the next evening with his nephew, Joey, in the working-class city of Somerville, pinched like a Fenway Frank between Medford (aka Med-fuhd) and Boston. Joey, chronically unemployed and twice-divorced, was the ne'er-do-well son of his late sister Edith. He lived with his girlfriend and her three truant sons in the ramshackle house he'd inherited from his mother. Unpleasant as it was, Jerry felt an obligation to check in on his last remaining relative.

Navigating his way through Somerville reminded him of why he'd left Boston. Choking traffic, impetuous drivers, audacious pedestrians, and death-defying bikers rekindled a vocabulary of epithets he'd largely abandoned since moving to Florida. Surviving the ordeal intact, he looked forward to the following day, his first visit to Fenway Park in ages.

It was sunny, breezy, and a pleasant seventy-five degrees when Jerry met Max outside Gate A on the corner of Brookline

Avenue and Yawkey Way an hour before game time. By prearrangement, Jerry donned his white David Ortiz jersey while Max sported a red Kevin Youkilis tee shirt. They found each other quickly despite the multitude of Ortiz and Youkilis impostors amidst the throng on Yawkey Way.

Inside the park, Jerry's first stop was the concession stand where he sprang for three Fenway Franks (a pair for him and the one he'd promised Max), an order of fries (for him), and a couple of beers (also for him). It cost as much as his night at the Richmond motel. Physically, they made a strange pair—like Santa out on the town with one of his elves.

"I was here the day Ted Williams hit his last homer," Jerry reminisced as they slithered past a half-dozen pairs of knees and legs and into their box seats halfway down the third base line and twenty rows up from the field.

"I sat *there*," Max said, pointing toward the left field grandstand, "when Bucky Bleepin' Dent hit that bleepin' homer in '78. Broke my bleepin' heart."

"Damn straight!" Jerry said, chuckling.

With the Sox up by two in the sixth, Red Sox knuckleballer Tim Wakefield, celebrating his two-hundredth Fenway Park start, surrendered a long homer to left by former teammate Manny Ramirez. "Goddammit!" Jerry hollered, rising from his seat, inadvertently sprinkling a few drops of his third beer on the beefy, twenty-something fan in the seat to his left.

"Watch it, asshole!" bellowed his aggrieved neighbor, punctuating his warning with a classic Fenway sneer.

Jerry ignored him, turning instead to Max. "The joys of Boston," he muttered sarcastically. Max smiled in acknowledgment. In the bottom of the inning, Sox first baseman Kevin Youkilis drilled a pitch over the Green Monster and onto Landsdowne Street, propelling Max from his seat in ecstasy.

"You're a big fan of the Youk," Jerry observed, as if it weren't already clear from the name plastered on the back of Max's tee shirt.

"Only Jew on the roster," Max explained with a grin.

By the ninth inning, the odd couple had become fast friends. Sharing a lifetime of Red Sox memories—most of them disappointments—they'd found a common bond. And when the Sox pulled off a victory in the ninth with a walk-off hit by Dustin Pedroia, they were on their feet cheering themselves hoarse with thirty-seven thousand other delirious fans.

Making their way through the concourse and onto the street, the duo scheduled a rendezvous at Max's apartment for Sunday afternoon. Within twenty-four hours, they'd begin their quest to unravel the mystery of the Cornelia Paintings.

Chapter Twenty-Two

Raindrops splattered against the windshield of Mike's ramshackle Chevy as they plowed through Indiana along I-74, just east of the Illinois border. Mike stole an occasional glance at his passenger, drawn by her haunting beauty and curious about her plight. Caroline sat silently beside him, peering wistfully through the rain-drenched window.

The young runaway contemplated her predicament as the landscape rushed past. She was drifting, her confidence rapidly evaporating. Caring for herself was one thing—she had the pluck for that—but the imminent addition of an infant complicated matters exponentially. She had no source of income and no prospects. How could she have been so cavalier, she wondered, leaving home seven months pregnant, reliant solely on fortune or fate? Yet what choice did she have? Home was no longer an option: she'd have been compelled to surrender the child she so desperately wanted to keep.

"Care if I turn on the radio?" Mike asked.

"Uh . . . no, of course not," she said, relieved to be liberated, at least momentarily, from her worrisome thoughts.

Mike rotated the dial until a familiar song emerged from the hiss of static. Caroline recognized the melodious tenor of Art Garfunkel, and the tune, *Bridge over Troubled Waters*:

When you're down and out
When you're on the street
When evening falls so hard
I will comfort you

The lyrics tugged at her, threatening to make her weep, but she resisted the impulse. Mike couldn't help but notice her change in demeanor.

Like a bridge over troubled water
I will ease your mind

The words were eerily apt. Whether driven by curiosity or impelled by the song's declaration, Mike resolved to probe, as gently as possible, into Caroline's dubious circumstances; to help her if he could, or failing that, as the song promised, at least to ease her mind. He'd engage her in conversation, trusting that by sharing his own story she'd be encouraged to reveal her own.

Twenty-three years old, Mike hailed from southeastern Pennsylvania, near Lancaster, where he'd spent the weekend visiting his parents and two kid sisters. He'd graduated from Purdue with a degree in English and had planned to pursue a masters in American Literature. But a growing disaffection with politics, war, and academia had eroded his determination.

"I needed a break," he explained, "and Andy offered the perfect opportunity." Mike described his friend and classmate at Purdue, and how he'd become enamored of Andy's self-sustaining, earth-based philosophy of life. "Andy dropped out three years ago when his grandfather died and left him a farm in Iowa," Mike related. "He and I connected, along with six others, and the eight of us have been living on the farm ever since."

Caroline was intrigued. "That's where you're going?"

Mike nodded. "With any luck, be there by late afternoon." Having primed the pump, he turned to Caroline. "I don't mean to pry," he said, "but I can't help but wonder why you're sitting here with me, hitchhiking, very pregnant, and with no particular destination in mind."

Caroline smiled grudgingly. Mike had been kind, open, and sensitive. He'd graciously offered his assistance when her prospects for the day looked grim. He deserved at least some explanation.

"It pretty much starts here," she said, patting her belly. "Something I hadn't planned on."

"What about the father?"

"It's complicated," she said. "Let's just say he's out of the picture and that's how I want it to stay."

Mike nodded. "Fair enough," he said, "but you seem awfully young to be on your own. Just how old *are* you, if you don't mind my asking?"

"Seventeen, going on thirty."

Mike pursed his lips. "What about your parents?"

"Demanded I give up the baby." Caroline shook her head dismissively. "Wasn't gonna happen." The bitterness in her voice was unmistakable. "Living at home was out of the question."

"What'll you do?"

She chuckled. "I'm open to suggestions."

Caroline didn't strike him as the classic teenage runaway. She impressed him as unusually mature and thoughtful, not one in the throes of an impulsive act of rebellion. Without a clear destination, he understood that her first priority was a place to stay, at least temporarily.

"Why don't you stay with The Family for a few days?" he volunteered.

"What family?"

"Sorry, that's how we refer to ourselves on the farm—the eight of us consider ourselves a family. We've made a commitment to care for each other, and we all pitch in toward a common goal of self-sufficiency."

Mike's offer was a godsend. "Wouldn't I be imposing?" she asked. "I'm sure The Family wasn't anticipating the arrival of a pregnant teenager."

"No, but we've got the room, and we're happy to help someone in need. Besides, as long as you feel up to it, you can make yourself useful around the house."

"I'd be a fool to say no," she said with a grateful smile.

Chapter Twenty-Three

Cambridge, Massachusetts
June, 2010

Max lived on a leafy street of stately Victorians a ten-minute stroll from Harvard Yard. His apartment comprised the first floor of a renovated two-family house with a driveway along one side and an manicured hedge on the other. Jerry maneuvered his SUV into the driveway, extracted himself from the driver's seat, and opened the hatch at the rear.

Hearing the commotion outside, Max glanced out his window. He hurried out to greet his new friend. "Let me help you with that!" he offered, bounding down the porch steps in a characteristic state of dishevelment. While Jerry carried a pair of bubble-wrapped canvases under each arm, Max hauled in the fifth painting and the portfolio of drawings and watercolors.

Awash with random stacks of art books, piles of old art journals, and mounds of yellowing paper, Max's apartment was an expanded version of the chaos of his campus office. The only difference was the presence of artwork: not only on walls but also propped or stacked against every conceivable surface. His taste was eclectic, from Regionalism and urban realism of the Thirties and Forties through Surrealism, Abstract Expressionism, Pop Art, and Minimalism. His residence was a veritable survey of mid-twentieth century American painting. Jerry deposited his canvases on the dining room table, the only surface in Max's apartment with a modicum of space.

"Tidy little place you've got here," Jerry deadpanned. "How do you find anything?"

"Got a sixth sense," Max said, smiling. "Whatever I need, I know it's here somewhere."

Jerry watched anxiously as Max unwrapped the first of the five canvases. It was a reclining nude, lying on her back, her hands cradled beneath her swollen abdomen.

"Now *this* is interesting," Max said. "Not a lot of precedent for pregnant nudes in American art history. Alice Neel did a few in the Sixties and Seventies, but I can't recall many others. Not a typical male artist's obsession . . . if it's indeed by a male." He gripped the unframed canvas gently at the edges, tipping it toward the sunlight filtering through the dining room window. "This is good. Very good," he declared. Jerry sat quietly, his spirits lifting in proportion to the professor's praise.

"No signature or monogram," Max noted before flipping the canvas over to inspect the back. *Cornelia* was inscribed in block letters, beneath which appeared the number 11 and the title *Soon.*

"The model's the same in all of the paintings," Jerry said. "She's pregnant only in the last two, numbers 11 and 12."

"She's exquisite, isn't she?" Max beamed. Satisfied that the reverse would divulge no further secrets, he turned the painting back over and laid it gently on the table. "Got a magnifying glass here somewhere," he muttered, scouring his desktop, rifling through drawers, peeking beneath piles of debris.

Glancing at the floor, Jerry caught sight of a reflective object. Crouching down, he retrieved the mislaid magnifying glass and passed it to the professor.

"See, I knew it was around here somewhere," Max chuckled.

Max inspected the brushwork for several minutes, withholding comment, while Jerry fidgeted. Finally, he set the glass aside. "The brushwork is remarkable," he opined. "Not unlike Wyeth and Elliott, but stylistically it looks more to me like the work Grant Elliott did in the Sixties and Seventies. Here," he beckoned Jerry, "come take a look."

Jerry circled the table and bent over the painting, peering tentatively through the magnifying glass Max handed him.

"Look at the handling of her skin, the delicacy of the brushstrokes, the cross-hatching and multiple layering of the egg tempera paint," Max said. Jerry stared through the lens, seeing now what he hadn't really noticed before. "See what I mean?"

Jerry nodded, even as he grew impatient. He sought to cut to the chase. "Is it by Grant Elliott?" he asked bluntly.

Max flashed an inscrutable grin. "Let's say, for now, that it certainly *could* be. But, as my old friend Marvin Dawes already told you, the lack of documentation is a critical issue with Elliott. Nothing ever left his studio without his wife, Becky's, imprimatur. She labeled and recorded everything and Grant signed everything—even studies. I'm not aware of a single exception."

"So it's *not* by Elliott?"

"I didn't say that either. But substantiating it as an Elliott presents some formidable obstacles." As Jerry groaned, Max raised a hand to temper his disappointment. "Let's take a look at the others."

Jerry unwrapped *Peonies*, the charming picture of the young lady cradling the white peony in the garden beside the barn.

"Stunning!" Max gushed. Again, he studied the brushwork, nodding in approval, before absorbing the limited information inscribed on the back of the canvas.

Next came the first painting in the series, the bust-length portrait entitled *Grief.* "Wow!" Max exclaimed. "This is wonderful! If this was the first in the series, I can see what motivated the artist to keep going." Max reclaimed the magnifying glass, leaned over, and scrutinized the painting. "And you know, it's not just the artist. The model is extraordinary! She exudes emotion. There's a real collaboration here between the artist and his model."

His excitement growing, Jerry unveiled the fourth painting, an engaging standing nude bearing the number 9 and the title *Reading.*

Max peered at the canvas, hopeful of isolating some clues. "An interesting contrast with the later painting, the one during her pregnancy," he said, rubbing his chin thoughtfully. "She looks younger somehow, certainly more innocent. Whoever this young lady was, she must've grown up fast."

Max stacked the four paintings beneath the dining room window, clearing space for the portfolio. Jerry unclasped the leather portfolio and withdrew a sheaf of drawings and watercolors. Max flipped through the stack slowly, oohing and aahing repeatedly as he worked his way to the bottom.

"These are wonderful. I wonder if there are any more paintings in the series beyond the dozen you own?" Max mused.

Jerry shrugged. "Wish I knew," he sighed. As Max continued to examine the drawings and watercolors, Jerry surveyed the room nervously. "I know I brought another," he said. "Where the heck is it?"

As Jerry began to hyperventilate, Max recalled that he'd left the final painting in the living room. "It's over there," Max said, pointing toward the fireplace.

"You could lose a truck in this mess," Jerry groused while

emitting a sigh of relief.

The last painting Jerry had brought, number 8 in the series, was inscribed *Lady Liberty* on the reverse. "This one's a bit of an outlier," Jerry pointed out, releasing it carefully from its cocoon of bubble wrap. The same model again, but draped this time in what appeared to be a toga, her right breast and left leg exposed, a branch clutched tightly in her right hand as she strode forward.

Max bolted upright. "I've *seen* this before! Same model, same garment, same pose! I'm *certain* of it!"

Jerry perked up. "In a painting by Elliott?"

"No, I don't think so. But . . . I can't place it just now." Max shook his head in frustration. "It'll come to me . . . eventually."

Max smiled. Jerry didn't know what to think. "We're gonna figure this out, Jerry," Max pledged, "if it takes all summer."

Chapter Twenty-Four

Mike steered the old Chevy down the pockmarked country lane and onto the muddy driveway that led to the farmhouse. Fresh puddles bore witness to a recent downpour. They were in rural Iowa, about thirty-five miles east of Omaha, totally off the grid.

Caroline's eyes lit up when she spied the farmhouse. It was an early twentieth century relic, a big, inviting home with a massive hip roof cleaved by a wide central dormer, like a Cyclops with an eyebrow. A covered porch hugged three sides of the building. Green shutters flanked the windows. It was elegant in its simplicity. About a hundred yards to the west, the Iowa River flowed lazily by while mature apple trees and fields of assorted fruits and vegetables held sway in random patches around the dwelling.

The storm clouds had receded into the distance revealing a bright, late afternoon sun. When Mike and Caroline arrived, several of Mike's housemates were picking vegetables on the east side of the house while others relaxed on the shaded porch. They came forward when they noticed a very pregnant young woman emerging from Mike's vehicle.

"Too pregnant to be your sister and too young to be your mama!" chirped Arnie, a slightly-built, curly-haired poster boy for the hippie era. A bulbous marijuana joint smoldered between the index and middle fingers of his right hand.

"She'll be *somebody's* mama before long," quipped Faith, a young mother herself judging from the infant she clutched to her breast. Mike hadn't mentioned anything to Caroline about a recent addition to The Family.

"Hey, everyone, this is Caroline," Mike announced as his housemates gathered around. "We met in Indianapolis. She needed a ride and a place to stay for a few days. Hope you don't mind." Presenting it as a *fait accompli*, it was impossible for his housemates to object.

Caroline greeted them warmly. "Hope I'm not imposing," she said with an appreciative smile.

"Not at all," Faith assured her, stepping forward to embrace the new arrival. "Lynette," she said, turning to a tall, slim young woman bearing a basket of freshly picked vegetables, "would you mind taking James for a few minutes while I show Caroline to the guest room?"

One of three females in the group, Faith was a short, round, olive-skinned woman in her mid-twenties, her frizzy brown hair tied into a neat single braid in the back. Like Lynette, she wore a snug tank top above a loose-fitting peasant skirt. After handing the infant to Lynette, Faith reached for Caroline's knapsack before Caroline could object.

"I can carry—"

"I've got it," Faith interrupted. "Come on, follow me."

Caroline shadowed Faith up the porch stairs and into the house. The dwelling was as unpretentious inside as it was out.

"When are you due?"

"Middle of May," Caroline answered as they passed through the dining room, already set for dinner, and then down a long hallway. "James is a beautiful baby," she said. "Is he yours?"

"I gave birth," Faith acknowledged, "but we're all James's parents."

Caroline shook her head. "I don't understand."

"We're a family in the truest sense of the word. Our sexual views are liberal," Faith explained as she opened the door to a small guest room at the rear of the first floor, "but consistent with our communal commitment. It doesn't matter whose particular sperm penetrated the egg," she continued. "The child's welfare is the Family's responsibility and its collective good fortune." Although Caroline was generally aware of the growing trend toward communal living, she'd never had occasion to consider its implications. The unqualified mutual commitment and support of The Family stood in stark contrast to the rejection she'd endured back home.

Faith urged Caroline to settle in and then join The Family for dinner.

The guest room was sparsely furnished but cozy, containing a bed in old red paint, a small antique bureau, and a stool. Much more welcoming than the Truck Stop Motel. Caroline emptied her knapsack on the bed, distributing its contents into the drawers of the dresser. Presumptuous, perhaps, but she hoped Mike's invitation would offer more than a day's reprieve. She changed into a pair of checkered maternity slacks and a long tunic top before joining her hosts for dinner. The prospect of a home-cooked meal with company and in pleasant surroundings lifted her spirits considerably.

Dinner comprised variations on a common theme. Eggplant ragu was served along with stuffed roasted eggplant and eggplant fries. The meal was a collaboration of the three women. "Bet you can't guess what we picked today," joked Lynette.

"Rutabaga?" Caroline ventured, laughing.

After abandoning Longmire, the last place Caroline imagined she'd find herself was back on a farm. Since her brother's death, the agrarian life had become anathema to her. But though the setting was similar, this was hardly the farm of her parents and grandparents. It felt kind and embracing rather than harsh and constraining. For the first time since her final session with Grant, she felt a sense of warmth and acceptance. She felt curiously at home.

Chapter Twenty-Five

Jerry had planned to return to Florida after his meeting with Max Winter, but Max had other ideas. As a semi-retired professor, his time was his own. What better way to kick off the summer than by investigating an art mystery?

"I've got a proposition for you," he said to Jerry that afternoon in his dining room. "Why don't you stay with me for a few days while we do a little more digging into this Cornelia conundrum?" He gave him a playful poke on the shoulder. "Got anything more exciting to do with your time?"

Although he feared what Max's guest room might look like, Jerry was game. What was the sense of running back to Fort Myers when he had a legitimate shot at solving the mystery of the Cornelia Paintings with the help of the foremost living expert on painter Grant Elliott and his circle? "I'm in!" he chirped.

Though he'd known him for only a few days, Jerry had no qualms about depositing his paintings with Max before enduring a final evening with his pot-puffing nephew in Somerville. But before leaving, he shamed Max into clearing away a corner of the living room to accommodate his cache, minimizing the risk of its dispersal into the general chaos of the apartment. Jerry packed his suitcase early the next morning, bid his wayward nephew goodbye (and good riddance), caught a bite (and then some) at a favorite local diner, and returned to Cambridge. Max was still in his pajamas when Jerry arrived at ten o'clock.

"It's driving me crazy," Max whined. Although it hardly seemed possible, his living room was in more disarray than it'd been a day earlier. Art books were scattered everywhere. Jerry glanced into the dining room where dozens of volumes lay open on the table, on the chairs, and on the floor. "I've seen that girl before," Max insisted. "I just can't remember where." He flipped pages furiously as he spoke. "The answer's somewhere in this house, I *know* it is."

Jerry rolled his eyes, then peered through the clutter toward the corner in which he'd left his paintings the day before. Satisfied they remained undisturbed, he asked Max how he could help.

"I've yet to go through the books on the lower shelf there," Max said, gesturing at a bookcase across the living room.

Jerry cleared a pile of books from a dining room chair and dragged it over to the relevant bookcase. He sat down, reached out, and fished out a random volume. "What am I looking for?"

"A reproduction of a painting with that figure of Cornelia in it—you know, the one where she poses as Lady Liberty. Should date from around mid-century or a little later. I seem to recall her image in the midst of a group of figures, but I can't, for the life of me, pinpoint the artist."

An hour later, as Max continued to pore through exhibition catalogues and monographs in his pajamas, Jerry picked up a weighty tome entitled *Brandon Blake: A Retrospective.* It was the glossy catalogue published by The Pennsylvania Academy of the Fine Arts in connection with its 1993 exhibition of the work of the Virginia artist Brandon Blake, who would pass away of a heart attack just four years later. Halfway through the book, over a two-page spread, appeared a full-color reproduction of a painting entitled *End of Time*, a powerful composition comprised of nine heroic figures emerging from the ruins of a post-apocalyptic landscape. At its heart stood a young woman clad in a white toga, her right breast fully exposed, a branch clenched in her right fist. Her expression was one of fierce determination.

"Max!" Jerry exclaimed. "I found her!"

Max leaped from his chair, books tumbling from his lap to the floor as he rushed to see what Jerry had discovered. "That's it! That's it!" he shrieked, more excited than he'd been watching Kevin Youkilis's home run sail over the Green Monster two days earlier. "I remember it now! Saw it at that show in Philly, at The Pennsylvania Academy," he cried breathlessly. "It had to be, what, maybe fifteen years ago! *Huge* canvas, covered a whole wall at the Academy. Fabulous painting, quite possibly Blake's masterpiece!" Max yanked the volume from Jerry's lap. "Hmmm. That's right, *End of Time*, painted in '69." He placed the open book on the dining room table, where the light was better. "Yup. Same angelic face. That's our girl! That's Cornelia!"

"So this means the Cornelia artist is . . . uh . . . Brandon Blake?"

"Possibly, Jerry, but I very much doubt it."

Jerry was thoroughly confused. "But I thought you just said—"

"That Cornelia was painted by Brandon Blake in 1969," Max said, excitedly, "but that doesn't mean that Blake is necessarily *our* painter."

"Slow down, Max. Tell me what exactly you're saying."

Max caught his breath, reclaiming his seat across the living room. "Blake was known for monumental paintings. I don't recall a single work in his retrospective under six feet in width. He habitually painted in oils. Scan the checklist of works at the end of the catalogue. Look at the dimensions, the mediums. What do you see?"

Jerry followed Max's instructions. He ran his finger down the checklist. Max was correct. Blake's paintings were all large-scale. And every last one was executed in oils. "You're right," he confirmed.

"Except for the watercolors in the portfolio, all of the paintings you've shown me are temperas. The artist's laborious, meticulous technique is completely consistent. Totally different from the broad brushstrokes Blake is known for. Does it make any sense that Blake would switch format, medium, even technique, just to paint and repaint *our* model?"

"I suppose not," Jerry conceded. Max's analysis was compelling. "I hear you, Max, but then how do you explain *Lady Liberty*?"

"What if," Max proposed, "our artist was present at the same modeling session during which Blake painted his own study of Cornelia?"

"Like they shared a model or something?"

"Something like that, yes," Max said. "Notice the angle from which our *Lady Liberty* is painted—it's more direct, more frontal. She's striding toward the artist. Blake's Cornelia is viewed more obliquely... she's marching off in a diagonal direction." Max paused, continuing to frame his hypothesis. "Maybe this was the *only* time Blake painted Cornelia. Maybe he was 'borrowing' our artist's model."

Jerry's head was spinning.

"You've been through a good portion of the catalogue, right?" Max asked. "Did you see Cornelia in any of Blake's other paintings?"

"Uh, no... at least not yet," Jerry acknowledged. He returned to the catalogue, pawing through the balance of the book while Max crept up behind him, peeking over his shoulder. The sound of flipping pages punctuated the silence of the morning. Then came the conclusive thump of the book's closing. "She doesn't appear again," Jerry confirmed.

"Okay, then," Max said, "let's summarize what we've got: two paintings, probably by different artists, of the same model in the same pose with the same garment but from different angles."

"Sounds like a game of Clue," Jerry quipped.

"That gives us two critical factors from which to extrapolate: time and geography." Max returned to his armchair, picking up the coffee cup on the adjacent side table. As he poised to drink, he realized it was empty. Clutching the cup, he retreated to the kitchen for a refill.

Max's abrupt disappearance, on the verge of a possible denouement, flummoxed Jerry. "What the..." he muttered to himself, rolling his eyes in exasperation. Unconsciously tapping his foot in anticipation, Jerry awaited the professor's return.

Max reappeared five minutes later. "So, as I was saying..." He paused, plopped down into his chair and took a deliberate sip of coffee. "Oh, I'm sorry," he said, interrupting himself, "I didn't even offer you a cup! Shame on me! Can I get you some coffee?"

"No, goddammit!" Jerry cried out. "Get to the fucking point, will ya?"

Max chuckled, realizing he'd left Jerry in suspense. "Sorry, Jerry," he said sheepishly. "Okay, then. *End of Time* dates to 1969, and Blake painted primarily someplace in the mountains of northern Virginia. But here's the really interesting part . . ." Max couldn't resist pausing for effect.

"Out with it, already!"

"Guess who Brandon Blake's mentor was?"

"I give up," said Jerry facetiously, "Carl Yastrzemski?"

"Grant Elliott!"

"No way!" Jerry was now fully stoked. "So what now? How do we tie these works to Elliott?"

"I suggest we start with provenance," Max said. "Figure out how these paintings managed to find their way to a storage locker in Fort Myers, Florida."

Chapter Twenty-Six

Rural Iowa, 35 Miles from Omaha
March, 1970

When Caroline awakened the next morning, the house and grounds were deserted but for Faith and baby James. Faith was at work at the kitchen sink while James slumbered contentedly in a baby carrier perched on the kitchen table. Faith explained the regular Monday regimen: the housemates awaken early, divide into two teams, load their Dodge van and a small pickup with excess fruits and vegetables, and embark on their weekly circuit of local groceries and farmers' markets to sell produce and stock up on provisions for the coming week.

As Caroline feasted on a bowl of Faith's house granola (containing, to her relief, no trace of eggplant), Faith scrutinized their young houseguest. At Mike's urging, the housemates had abstained from further inquiry into Caroline's circumstances, deciding that Faith should pursue the matter alone—that Caroline might be more willing to talk freely with a woman who'd recently given birth to a child of her own.

Faith plunged right in. "What are your plans?" she asked bluntly.

Caroline's lips tightened. "I don't really know."

"That won't cut it, Caroline," Faith said sharply. "Mike brought you here out of concern for your welfare. You're seven months pregnant, you've run away from home, and you have no plan?" Faith shook her head. "You *have* to do better than that—if not for your sake, then for the baby's."

Faith struck a chord. Caroline put her spoon aside and looked blankly into her half-emptied bowl. She'd considered herself tough, almost impregnable, but was she, really? Or was she just another troubled teenager who'd painted herself into a corner? Tears threatened to flow but she held them in check.

Faith put aside the pot she was washing, removed her rubber gloves, and sat at the table beside her. "You need a plan, honey." Her tone was sympathetic.

"I know," Caroline acknowledged. She inhaled deeply. "I couldn't stay home and give up my baby and I can't ask the father—"

"Why can't you ask the father for help?" Faith interrupted. "Is he still in high school?"

"Hardly," she snickered, "he's a . . ." Caroline caught herself. Even as she continued to shield Grant's identity, she balked at describing their relationship. How could she possibly convey the emotional connection between a seventeen-year-old high-school senior and a sixty-year-old married man without it sounding creepy, foolish, abusive, or worse? "He's an older man," she allowed, "but one I'm proud to have as the father of my child."

Faith read the determination in Caroline's expression. "And he knows?"

Caroline shook her head in the affirmative, brushing a nascent tear from her cheek.

"What about your parents?"

"They couldn't even *look* at me!" she stammered. "Demanded I give up the baby for adoption. There's no way in hell I'd do that!"

Faith placed a reassuring hand on Caroline's shoulder while James gurgled in his sleep.

Caroline felt compelled to explain herself further. "I left home not only to escape my parents and keep my baby," she said, "but also to prevent the father from sabotaging his marriage and career. Staying home or revealing the father's identity would only have made things worse—much worse—for everyone." What felt rational to her, Caroline understood, might seem less so to others. "I know how this must sound, but I can't include him in our future, for everyone's sake." She looked down grimly, caressing her belly.

Faith had listened intently, choosing neither to challenge nor debate the choices Caroline had made. She appreciated Caroline's conundrum, even without all the facts. "Okay," she said calmly, "let's just talk about where you go from here."

Caroline heaved a sigh of relief. "You're the first person," she said, meeting Faith's eyes with a look of gratitude, "willing to listen without judging me." She reached out and clasped Faith's hand. With that gesture, the dam broke: Caroline cried harder than she'd cried since the death of her brother. Faith pressed Caroline's trembling hands between her own, then reached out to embrace her. "It's gonna be alright," she said, gently stroking Caroline's hair. "We'll figure it out, honey."

Chapter Twenty-Seven

Cambridge, Massachusetts
June, 2010

Following their breakthrough that morning, Jerry devoured the Brandon Blake catalogue, searching for clues to jumpstart their investigation into the provenance of the Cornelia Paintings. The biographical essay confirmed that Blake had been Grant Elliott's longtime friend and protégé, their relationship beginning in the late 1960s and continuing until Elliott's death almost three decades later. They were also neighbors. In 1967, at Elliott's urging, Blake had relocated from the Philadelphia suburbs to Longmire, Virginia, a picturesque colonial village at the northern end of the Shenandoah Valley, where he rented a farmhouse with a barn he converted into a studio. Blake's home and studio were no more than a half-mile from those of his mentor.

Jerry's first order of business was to seek a link between the deceased Florida attorney Martin Becker and Brandon Blake, Grant Elliott, or the town of Longmire, Virginia. At Max's suggestion, he slogged up Broadway past Harvard Yard and across campus to the Harvard Law School Library. A reference librarian directed him to a shelf of bulging beige volumes with red and black labels comprising the 2006 edition of the Martindale-Hubbell Law Directory. In the volume containing the roster of Florida attorneys, Jerry found a listing for a Martin S. Becker, Jr. in Fort Myers. The information it offered was scant: the years of his birth (1961) and admission to the Florida bar (1998), an office street address, and codes identifying the college and law schools from which he graduated and the degrees conferred. Consulting the index of colleges, universities, and law schools, Jerry found an encouraging clue: Becker had attended both college and law school in Virginia, at The College of William & Mary in Williamsburg.

Pursuing a hunch, he requested the corresponding volumes for the year 1990, testing his theory that Becker practiced law in Virginia before moving on to Florida. Twenty minutes later, he found his answer.

"Bingo!" he shrieked, drawing disapproving looks from every corner of the library. Becker, he discovered, had been a member of the law firm of Becker & Becker in Longmire, Virginia!

Barely able to restrain his excitement, Jerry scampered back to Max's place to share his findings.

"Now we're getting somewhere!" Max exclaimed, glancing up from the Blake catalogue on his lap. He rose abruptly, dumping the book unceremoniously to the floor. "Come on, we're going for a ride."

Max dashed out the door with Jerry panting in his wake. Since Max didn't own a car, Jerry'd have to drive them in his Blazer.

"Where are we going?" Jerry asked.

"The Rose Art Museum at Brandeis."

"How do I get there?"

"How would I know?" Max chuckled. "You're driving."

Jerry shook his head. He fished a tattered map out of the glove compartment, unfolding it over the steering wheel. He spent the next five minutes sifting through a tangled knot of arteries, pondering possible routes.

"Can't you at least *talk* me from here to the Mass Pike?" he asked in frustration.

"No, but I could use the Maps application on my iPhone," Max said.

"Why didn't..." Jerry sighed, rolled his eyes, and backed out the driveway while Max activated his cell phone GPS.

Jerry waited until they'd reached the Mass Pike before inquiring as to the purpose of their journey.

"The Rose has a painting by Brandon Blake in storage. The curator there is an old friend. She offered to let us take a look at the signature and any inscriptions on the back. I took a photo of the Cornelia inscription on my iPhone. If my hunch is correct, they won't match—offering more evidence that Blake is *not* the artist and making an attribution to Elliott a little more likely."

Arriving at the Rose, Max made a beeline for the front desk, asking for someone named Julia. A few minutes later, a petite, curly-haired, middle-aged woman appeared.

"How the hell are you, you old bastard!" Julia cried, embracing Max like a long-lost paramour. Maybe he was, Jerry speculated.

Max returned the greeting and introduced Jerry. Still engaged in animated conversation, the old friends left the main gallery for a cavernous storage area in the bowels of the museum, with Jerry tagging along behind them.

Julia led them to the back of the room where she grasped a heavy, picture-laden storage rack, drawing it out slowly along its metal runner. "Here it is," she said, pointing to a large canvas secured to the ponderous wire-mesh rack. The painting depicted a handful of shabbily dressed figures assembled around a campfire against a background suggesting devastation.

Jerry remembered the painting from the catalogue. "Part of Blake's *Post-Apocalyptic Series*," he said proudly. Max smirked in amusement.

Max focused on the signature and date in the lower right corner of the canvas. "BRANDON BLAKE" was inscribed in large block letters beneath which appeared the date, 1968. "Hmm," he murmured, but in a way that made Jerry uneasy. Max opened the photo app on his iPhone, swiped a few frames, and stared at the photograph he'd taken of the Cornelia inscription on the back of the painting *Grief.* "Take a look for yourself," he said.

Jerry circled behind Max, who remained crouched opposite the signature on the painting, holding the iPhone image in his left hand. Although the inscriptions looked eerily similar, the Blake signature was all upper case as compared with Cornelia, which appeared with only an initial capital letter.

"Is there anything on the reverse?" Max asked Julia.

"Quite possibly," she said, stepping around the edge of the rack and glancing through the wire mesh at the back of the enormous painting. Max and Jerry followed. Looking up, all three detected an inscription on the middle of the top wooden stretcher, at least eight feet off the ground.

"Got a ladder?"

"I do," Julia said, turning toward the back of the room where a six-foot wooden ladder stood propped against the back wall.

"Let me," Jerry offered, rushing to retrieve it.

"Careful," Max cautioned, fearful that his friend, in his haste, might poke a hole through a Pollock or Picasso.

With Jerry's assistance, Julia positioned the ladder behind the painting. With his iPhone in hand, Max ascended. Fortunately, the overhead lighting was sufficient to illuminate the inscription. "Remarkable," Max muttered after a few moments. "Plenty of lower-case lettering," he said. "And I'll be damned if it isn't a match."

Was this good news or bad, Jerry wondered? "Can I take a

gander?" After Max descended, Jerry grabbed the iPhone from Max and climbed the ladder himself, its joints creaking with his weight. After a few seconds of study, he nodded. "He makes his lower-case "a's" the old-fashioned way, with the overhanging cap, the way you see it in typeface. It's the same as it appears on the Cornelia Paintings." At Max's direction and with Julia's approval, Jerry snapped some photos of the inscription.

Jerry swore at the traffic all the way back to Cambridge. Between epithets, he peppered his colleague with questions.

"If Brandon Blake didn't paint the Cornelia pictures, as you've hypothesized, why would his handwriting appear on their backs?"

"Pretty intriguing question, isn't it?"

"How can you be so sure Blake *didn't* paint them?"

"You've just seen a prime example of his work, Jerry. It's not even *close* to the style of your pictures."

Jerry pinched his lips. "So, what've we got, then?"

Max was constantly amused by Jerry's impatience. "What we've got is a pile of really great paintings in the style of Grant Elliott with no documentation, and inscriptions quite possibly by his friend, Brandon Blake. And we have an owner you've traced back to Longmire where both of them lived and worked. Frankly, Jerry, we've got a lot."

"Which amounts to . . ."

"A riddle, wrapped in a mystery, inside an enigma."

"What?"

"Winston Churchill."

"Fuck me," Jerry said, his frustration mounting. "What do we do next?"

"We look for Cornelia."

Chapter Twenty-Eight

Rural Iowa, 35 Miles from Omaha
May, 1970

It happened almost imperceptibly. Caroline's temporary stay stretched to a week, two weeks, and then a month. Faith took her under her wing, counseling her on the vagaries of late pregnancy and routines of the commune. Sharing responsibility for the care of baby James, the expectant mother received a crash course in the fundamentals of early parenting.

Caroline pitched in eagerly both in the farmhouse and in the fields, unwilling to let an eight-month bulge temper her enthusiasm. A farm girl herself, she was an asset from the strawberry patch to the vegetable garden, denied only the assignments clearly inappropriate for a woman in her condition. In the kitchen, she parlayed her existing skills with those imparted by Faith, Lynette, and Susan, the third distaff member of The Family.

From six to ten years older than she, Caroline perceived the three women as the big sisters she never had. Their male counterparts were unfailingly solicitous, infatuated by her charm and her beauty. So long as they allowed her to remain, she was content to stay. Her lack of a plan had become the key to her salvation.

Mike, in particular, found Caroline as irresistible as he had on the day he discovered her at the Truck Stop Café. Recognizing her intelligence, he plied her with a steady diet of books, from classics such as *The Great Gatsby* to more contemporary fare like

Portnoy's Complaint. She was more than receptive, both to his attentions and his literary advice.

It was Mike who'd volunteered to remain at the farm with Faith and Caroline on that third Monday in May, while the others conducted their weekly rounds at the farmers' markets and grocery stores. With Caroline fast approaching her due date, Faith and Mike were poised to handle the inevitable should it occur on their watch. To avoid any unnecessary complications, Little James did the rounds with Susan and Lynette.

The girls were at work in the kitchen. Mike had begun the strawberry harvest on a patch immediately behind the farmhouse. At about eleven in the morning, an ear-piercing shriek rang out from the house. Mike bolted up the back steps and into the kitchen. He found Caroline shaking, clutching a kitchen chair in terror, a puddle of water at her feet and Faith by her side.

"Her water broke," Faith announced calmly.

Caroline was anything but calm. "Oh my God!" she cried. "I'm gonna have it here on the kitchen floor!"

"No you're not," Faith assured her. "Mike's gonna drive us to the hospital. Everything's gonna be fine."

Faith walked her to the front door and down the porch steps while Mike brought the Chevy around.

Faith helped Caroline into the back seat. She sat beside her, grasping her hand to soothe her, rendering her as comfortable as possible. "Everything's gonna be just fine," she repeated. When the car door closed, Mike floored it.

"Take it easy, Mike!" Faith scolded as the car bounded over the gullies and potholes along the driveway.

Faith had prepared Caroline for this day, drawing on her recent experience with James. But the intensity of the moment had reduced the expectant teenage mother to tears. She'd been through more than her share of emotional stress, but the sudden loss of control of her body traumatized her.

Caroline trembled, doubling over in pain.

"Contraction?"

She nodded. "Second in the last couple of minutes."

Mike glanced at her warily through the rear-view mirror. Her pain and anguish twisted his stomach into knots.

"How far to the hospital?" she asked, panting.

"Forty minutes," Mike shouted from behind the wheel, the old Chevy's tires screeching as the car flew off the driveway and onto the road.

"You've gotta be kidding!" Caroline was panicking, unable to imagine holding out even half that long. "Shit!" she screamed a second later, wracked by yet another contraction. She winced, clutching her abdomen in obvious discomfort. "It won't fucking end!"

"Breathe!" Faith implored her.

"What the hell do you think I'm doing?" She barked at Mike: "Can't you drive this damn heap any faster?" Meanwhile, the contractions kept on coming. Caroline grimaced in agony.

The contractions were now a minute apart. Mike chewed on his lower lip as he steered the car frantically down the snaking two-lane road, stealing an occasional glance through his mirror at the drama unfolding behind him.

"Watch the road!" Faith grumbled.

"Another one! Oh, my God!" Caroline wailed. "Feels like a hippo on my bladder!"

"Shit," Mike moaned under his breath. They were barely halfway to the hospital.

"Pull over!" Faith demanded.

"What?" Mike sputtered.

"Pull over! Now!" She bored into Caroline's eyes. "We're gonna have to do this now, Caroline. Let's just take it easy and let it happen naturally."

Mike pulled the car to the side of the road. Caroline's face was seared with panic.

"Any towels in the car?" Faith asked him.

"What do you think this is, a linen closet?"

"How about a blanket?"

"Might be one in the trunk. I'll look."

Mike exited the car and searched the trunk.

"I'll have to remove your underwear," Faith said to Caroline. "Try to relax."

"Oh my God!" Caroline shrieked in the wake of another contraction.

"Here's the blanket," Mike said, showing little disposition to delve more deeply into the bedlam of backseat birthing.

It was too dark in the back of the car for Faith to clearly see what she had to do. "Got a flashlight?"

Mike nodded. "I think so." He reached into the glove compartment, drew out a flashlight, and flipped it on, sighing with relief when he saw that it functioned.

"Okay," Faith said, yanking the flashlight from his hand. "Have any soap, water, or alcohol of any kind in the car?"

"No!" Mike said with growing alarm.

"Windshield washer fluid?"

"There's some in the trunk. What the fuck for?"

"It's mostly alcohol," Faith said. "Have to clean my hands as best I can." Mike returned from the trunk with the washer fluid and poured it over Faith's outstretched hands. The back seat of the old Chevy was never going to be the same.

Caroline was now yelping and moaning incessantly, thoroughly consumed by fear.

"Breathe," Faith instructed. "Are you comfortable?" Caroline's expression indicated otherwise. "Try lying down. Put your head on that seat cushion there and get as comfortable as you can. Stay calm, honey. We're gonna do this."

Mike stared at them rigidly from the front seat, his eyes filled with trepidation. "Mike," Faith said, "try flagging down a passing driver. Someone who can get to a phone to call an ambulance." Mike leapt from the front seat, glad for the excuse to escape. "But stay within earshot in case I need you."

Faith lifted Caroline's skirt, aiming the flashlight between her legs. A blood-tinged patch of hairy skin began to poke its way through.

"I can't hold back any longer," Caroline grunted. "I feel like I have to push!"

"That's fine," Faith said. "Push. That's it. Keep going. Breathe. You're doing great. I can see the baby's head!"

Voices drifted in from the road. Mike had flagged down a local who'd sped off to seek help.

Caroline pushed between her rapid contractions. Soon, the baby's head poked all the way through. Faith cradled the head and let Caroline's contractions push the little booger farther and farther until *he* ("It's a boy!" Faith declared triumphantly) slid into her waiting hands. Caroline issued a mammoth sigh—signifying both relief and euphoria—as the reality of the momentous event took hold. She was physically and emotionally spent. Tears of joy flowed like rivers from her bloodshot eyes.

Faith wrapped the baby in the blanket, careful not to tangle his umbilical cord, and handed him gently to Caroline. She drew him to her chest and cuddled him. The baby began to cry, softly at first and then with more vigor. "Welcome to the world, Elliott Grant McKellan," Caroline purred, smiling broadly, almost uncomprehendingly, at her newborn son. "You're beautiful, Eli!"

The sound of an approaching siren interrupted her reverie. An ambulance screeched to a halt. Two paramedics emerged and hustled to the car. Faith stepped out to let them attend to mother and newborn son. Mike gave Faith an enthusiastic bear hug.

"You were wonderful back there," he told her. They both smiled, only now fully appreciating the enormity of what had occurred. Through the ensuing commotion, Caroline beamed and Eli gurgled.

Chapter Twenty-Nine

*Longmire, Virginia
and Points North
June, 2010*

"Road trip!" Max screeched in delight after they'd shut the rear hatch and mounted the front seats of Jerry's SUV. The odd couple had packed their bags, two of the Cornelia Paintings, and a handful of photos for an art-sleuthing expedition into the Shenandoah Valley of Virginia.

Summoning faded memories of their younger days, Jerry and Max wound their way south in the spirit of adventure. They challenged each other with tidbits of baseball trivia as oldies blared from the car radio.

The pair spent their first night in Harrisburg, Pennsylvania. To pass the evening, they attended a minor league baseball game between the Reading Phillies and the Harrisburg Senators in a ballpark plunked onto an island in the middle of the Susquehanna River. "Heard it floods when the river rises," Jerry laughed. "What a dumb place for a ballpark!"

"Shoulda called themselves the Harrisburg Amphibians," Max chuckled.

Jerry helped himself to three ballpark franks and a couple of beers while Max, vexed by the absence of Jews on the roster, chose to cheer on players with animal names instead. He rooted wildly for Brad Hogg (two hits, two RBIs) and hooted lustily when Moose Mullins fanned on three pitches.

Max and Jerry arrived in Longmire early the following afternoon. They made their initial inquiries at the local newspaper, the *Longmire Ledger*, whose offices were nestled in a Georgian-style building in the city's historic district. Jerry marched up to the front desk like a cowboy bursting into a western saloon.

"Hi, there," he boomed at a bespectacled, gray-haired woman behind the counter. "Somebody here we can talk to for some background on a fellow named Martin Becker? Was a lawyer here in town a few years back."

The woman nodded in recognition. "Senior or junior?"

"Both," Max interjected.

"Why do you ask?" she inquired, a look of suspicion creeping onto her face. As a former IRS auditor, Jerry was accustomed to that reaction.

"Just doing our jobs, ma'am," he said. Though no longer able to flash his government credentials, his manner was sufficiently authoritative to command cooperation.

"Give me a minute," she said, dialing an extension. Soon, a stocky, silver-haired gentleman emerged from a nearby office. The way he wore his half-glasses—perched on the bridge of his nose—and rolled up the sleeves of his open-collared white shirt reminded Jerry of Lou Grant, the cranky newsroom boss played by Ed Asner on the old Mary Tyler Moore show.

"Ned Brady," the man announced, extending his hand graciously to each of his visitors in turn. He appeared to be of similar vintage to Jerry and Max. "I'm sort of the editor emeritus here. Told you've got some questions about Martin and Marty Becker," he chuckled. "Two very different kettle o' fish." Brady beckoned them to his office, pulling up a chair for each of his visitors before reclaiming his position behind an old oak desk.

"Martin Becker—Senior, that is—was a god in this town. War hero, highly respected attorney, mayor for something like four terms. Practiced law here from mid-century till the early 1990s when he passed away suddenly." Brady leaned back in his chair, happy for the opportunity to reminisce. But his demeanor changed when he turned his attention to Marty, Jr. "Now Marty, Junior, he was a totally different story. Not quite up to the old man's standards. Didn't have the fire in the belly. Joined his old man's law firm not long before his father died, then ran it into the ground after the old man's death. Started drinking. Wife left him. Finally absconded south, somewhere in Florida, I think. Left a trail of unhappy clients in his wake. Rumor is, stole some client trust funds on his way out the door. Someone told me he killed himself in a drunk-driving accident not too long ago."

"Quite a contrast," Max acknowledged.

"Would you happen to know," Jerry inquired, "if there was any connection between the Beckers and either or both of the artists Grant Elliott or Brandon Blake?"

Brady removed his spectacles and rubbed his chin. "You know, I think I recall some connection between Becky Elliott— she was Grant's wife—and Martin, Senior. She was the one who handled all of Grant's business affairs. I wouldn't be the least bit surprised if he'd been the Elliotts' personal attorney. No idea, though, with regard to Brandon Blake."

"Does Marty, Junior, have any other living relatives that you know of?" Max asked.

"Mother passed away about ten years ago. As best I can recollect, Junior was an only child. So far as I know, he never had kids."

"You mentioned that he had a wife. Is she still in the area?" Max inquired.

"Sure, she remarried. Another lawyer. Mary Daniels is what she goes by now. Husband's name is Jim. Practices here in town, just a couple blocks down Main Street, over by the courthouse."

Jerry glanced at Max, eyebrows raised. "Anything else, Max?"

"Show him the photograph."

Jerry nodded, withdrawing a photo of the painting *Grief* from his back pocket. "Any idea who the young woman in this painting might be? First name's Cornelia. It was painted maybe forty years ago."

Brady shook his head and shrugged. "What prompts all these questions, if I may ask."

Max and Jerry looked at each other before Max spoke. "Trying to track down the provenance of a painting we think is by Grant Elliott."

"I see. Let me know if there's a story in it."

"Sure," Max said. "Appreciate your help."

Chapter Thirty

Dear Grant:

It's been way too long. I'm sorry for that. I've often had the urge to write you, but always hesitated, afraid to shatter your reverie. Big word, I know, but you'd be surprised how much I've learned over the past couple of years.

I'm living on a farm in the Midwest. I know, I swore I'd never spend another day on a farm. Well, things change. And actually, it's a commune. There are ten of us here, including two children. We share responsibilities, grow our own food (and then some), take care of each other.

Amazingly, I've been here since the day I mailed you my first letter. I was having breakfast in a truck stop café when a really nice guy (I'll call him "M") offered me a ride and, later that day, a place to stay—here at the farm. I couldn't have asked for better luck. M, and everyone else here, has been wonderful to me. M studied literature in college, and has opened my mind to a world I'd barely known. I probably devour a book a week. Fiction, mostly, both living authors and the classics. I'm hoping, when things settle down in a year or two, to get my GED, and maybe even someday go to college. But for the moment, life is good.

Today is an important day. It's Eli's second birthday. That's right, Old Man, your son, Elliott Grant McKellan, is two. I'm enclosing a snapshot taken with one of those cool new Polaroid instant cameras. A couple minutes after this picture was shot, he nearly dove into that birthday cake! He is so cute! I can't tell you how happy I am to have him, and how proud I am that you're his dad.

I read about you occasionally in ArtNews. They get it in our county library. I see where you had a big exhibition at the Detroit Art Institute. Wish I could have been there. I sent away for the catalogue. Our paintings aren't in it, so I gather you've maintained our secret. Maybe one day that will change, but not to worry, I'm in no hurry.

You'll be pleased to hear that Eli has some real artistic talent. He draws like a kid at least twice his age. Not just scribbles, but human and animal forms, trees, houses. He's even got a keen sense of color. And, of course, I encourage him.

In case you're wondering, I've communicated with my parents. They know I'm fine, but not where I'm living. I've sent them pictures of Eli. They were pretty damn anxious to shunt him off to an adoptive family, so I don't really know how they feel about having a grandson. But I didn't think it right to keep them completely in the dark. Anyway, you won't have to feel guilty that my parents are uninformed. They know what you know, except, of course, for that pesky little matter of paternity.

    I hope you and Becky are well. And give my regards to Brandon, too. I sure hope he's still around, since I'm mailing this to you at his address.

Love,
Caroline

P.S.- M mails this to you from a post office near his parents when he goes to visit them. See, I'm as good at keeping secrets as you are!

Chapter Thirty-One

Longmire, Virginia
June, 1972

Brandon appeared at Grant's studio door on a hot and sticky June afternoon. The younger artist had just returned from a two-week trip to New York where he'd mounted and hosted his second solo exhibition.

"How'd the opening go?" Grant asked.

"A good crowd and two major sales," Brandon reported, "so I can't complain. But I much prefer the peace and quiet of my studio to the chaos of the city."

"Guess that's why we're hunkered down in these hills."

Brandon drew a small, white envelope from his back pocket. "I've got something for you," he said. "Probably been lying around the studio for a week or two, but better late than never." He pinched his lips. "I think I know who it's from."

Grant turned ashen. He, too, recognized the handwriting on the envelope. Caroline had never been far from his mind. After her farewell letter two years earlier, he'd expected to hear from her again. Her silence tormented him. He longed to know how she was, how the child was—he'd be a toddler now. He held the envelope in his hands anxiously, hesitant to open it.

Brandon stroked his beard impatiently. "For Chrissake, Grant, open it!"

The older artist grabbed a Windsor chair and sat down, motioning Brandon to do likewise. Inhaling deeply, he tore the envelope open with his index finger. A photograph fluttered to the floor. Brandon bent down to retrieve it, smiling broadly as he returned it to Grant.

The Polaroid captured Caroline and her son posing gleefully before a birthday cake surmounted by two jumbo candles. Grant's eyes moistened. Caroline, dressed in shorts and a flowery peasant top, was radiant. She looked older than he remembered, more mature—she'd be almost twenty by now—but no less beautiful. And the child was adorable.

Brandon leaned forward for a better view. "He's got her eyes," he observed, "but he looks more like you." Grant was speechless.

Grant read the letter aloud, stopping occasionally to compose himself. His voice trembled when he articulated his son's name for the first time. "Elliott Grant," he said softly. "Calls him Eli." He sighed. "What a beautiful child."

"She's proud of his connection to you," Brandon noted.

"I don't deserve that," Grant confessed. "But at least I know she's well, her son's wonderful, and they're happy. I can't tell you how much I've worried over the past two years."

"You can relax now. It all turned out fine. What more could you ask?"

"I've no right to ask for anything," Grant conceded, "but I'd love to meet him some day."

Chapter Thirty-Two

Longmire, Virginia
June, 2010

Jerry dug into his porterhouse steak like a lion attacking a hyena. Max sat across the table picking at a salad. They were in Old Town, the historic center of Longmire, consuming a mediocre dinner in a tourist-trap restaurant with overblown Colonial pretensions. A waiter dressed in a frilly white shirt and zipperless black breeches refilled their water glasses.

"How the heck does he pee?" Jerry pondered between bites.

"Sitting down," Max deduced.

"Fuckin' shirt reminds me of the puffy shirt episode of Seinfeld."

"Didn't see it," Max said.

"Need to get your head out of the clouds, Professor," Jerry chided him.

Duly chastened, Max took a sip of water, replacing the glass heavily on the table. "So, we know our Marty Becker was a drunk and a rogue," Max said, redirecting the discussion to the matter at hand. "What does that tell us?"

"Nothing about the artist of our paintings," Jerry growled.

"No, but it does at least raise a possibility that you're probably not too keen on contemplating."

Jerry's eyes narrowed, though he continued to chew. It wasn't as if the thought hadn't already crossed his mind. Still, he wasn't ready to articulate it. So, much to his dismay, Max did.

"He probably wasn't a collector. A collector would've framed the paintings, maybe even kept one or two at home to enjoy. A thief, on the other hand, is more likely to hide them in a storage locker, don't you think?"

Jerry put down his knife and fork and glared at his dinner companion. "Look, Max, we're not the F.B.I. here. I'm not gonna assume Becker was a thief. And there's no reason to go around blabbing that I bought this stuff out of some dead bastard's storage locker. If anyone asks, let's just say I bought it at an estate sale, cause that's essentially what it was. All right?"

Max could see Jerry was peeved. "Sure," he said, hoping to put the matter at least temporarily to rest.

"So, what now?"

"We try to figure out who Cornelia is."

"And how do we do that?" Jerry lifted the largely denuded steak bone from his plate and gnawed on it, hoovering the last specks of meat into his gullet.

"Well, what do we know about her so far?" Max's habitual resort to the Socratic method irritated Jerry almost as much as Jerry's insatiable appetite irked Max.

Jerry put down the bone, awaiting enlightenment. Rather than act as Max's foil, he chose to let him answer his own question.

"We can tell, by her clothes—when she's wearing them— that she was probably painted somewhere within the Sixties/Seventies time frame. So, for argument's sake, let's presume 1970. She looks to be, what, seventeen, eighteen . . . no more than twenty, right?"

"Mmm hmm," Jerry muttered, slathering butter onto the fourth of the dinner rolls he'd fished from the breadbasket.

"So, let's say she was born around 1950 or a year or two thereafter."

"That'd make her sixty now, poor kid."

"Speaking of kids," Max continued, "we presume she had one in the early Seventies."

"Be close to forty by now," Jerry mumbled, his teeth tearing away at the crust of his dinner roll.

"Right. But here's a clue," Max said. "If Grant Elliott is the artist, then it's most likely that our model lived nearby. Almost all of his portrait sitters were locals, most of them neighbors."

"So, what, we go knocking on doors? Shit, that was forty years ago! Who's gonna still be around in the same place they were living forty years ago?"

"You have a better idea?"

"Nope," Jerry acknowledged. He stared at the plain white shirt Max was wearing above a nondescript pair of black trousers. "Let's just not go out dressed like Jehovah's Witnesses, Max, or we'll never get anywhere."

Their pursuit of Cornelia began in earnest the following morning. At least they had a place to start. After Becky Elliott's death in 2005, the Elliott house and studio were bequeathed to the local historical society and opened to the public as a museum. Although Max had been there before, it was Jerry's first visit. They paid the modest admission fee and toured the house and studio in search of clues.

"Observe the studio carefully," Max charged his companion. "Compare the indoor and outdoor settings with the backgrounds appearing in the paintings."

Jerry did as instructed, scanning every square inch of the studio while referring to his photos. He strained in search of an epiphany that never materialized.

"Shit," Jerry muttered when the tour ended. "Nothing looks even remotely familiar." He noticed the smug look on the professor's face. "You knew it all along, you bastard."

"Right, but I needed to see it again. Besides, you could've picked up something I missed."

Jerry shook his head in frustration. "Okay, so now we knock on doors?"

"Lighten up," Max counseled. "Research takes patience."

Patience had never been Jerry's strong suit.

A couple hundred yards north of the Elliott Homestead stood a nineteenth century farmhouse. A freshly carved dirt road divided the two properties. At the end of the road was a busy construction site. Jerry had noticed the sign when they'd approached the Homestead from the main road. "Luxury Homes From the $300's," it proclaimed.

Serenaded by the groaning and clanging of tractors and steam shovels, the sleuths trudged through a meadow of wildflowers. They crossed the new access road for the fledgling subdivision, then ambled down an old dirt path to the farmhouse. The sign in front read: "Sales Office/Carrell Construction Company."

"Looks like this neighbor's long gone," Jerry groused.

"Let's find out what we can," Max said.

The door was open. Inside, a short entry hall opened to a pair of rooms. On the left, in what had evidently once been a dining room, a large model of the rising housing development rested on a pair of sawhorses. To the right was the living room, now repurposed as an office. A middle-aged man with dark hair and a dark complexion sat behind a desk in the center of the room.

"How can I help you gentlemen?"

Max spoke up. "We were hoping to locate the prior occupants of this building."

The man snickered. "Nobody's lived here for years. It was a

near-wreck when Carrell Construction bought the full hundred-acre parcel back in '07. It'd been in the same family for generations. Bought it out of a sheriff's sale."

"I see."

"Thanks for nothing," Jerry grumbled, grabbing Max's arm and exiting the front door.

"Come again!" trilled the salesman mockingly.

Max and Jerry spent the next few hours canvassing the rest of the homes nearby. They knocked on at least a dozen doors. No one recognized Cornelia from the photos they displayed; most had arrived within the last twenty years.

"Well that was a fuckin' waste of time," Jerry declared as another door slammed shut. "We sounded like perverts looking for a favorite young girl to abuse."

"Occupational hazard," Max said, smiling as always.

"What next?"

"First we have lunch, and then we go to school."

Jerry heard only the part about lunch.

Chapter Thirty-Three

Rural Iowa, 35 Miles from Omaha
May, 1982

Caroline heard the familiar roar of the approaching school bus as she planted the fragile eggplant seedlings in the raised beds behind the farmhouse. Mike worked the row beside her while Faith trailed behind them, staking the seedlings to provide support. It was a glorious May afternoon, warm enough to erase the memory of April snow squalls and incessant spring rains. The ladies glanced in unison toward the road, where their rambunctious twelve-year-olds vaulted from the bus and began their daily foot race down the long, unpaved driveway that led to the farmhouse.

As she watched, Caroline's eye caught something unusual: a plume of smoke curling up from the kitchen window. "What's that?" she asked Mike, pointing anxiously toward the house.

Mike and Faith dropped their implements and sprinted toward the house. Caroline ran toward the boys, hollering for their attention, warning them to stay clear. Alarmed by Caroline's screams and the billowing gray smoke, their housemates dashed up from the vegetable patch near the river. By now, flames had burst through the windows of the kitchen and were spreading to the bedrooms above.

Mike circled to the front of the house, wary of the fire engulfing the kitchen and back entrance. Andy and Arnie joined him. Caroline, Faith and Lynette remained with James and Eli.

"What's happening?" James cried, an uncomprehending look on his face. Caroline drew Eli into her arms, clutching him tightly.

After a moment of indecision, Andy lunged toward the front door, desperate to salvage his grandfather's legacy. Mike and Arnie sprang forward, grabbing his arm and yanking him back. "It's too late," Arnie hollered. By now, the blaze had spread to the side porch and began to penetrate the roof. Calling for help was impossible: the telephones, in the kitchen and upstairs hallway, were no longer accessible. But it wouldn't have mattered anyway—they were too far off the grid.

Helpless, the men retreated to a safe distance, joining the women and children. Their hearts were stabbed by the acrid smell of smoke and the mournful wails of crashing timbers and shattering glass. Their faces were etched with resignation. Mike wrapped his left arm across Caroline's shoulder while she wept, her arms enfolding her son as he stood before her, staring at the inferno, tears descending his cheeks. Not a word was spoken; there was nothing they could do.

The Family had lived there contentedly for more than a decade, their idyllic life a palliative for the political and emotional turmoil gripping the nation through the tumultuous Sixties and Seventies. But the tide had turned. Nixon had resigned in disgrace, the Vietnam War had mercifully ended, and Ronald Reagan had ascended to the presidency. The counterculture fed by youthful rebellion had lost its steam. The conflagration, it seemed, marked the end of an era.

As she watched the flames ravage their home, Caroline understood that the life she'd known for the last dozen years had come to an abrupt, if inevitable, halt. She'd reached another crossroads, much as she had when she'd arrived, pregnant and clueless, on the doorstep of this once proud farmhouse, now disintegrating before her eyes.

Mike found Caroline sitting alone in the guest bedroom of the old Victorian occupied by the Johnsons, one of several area families offering temporary accommodations to the displaced victims of the fire. Though disapproving of their communal lifestyle, they'd nevertheless extended a lifeline, graciously offering them food and shelter while they pondered their options.

Caroline sat glumly on the bed. Her sadness was palpable. Mike sat down beside her, stroking her hair tenderly, comforting her as best he could.

Mike squeezed Caroline's hand. "I love you," he said warmly. It wasn't the first time he'd said it. He'd fallen in love with Caroline on the day he rescued her from the Truck Stop Café in Indianapolis. He recalled every detail of their drive that day, from the pounding rain to the lyrics of Simon & Garfunkel. From that very first day, he'd taken her under his wing. They'd made love for the first time a year later, and many times since. He'd bonded with Eli, amusing him, reading to him, comforting and encouraging him as a real father would.

"What are we going to do?" she sniffled.

Mike brushed his fingers tenderly against her cheek. "If you'll let me," he said, "I'll marry you. We'll live like normal people—just the three of us." He gathered her hands into his. "I've got enough money saved. I'll go back and finish my degree, get a teaching job somewhere. You can do whatever you want. Get a job, or, if you prefer, stay home with Eli. We'll make it work."

Caroline smiled. "Was that a proposal?"

"I suppose it was," he said, grinning.

She embraced him, kissing him deeply. But before she delivered her response, she sought an assurance. "I'd want you to treat Eli as if he were your own son," she said, hoping to dispense with the vague, 'we're all one big family' fabrications with which she'd mollified her son for years, replacing them with the more convenient fiction of Mike's fatherhood.

Mike closed his eyes gently and smiled. "I'd like nothing more."

"Then my answer is yes."

Chapter Thirty-Four

Jerry and Max parked themselves in a corner of the Longmire High School library, thumbing through old yearbooks. "That's the year I was born!" giggled the tall, redheaded woman manning the visitor's desk when Max had inquired about the availability of yearbooks from the Class of 1965 on. Fortunately, she knew where to direct the would-be gumshoes.

While Max scanned the black-and-white head shots from the class of 1970, Jerry perused a dog-eared copy of the '71 yearbook.

"Ah, the carefree days of high school," Max said wistfully, studying the playful poses and the smart-ass captions plastered across the glossy pages.

"Sort of like retirement," Jerry shot back, "but without the arthritis."

They'd already eliminated the members of the graduating classes of 1965 through 1969. There was nary a Cornelia among them. "Half of the girls are blondes," Jerry muttered as he turned the pages, studying the endless rows of photos. "They all look alike."

"You'll know her when you see her," Max laughed. "Look for the pregnant one."

Jerry rolled his eyes. "What if she's not here?" he said. "Pregnant girls don't always make it to graduation. Might not have even made it to photo day."

Max sneered. "Or maybe she went to private school. Or maybe she was home-schooled," he said, mimicking Jerry's whine. "Who the hell knows? Do you have a better idea?"

Jerry sighed, continuing to flip pages, his eyes glazing over. When they'd collectively slogged through every yearbook from 1965 to 1975, he proposed they call it a day. "No matches and only one Cornelia," Jerry moaned, "but she's black."

"Okay," Max said. "But you said something earlier that makes sense, now that I think of it."

Jerry snickered at what he perceived as a backhanded compliment, uttering a facetious "Hallelujah!"

Max pressed on. "I noticed that one of the yearbooks included a notation at the end listing students without photographs." Max retrieved the 1970 yearbook. He pointed to a note at the bottom of the last page of photos. "Look here," he said, reading the caption. "Students Without Photographs: Edward K. Burke, Caroline McKellan."

"Well, we can rule out Edward," Jerry said.

"Which leaves Caroline."

Jerry puckered his lips. "Come on, what are the chances that the only female not pictured in ten years' worth of yearbooks is our subject? Besides, her name's not even Cornelia!"

As the words came out of Jerry's mouth, Max had an epiphany. "Jerry," he said excitedly, "what do you get when you rearrange the letters in Cornelia?"

"Gee, Max, I don't know, what *do* you get?"

"Caroline."

Jerry rocked back in his chair. "Let me get this straight," he said. "Because Cornelia and Caroline are . . ."

"Anagrams," Max interjected.

"Right, anagrams, you think the girl without a picture is our model?"

"You said as much yourself!" Max responded. "Maybe she left school due to pregnancy."

"Right. I did say that. And the anagram?"

"An effort to further obscure the trail."

"Hmm," Jerry sniffed. He remained dubious, but at least they had a straw to grasp. "Maybe they've got a file on her back in the office."

Jerry and Max reshelved the old yearbooks, nearly galloping back to the visitors' desk. They asked for all available files on Caroline McKellan, Class of '70.

"Oh, those records are no longer onsite," the redhead explained. "But even if they were, they're confidential."

Jerry turned to his colleague. "Now what?"

Max rubbed his chin. "I've got a hunch. Where's the town library?" he asked the woman.

Armed with directions, the pair hopped back into Jerry's SUV and made a beeline for the library. Passing through its faux-colonial entrance, they found their way to the reference desk.

"Where would I find a local telephone book from the 1970s?" Max asked the reference librarian.

"In the landfill," she said.

Max scowled. "Fine. I've got another idea."

Jerry shuffled behind Max as he hustled out the door and back to the Blazer. "Where to now?"

"Town Hall," Max said.

Wearily, Jerry unlocked the car, wriggled inside, and flipped on the ignition. "What's there?" he asked Max, grateful they weren't headed for the landfill.

"Real estate tax records."

"Okay..." Jerry muttered, hoping for more elucidation. None was forthcoming.

Max led the way as they barreled into Town Hall, located the tax records office, and secured the attention of a clerk.

"Looking for real estate tax records under the name McKellan," he said to the gaunt, gray-haired man behind the counter, spelling it out to avoid confusion.

"Hmm. Let's see what we've got," the clerk responded, retreating to a massive library-style card catalogue. He returned a couple minutes later bearing an index card. "I've got an old reference to James and Alice McKellan at 254 Plain Ridge Road, but the property passed to a development company three years ago."

Max flashed a smug grin. "That's the house next door to the Elliott Homestead," he said to Jerry, "the one that's now a real estate sales office. It would be an incredible coincidence if their daughter's name *wasn't* Caroline McKellan!"

"We've found the needle," Jerry quipped. "All we have to do now is find the haystack it's buried in."

Chapter Thirty-Five

Eli sensed that there was something momentous about this day. Sure, it was his twenty-first birthday. That was certainly a milestone. But there was something else in the offing—something suggested by the curious reserve he'd noted in his parents' demeanor at the restaurant where they'd gathered to celebrate the occasion.

Classes at Purdue were over, graduation a week away. Though still living on campus, Eli had elected to spend the evening with his parents rather than endure the traditional drunken initiation into adulthood with his peers. He adored his parents; the bacchanal could wait one more night.

Mike, in particular, looked anxious when they'd returned home from dinner. He proposed a toast. While he fetched a special bottle of cognac and a trio of snifters, Caroline sat quietly across from her son on the living room sofa. Eli thought he detected tears in her eyes as she awaited her husband's reappearance.

Mike poured an inch of the golden liquid into each of the snifters before distributing a pair to Caroline and Eli. "To our son on his twenty-first birthday," he said, lifting his glass. "May your adulthood be blessed with love, good health, and happiness!" They clinked glasses and sipped in unison. But the smiles quickly evaporated from his parents' faces.

Eli was spooked by the uncharacteristic silence that followed.

"What's up, you guys?" he asked with growing concern.

Mike removed his spectacles and rubbed his eyes. "Your mother has something to tell you," he said.

Eli looked at Caroline apprehensively. "What is it? You're scaring me."

Caroline fortified herself with a sip of cognac. "We haven't been entirely honest with you over these past twenty-one years," she said. "But now it's time we told you the truth."

A host of possibilities careened through Eli's mind. They'd lived a dozen years in a commune. Were they criminals on the lam? Hippie radicals evading capture by living off the grid? In witness protection programs, living under false identities?

Calmly, Caroline told the story of the teenager who'd run away from home, Mike's serendipitous offer of transportation, her acceptance into the commune. Eli had assumed they'd met elsewhere, but no matter, he thought.

"I was pregnant with you when Mike and I met," Caroline said.

"You were . . . then how could . . ." Eli sputtered as the import of the revelation took hold.

She told him about the heady year and a half spent modeling for Grant Elliott and Brandon Blake. During her son's teenage years, she'd exposed him to the artwork of both. "Eli," she said, reaching for his hand, "Grant Elliott is your biological father."

Eli felt as if he'd been slammed in the gut with a two-by-four. He slumped into his chair. Elliott, he knew, was decades older than his mother. "But—"

"It was fully consensual, Eli," she assured him. "I was only seventeen, a senior in high school. Foolish, maybe, but I loved him. He was, and still is, married. I never revealed your father's identity, not even to my parents."

"I thought you said my grandparents were dead."

"They are now; they weren't then." Caroline drained the last of the cognac from her snifter. "They didn't handle it well. Demanded that I give you up for adoption, which I refused to do."

Eli was almost swooning. "I can't believe this," he said, still struggling to get his head around his mother's earthshaking revelation.

"I had no choice, Eli, but to leave home. Your father—er, Mike—discovered me the following day, eating breakfast at a truck stop café in Indianapolis. I'd hitchhiked from home without even a glimmer of a plan."

"I fell in love with your Mom the day I met her," Mike said, squeezing Caroline's hand.

"And I guess you pretty much know the rest," she said.

"We decided it would be easier for you, for all of us, if you believed I was your father," Mike interjected. "I've known you since the day you were born, so it was no stretch for me. It's been a privilege to be your dad. I'm proud of you and love you no less than if I'd been your actual biological father."

"I don't know what to say," Eli murmured, sinking back into his chair.

"You needed to know the truth," Caroline said. "We decided that now was the time. You're old enough to understand and mature enough to be trusted to keep our secret. I never wanted to hurt Grant Elliott's wife or tarnish his legacy. I hope you'll forgive our deception and try to understand and accept the decisions we've made."

Eli maintained a stunned silence. He was thoroughly surprised, completely blindsided. To learn the man you thought was your father isn't your father is one thing. But to learn your father is a world-famous artist is quite another.

"Does . . . Grant Elliott know?"

"Yes." She told him of her letters and why she stopped writing. "I didn't want him to come looking for us. You and Mike were already father and son. I didn't want anything to upset that."

"Grant Elliott," he said softly, shaking his head in disbelief. "It was always right there in front of me," he said, finally appreciating the full significance of his given name.

"And now you understand why you grew up handsome like him and not ugly like me," Mike laughed, in an effort to lighten the mood.

Eli managed a halfhearted smile. It was not as if he was losing a father, he told himself, he'd simply gained another.

"Give it time," his mother said. "It's a lot to absorb. But understand, above all, that nothing changes among us. We love you and always will."

"Not your conventional birthday present," Eli declared wearily. He rose from his chair and hugged his mother as Mike stepped forward to join the embrace. "I love you both," he said as they shared a cathartic cry.

Chapter Thirty-Six

The circumstantial evidence was mounting. Though there was no photo to confirm it, Max and Jerry had every reason to believe that Caroline McKellan was Cornelia. Her proximity to the artist and the compelling stylistic similarities between Jerry's paintings and Grant Elliott's known works made the attribution to Grant Elliott a near certainty. Yet questions remained.

Why were they inscribed in Brandon Blake's hand? Where were they painted? Why were they apparently hidden away for forty years? Why didn't Becky Elliott record them? How did they get into the hands of Marty Becker? And most troubling: is Jerry the rightful owner or did Becker, a known scoundrel, obtain them illicitly?

In his usual methodical fashion, Max ran through the questions with Jerry at breakfast the next morning. "Let me be clear," Max said, pausing between forkfuls of scrambled eggs, "I'm down here sleuthing with you for two reasons. First, to prove these paintings are lost works by Grant Elliott. And second, if at all possible, to arrange for their exhibition and documentation." He lowered his voice as he laid the rest of his cards metaphorically on the table. "And it would be disingenuous of me not to admit," he added with a smirk, "that presenting this discovery—maybe even writing that exhibition catalogue— would nicely cap off my career as an art scholar."

Jerry had no idea what 'disingenuous' meant and didn't care. "Listen, Professor," he said with a noticeable edge, "none of that's worth shit to me if I don't get to keep the damn paintings. So let's not go looking for trouble on that score, okay?"

Max nodded, but without enthusiasm. While Max wasn't 'looking for trouble,' as Jerry put it, neither was he willing to compound any shenanigans that might have led to Jerry's possession of the artwork. He genuinely liked and trusted his new buddy, but was loath to imperil his reputation for Jerry's sake.

As Max watched Jerry blast away at a prodigious stack of pancakes, he reconsidered the facts. "So, here are some of the tentative conclusions we can draw from what we know or think we know," he began. Jerry speared a sausage.

"First, it's likely that Grant Elliott didn't paint the Cornelia—let's amend that, the *Caroline* Paintings—in his studio. The backgrounds don't match, so we can assume he executed the paintings, or at least his preliminary studies, somewhere else." Jerry devoured another sausage.

"Second, Brandon Blake is implicated in all this. His handwriting is on the back of every work.

"Third, these paintings were a closely guarded secret. Why would the artist paint his neighbor's beautiful daughter and hide the results? How does her eventual pregnancy, documented in only a few of the works, figure into the secret? And was Becky Elliott a co-conspirator or was she ignorant of the entire affair?"

"*Affair*," Jerry mumbled, his mouth stuffed with flapjacks. "Not sure if you meant it that way, but it ties it all together, doesn't it?" As was his wont, Jerry cut to the chase. "He painted them behind his wife's back from the get-go," Jerry hypothesized. "If his wife knew about it, then there'd be no reason to hide any but the last paintings—the ones where she's pregnant. And, duh, of course the old guy knocked her up! Isn't that the M.O. of all the great artists?" As Max cringed, Jerry swept his fork through the puddle of syrup remaining on his plate before licking it clean with his tongue.

"Okay," Max said, "but why didn't it all come out? Wouldn't the parents of a girl that young be livid about his 'knocking her up' as you so artfully put it?"

"Probably, but maybe they didn't know it was him. Maybe she's part of the conspiracy."

Max scratched his ear. "Then why not destroy the lot of them, save everyone from embarrassment."

"Because," Jerry posited, "they were too damn good!" Jerry leaned back in his chair, either impressed with his analytical prowess or too stuffed to sit upright. "Maybe he didn't give a rat's ass what people thought when he—and probably Becky—were gone. Then the paintings could be revealed without harming a living soul."

Max pondered Jerry's theory. "If Caroline's still around somewhere, wouldn't *she* care?"

"She'd probably *love* to see them," Jerry posited. "She clearly wasn't ashamed of her body. She'd finally have her fifteen minutes of fame, now, wouldn't she?"

"So why didn't the paintings reappear after Becky died? That was in 2005, if I recall."

"Maybe Grant gave them to his buddy, Brandon Blake," Jerry suggested.

"Blake died in the late 1990s," Max reminded him. He sighed deeply, flexing his fingers. "Maybe *that's* where Marty Becker takes the stage."

Jerry turned suddenly silent. The premise seemed credible,

but the consequences for Jerry were potentially disastrous. Jerry knew in his heart that the status of Marty Becker as the rightful owner of the Caroline Paintings was subject to question. He'd driven his father's law firm into the ground. Facing financial challenges, it was hardly likely he could have afforded to legitimately purchase the paintings. He died shortly after Becky Elliott. Had he stashed the paintings with the intention of cashing in on them after her death? Maybe his access was legitimate. Maybe he breached some fiduciary trust. Maybe the paintings aren't Jerry's to keep. As he fit the pieces together in his mind his stomach began to churn, abetted in no small measure by the influx of a half-dozen pancakes.

Chapter Thirty-Seven

Longmire, Virginia
November, 1994

A cold draft whipped through Grant Elliott's studio as he labored over a still life. He'd dragged his easel in front of an old, scrubbed-top wooden table on which he'd placed a brown stoneware jug with a chipped lip, a rumpled cloth napkin, a blemished pear, and a spray of dried flowers. It was an apt metaphor for what his life had become. He was eighty-four. His health was steadily declining. Life was a series of ailments, each more worrisome than the last. He painted infrequently now, and only on those rare occasions where his arthritis was tolerable. His hand was unsteady and his eyesight unreliable. He'd been reduced to churning out still lifes, compositions of artifacts illuminated by the brightest possible light, so he could see what he was painting.

Grant thought often about his mortality. He'd achieved more than he'd dreamed possible. Beloved by an admiring public, his work appeared in virtually every major art museum in the country. Next year, there'd be one more retrospective, the most comprehensive yet. It would open in Boston and travel to five other venues before crossing the Atlantic for a final appearance in Paris. He doubted he'd live to see it.

A journalist once asked him if he had any regrets. "No," he'd answered, "I've had a wonderful life, I have a wonderful wife, and I've been able to do what I love the most—to paint." He was lying, of course. Little could he know that this would be the day on which one of his greatest regrets would be rectified.

It was late afternoon. The light outside was fading. Having fallen asleep at his easel, the artist was aroused by a banging at the door. He thought of the teenaged Caroline, whose brazen pounding had interrupted him in that very studio a quarter of a century earlier, igniting his secret obsession with the young model and muse. "I'm coming," he croaked. "Hold your damn horses!"

Leaning on his cane, he wrenched himself from his chair. He hobbled to the door, opening it with considerable difficulty. "Who are you?" he said, with more than a hint of annoyance, to the young man standing before him.

"My name is Eli Grainger," he said. Then, after a moment's pause: "I'm your son."

The old man staggered. Eli sprung forward to catch him. He grasped the artist's elbow and steadied him as he crossed the threshold into the studio. "Are you all right, Mr. Elliott?"

Grant's mind spun somersaults. "Fine, fine," he stammered, "you . . . uh . . . you startled me. Come in. Come in, please."

Eli was tall, well over six feet, with a square chin, lush brown hair, and well-defined features. He was ruggedly handsome, his good looks enhanced by his piercing blue eyes. Grant was mesmerized—he was gazing at a twenty-four-year-old version of himself, but with Caroline's eyes and broad, toothy smile.

"I didn't mean to startle you," the visitor said. "I'd read you'd been ill, and I wanted to meet you before . . ." Eli caught himself. He hadn't meant for it to come out that way. He looked at his father with distress. "I'm sorry, I didn't—"

Grant shook his head. "Don't give it a second thought, young man," he said, smiling weakly. "Come in, sit down. Can I offer you something?"

"No, no, Mr. Elliott, I'm fine, thank you."

"You have your mother's eyes," Grant said wistfully, bracing himself on the arms of his old Windsor chair as he lowered himself into the seat. "And her glorious smile."

"I've been told that before." His voice was strong and melodious.

"How," Grant inquired haltingly, hopeful that his visitor hadn't come bearing bad news, "is your mother?"

His doppelganger smiled. "She's terrific," he said, "couldn't be better!"

"Ah . . . I'm so glad to hear that." Grant paused, as if to savor the magnitude of the moment. "For a few years, she sent me a letter on your birthday, with a photograph," he recalled. "I cherished those letters. Seeing you grow up, your mother looking so proud and happy . . ." His voice trailed off. "But then the letters stopped coming. I didn't know . . ." He removed his spectacles, rubbing the bridge of his nose.

"It was because of Dad—uh, Mike—I call him that because that's what he was—and is—to me," Eli said without rancor. "It wasn't until my twenty-first birthday that Mom told me the truth. It was quite a shock. I'd always believed that Mike was my biological father." The old man sighed, unable to suppress his remorse. "Mom told me about the letters and why she stopped writing. It was around the time she and Mike decided to marry. She thought it best that I continue to believe that Mike was my father." The old Windsor creaked as Eli shifted forward. "She feared her letters might encourage you to find us and pursue a relationship. She was afraid it would hurt Mike and crush me," he said. "Besides, she couldn't be certain that I wouldn't reveal her secret, inadvertently or otherwise. She was adamant about protecting you and Mrs. Elliott."

Grant's weary eyes glistened with emotion: a curious cocktail of sadness, resignation, and gratitude. He understood and appreciated Caroline's motives, but the years of silence and uncertainty had taken their toll. "I worried," Grant acknowledged. "I didn't know where you were . . . or how you were faring." He reached into his pocket for a handkerchief, drying his eyes unabashedly. Then, mustering the hint of a smile, he motioned toward the pot of coffee warming on the coffee machine on his worktable. "Pour yourself a cup—and another for me, if you don't mind—and fill me in on your lives all these years."

Eli rose, filled two mugs, handed one to his father, and returned to his seat. He told Grant of his carefree childhood on the Iowa farm, the camaraderie of its residents, the warmhearted woman he came to know as his Aunt Faith, and his best friend, James, Faith's son, the boy he considered a brother. He spoke fondly of those years, and how the others so warmly embraced his mother and him.

"Tell me about Mike, the one you call your Dad." Grant surmised this was the man Caroline had referred to in her letters as "M."

"The residents of the farm considered themselves a family," Eli explained. "The males took on shared responsibility as fathers to James and me. But Mike—Mike Grainger—was different. He loved Mom from the moment he met her at a truck stop café in Indianapolis, the day after she'd left home." Eli chuckled. "I heard that story for the first time on my twenty-first birthday, too."

The old man listened intently as his son described the near tragedy that disrupted his idyllic life.

"It was in May of '82. I was twelve. The wiring in the old

house hadn't been updated. A random spark ignited an inferno. The place was long gone by the time the fire engines arrived. Everything inside was lost, but thankfully, no one was injured."

Grant raised his mug to his lips with a trembling hand. He shook his head sympathetically. "What did you do after that?"

"We stayed a few weeks on a neighboring farm, then moved to an apartment in Lincoln, Nebraska. It was hard to leave, but there was nothing left. Mike and Mom married a few months later. Mom took a part-time job as a receptionist that fall while Mike enrolled in a master's program in American Lit at the University of Nebraska."

Grant was heartened by Eli's account. It erased years of uncertainty and assuaged, at least marginally, his deep-seated guilt. He urged his son to continue.

Eli took a sip of his coffee. "Mike got his masters in '84. We moved several times over the next few years. He got jobs at Ohio University, Iowa State, and finally Purdue, in West Lafayette, Indiana, where we've lived for the past seven years. Mom found jobs at each of those schools. She's working at one of Purdue's art galleries now."

Grant was particularly pleased by that revelation.

"She loves art," Eli laughed. "She took me on a tour of the gallery not long ago. You should have seen how her face lit up when she showed me their Grant Elliott landscape!"

The old man smiled.

"She loved posing for you," he told his father. "Over time, I think she's described to me each and every painting you did of her. Even the nudes!" Eli laughed heartily. "Last year, she insisted I join her for a trip to Philadelphia to see a painting by Brandon Blake called *End of Time.* There she was, right in the middle of the picture. She was so proud of that! But she'd always say, in the same breath, that your paintings were better, and that she hoped to see them again someday." Eli paused, his memory harkening back to the fire. "She had a drawing you'd done of her the first time she posed for you. It was all creased and worn, but she cherished it. She lost it in the fire. I remember how heartbroken she was, though I didn't realize its significance at the time."

Grant listened intently. He expressed his regret over the concealment of the Caroline Paintings, confessing both his quandary and his shame.

"No need to explain," Eli interrupted. "Mom understands, and so do I."

Grant leaned back in his chair. His son's revelations elicited an unexpected wave of relief, chipping away at years of guilt and misery. "Tell me about yourself. You're, what, twenty-four now? What are you doing with your life?"

"Attended college at Purdue, where Mike teaches American Lit," Eli said. He told him of the graduate degree in architecture he anticipated from UCLA in the spring and the post-grad fellowship he'd been seeking at the University of Virginia. "I was in Charlottesville for an interview," he said. "Figured it was my best chance to swing by to meet you."

"Caroline must be so proud of you. Have you brothers or sisters, or a wife?"

Eli shook his head.

Grant sighed. He leaned forward, lowering his voice conspiratorially. "Does your mother know you're here?"

Again, the young man shook his head. "I wasn't sure how she'd react—or how *you'd* react, for that matter—so I decided it was best to say nothing. Besides, I came here for *me*," he emphasized, softly patting his chest, "to satisfy an itch that's been building for the past three years. I hope you don't mind—"

"Mind? I'm *thrilled* to meet you!" The artist suddenly choked up. "I'm sorry," he said, retrieving his handkerchief to wipe his tears. "I've borne years of conflicting emotions about this. But now," he declared, a smile of satisfaction settling upon his weathered face, "I'm ecstatic for you and for Caroline."

There were many more questions Eli wanted to ask. And others too delicate to address. But his father's strength was waning. Cognizant of his frailty, Eli prepared to take his leave. "It's getting late," he said. "I should leave you to your painting now. Thank you so much for seeing me."

Grant placed his hand on Eli's knee. "Before you go, there's something I want you to know," he said.

"What's that?"

"Those paintings of your mother," he said with a glint in his eye. "I have a plan in place."

Eli gave his father a quizzical look.

"After Becky and I are gone, I want your mother to have all of the paintings in the Caroline Series. I want her to tell her story, if she wishes, and arrange for their exhibition." He rubbed his tired eyes. "She always wanted them to be seen, and indeed they should be."

Eli's jaw dropped as he grasped the import of what his father had just told him. His mother would realize the dream she'd clung to for a quarter of a century: to have "her" paintings revealed to the world. But to own them would be a life-changing event. She never could have imagined that.

"Caroline sacrificed everything when she left Longmire. That was on me," Grant declared, thumping his chest in acknowledgment of his responsibility. "She assumed a heavy burden, but she did so with greater regard for you and me than for herself. It was a courageous act. I've many regrets over what happened then, and what followed, but as I see you sitting before me, I'm heartened beyond words." His voiced quaked. "The gift of the paintings can't replace what she lost, but it can begin to repay my debt to her, as an artist and as an absent father."

Eli pressed his lips together, shaking his head slowly as he processed Grant's revelation. "I don't know what to say."

"I'll need Caroline's address, as well as your own. When Becky and I are gone, my good friend, Brandon Blake, will contact your mom and make the necessary arrangements."

"I can't tell you how—"

"It's the very least I can do, but I'm happy to do it." The artist smiled. "And one more thing, if you've got the time." Eli nodded. "If I can arrange it right now, would you like to see your mother's paintings?"

"Absolutely!" he said. Grant laughed, recalling Caroline's fondness for the very same exclamation.

"I need to warn you—"

"I know," Eli said. "She's not always clothed. I won't stare," he laughed. He rubbed his forehead thoughtfully. "She's still a beautiful lady."

"I wouldn't doubt that for a moment."

While Eli scribbled his and his mother's addresses on a scrap of paper, Grant reached for the telephone on the table beside him, dialing Brandon's number. A brief conversation ensued.

"Mr. Blake would be delighted to meet you and show you the pictures," he reported, offering directions to Brandon's studio.

Grant took hold of the arms of his chair, preparing to rise. Eli reached out to assist. Lunging forward with the aid of his cane, he embraced his son, tears flowing down his dry, brittle cheeks. His son returned the embrace with equal enthusiasm.

The two men shook hands and smiled at each other. It was a bittersweet moment, one for which both men were deeply grateful. It would, each of them recognized, be unlikely to happen again.

Chapter Thirty-Eight

Chicago, Illinois
and Longmire, Virginia
August, 2006 – April, 2010

It had been almost a year since he'd read of Becky Elliott's passing; almost a dozen since he'd met his father, the year before he died, and saw the Caroline Paintings for the first time in the studio of Brandon Blake. Grant Elliott had assured Eli that the paintings would pass to his mother upon the death of his wife. So why hadn't he heard anything?

Eli had cherished his only meeting with his father. And the paintings were a revelation. The rapport between the painter and his muse was unmistakable. Caroline was radiant, almost otherworldly. Her eyes conveyed her adoration for the artist. And despite his uneasiness in so perceiving his mother, he could hardly fail to recognize her allure.

But as much as he appreciated the pictures, they also unnerved him, chronicling as they did the time and place of his own beginnings as the illegitimate offspring of a clandestine union he still couldn't quite comprehend.

Eli had longed to tell his mother about his visit to the dying artist and his promised gift of the paintings. But he harbored misgivings. What if Grant changed his mind? What if the promises were meant merely to send him away happy, to keep him from divulging the existence of the artworks? If the story came out, all bets might be off. His mother might receive nothing. His apprehensions convinced Eli to maintain the secret, even from his mother. Secrets, it seemed, were the currency of his family. But why raise her hopes if he couldn't be certain?

Now, his fears were multiplying. While he'd read of the death of Brandon Blake only a few years following his visit to Longmire, Eli presumed that precautions had been taken, that a plan was "in place," as his father had indicated, to carry out his intentions. But who was responsible for executing the plan? He decided it was time to investigate.

Eli began by contacting the probate office in Longmire. He identified the attorneys for the estates of both Grant and Becky Elliott.

The records revealed that local attorney Maynard Davis had handled the probate of Becky Elliott's estate in 2005. Eli wrote Davis a letter detailing his 1994 conversation with Grant Elliott and his understanding that his mother was the intended beneficiary of what his father had referred to as the Caroline Series. After weeks of waiting came a terse reply. "We've carefully reviewed your inquiry as well as our files on the probate estate of Mrs. Elliott," Davis wrote. "We regret to inform you that we find no evidence of the existence of the artworks to which you refer."

Dissatisfied, Eli phoned the attorney. Every painting in the Elliott estate had been labeled and documented by Becky Elliott, Davis informed him, leaving no room for confusion or error. "The paintings you refer to do not appear in the artist's catalogue raisonné," Davis added, "so I can assure you, with one hundred percent confidence, that they were not part of Mrs. Elliott's estate."

Eli knew his father had hidden the paintings from Becky Elliott, so he wasn't surprised by their absence from her estate. How would Grant have bypassed Becky to arrange for their ultimate disposition to his mother? Eli could conceive of only two possibilities. Either they were placed into a trust or other legal arrangement while Grant was alive, or he'd entrusted them to his friend, Brandon Blake, to deal with informally after his death.

His pursuit of the first hypothesis was doomed from the start. His examination of his father's probate records revealed nothing. All of his artwork passed to his wife. It was recorded in scrupulous detail by title, reference number, and subject matter. Nothing even remotely matched the Caroline Paintings. There were no unusual will provisions; no trust indentures included or referenced in the file.

Eli's inquiry was further complicated by the dissolution of Becker & Becker, the Longmire law firm that had represented his father's estate. The files of the firm had simply vanished. Even worse, both Beckers were deceased. Eli went so far as to obtain copies of the probate inventory of Marty Becker, Jr., in Fort Myers, Florida. It proved just another in a long line of dead ends.

Eli's second hypothesis, that the paintings had been entrusted informally to Brandon Blake, was equally fraught with complications. Blake died *before* Becky Elliott. Absent a trust arrangement, had the Caroline Paintings been in Blake's possession at the time of his death in 1997, Eli reasoned, they could have passed through his estate. A fresh spate of correspondence yielded additional helpings of frustration. While Blake's own paintings had passed to a trust managed by his dealer in New York, his personal effects, including artwork of others, had been sold upon his death, with the proceeds distributed to his beneficiaries. A copy of the estate inventory identified several works, even a few by Grant Elliott, but the descriptions didn't match the paintings of his mother. He recalled noticing the absence of signatures on the Caroline Paintings when he'd viewed them in Blake's studio. Could they have been somehow mistaken for Blake's own work and conveyed to the trustee of Blake's trust?

In the spring of 2007, Eli flew to New York City to meet with Aubrey Chase, proprietor of Chase Gallery, Brandon Blake's longtime dealer. Eli'd been coy in arranging the meeting. He expressed an interest in Blake's art, making no mention of the Caroline Paintings. The last thing he wanted was to alert the dealer to the possibility of a competing claim to works that might reside in his inventory.

Chase Gallery occupied the ground floor of a meticulously restored nineteenth century mercantile building in the heart of New York's historic SoHo district. With an elaborate cast iron facade, the edifice stood proudly in a trendy neighborhood of art galleries, wine bars, and pricey boutiques. Passing through a pair of etched glass doors, Eli entered an expansive, high-ceilinged space with brick walls, polished wood floors, and large, airy windows.

Eli introduced himself to the young woman at the reception desk. The color of her lipstick perfectly matched the candy-red hues pulsating from a series of large, abstract canvases hanging from the walls.

"Mr. Chase will be with you shortly," she informed him. She directed Eli to a wide, backless sofa behind an antique industrial cart repurposed as an oversized coffee table. Copies of *Architectural Digest* were splayed across its surface.

Soon, a stocky, bald-headed gentleman approached. Well into his seventies, he wore a finely tailored dark blue suit with a silk handkerchief elegantly placed in the breast pocket. It, too, was cherry red. "I'm Aubrey Chase," he said, graciously extending his hand. "I understand you have an interest in the work of Brandon Blake."

Eli nodded as Chase beckoned him into the gallery. "We have several of his pieces here in the gallery," he said, "but the larger paintings are in our storage warehouse in Brooklyn. Was there anything in particular you cared to see?"

"Actually, there is," Eli replied. "I saw the artist's retrospective at the Pennsylvania Academy back in 1993," he began, as if reciting lines from a script he'd committed to memory. "*End of Time* has always been my favorite. I greatly admired the model at the heart of the picture. I know it's a long shot, but I wondered if you had any other paintings or drawings featuring that particular model." Eli studied the older man carefully for his reaction.

The dealer chuckled. "You're not alone. That model has never actually been identified, but she's infatuated viewers for decades." He paused as they approached his office, a spacious, art-filled room carved into the rear of the gallery. He directed Eli to an armchair while he slid behind a carved mahogany desk.

"I've represented Brandon, and subsequently his estate, since 1967," Chase said. "I've seen hundreds of his paintings, including a large number of preparatory works that we received after his tragic passing. I'm sorry to say that none of them features that delightful young model."

Eli's shoulders slumped. Had the dealer been harboring any of the Caroline Paintings, whether denominated as Blakes or Elliotts, he'd almost certainly have made them available in response to Eli's inquiry. Thoroughly discouraged, he rose, thanked the dealer for his time, and departed. Yet another blind alley.

Months passed, and then years. In retrospect, Eli was relieved he'd revealed none of this to his mother. She'd have been crushed.

In the spring of 2010, still despondent over his failure to make even marginal headway, Eli took a detour to Longmire after a Washington business trip to pursue one last hunch. On the internet, he'd located Mary Daniels, Marty Becker's former wife. Perhaps she could shed some light on the fate of the Caroline Paintings.

Haggard and pale, Mary Daniels had that look of resignation one might attribute to a woman who'd regretted her choices in life. The deep crevices etched into her weathered face made her appear considerably older than her fifty years. A half-emptied pack of Chesterfields and a red plastic lighter lay on the table beside her as she peered at Eli from the living room couch. She offered him one as she lit up; he politely declined.

Eli asked what she knew of her ex-husband's involvement with Grant Elliott, and whether she knew of the Caroline Paintings.

"Marty bragged about meeting him, doing some work for him," she remembered. Her voice was throaty and raw. "It was sometime in the mid-'90s, I think, about the time our marriage was beginning to unravel." She drew deeply on her cigarette. "He was a heavy drinker, you know," she said, flicking ashes into a ceramic ashtray on the coffee table. "But no, the paintings you describe don't ring any bells." There was nothing in her demeanor to cast doubt upon her veracity.

"Do you know what became of his client files?"

"Hmm," she snorted. "The bastard was one step ahead of his creditors when he abruptly shut down his practice back in '98, I think it was. I'd already divorced him by then. From what I've heard, he filled a U-Haul with all his possessions and took off for Florida. Maybe the files were among them," she said, greedily inhaling her Chesterfield.

"What happened to the clients he left behind?"

"Screwed 'em over, for the most part," she said with little emotion. "Rumored to have absconded with some of their funds as well, but he was probably judgment proof by then anyway. I doubt anything came of it." She extinguished her cigarette in the ashtray.

He didn't have to ask the crucial question. It was clear from what she'd said that it wouldn't have been beyond Marty Becker to misappropriate the Caroline Paintings, assuming they found their way into his possession after Brandon Blake's death. Eli speculated that they, too, may have been among the items Becker had piled into his U-Haul when he absconded to Florida.

"Thanks for your time," Eli said, rising from his chair. "You've been helpful." She smiled meekly and followed him to the door. Before departing, he reached into his wallet for a business card. "Please take this," he said. "If anything else comes to mind regarding the files or the pictures, please give me a call."

Mrs. Daniels nodded, accepting the card as he let himself out. Though his visit spawned theories, it yielded no leads. But it would soon pay off in a way he could never have anticipated.

Chapter Thirty-Nine

A thick frosting of fresh snow blanketed the Shenandoah foothills where Grant had lived and worked for nearly half a century. The evergreens along the ridge behind him glistened in the muted sunlight. He'd painted that scene more times than he could remember. He'd been heartier then, able to withstand the whistling wind and biting cold that rumbled down the mountainsides and into the valleys. He savored the majestic beauty as he hobbled, with the aid of his cane, from the house to his studio along the path shoveled earlier that morning by an enterprising neighborhood youngster. Once a daily routine, the short walk was now an infrequent and challenging adventure.

Grant knew it would be his last winter. He'd had a good run. His artistic legacy was as secure as the secrets he'd take to his grave. But that legacy lacked a critical chapter.

The revelation of the Caroline Paintings would transform his image as an artist, displaying a range of sensuality and emotion not previously seen in his work. It would come at a personal cost, exposing a long-buried and thoroughly indefensible indiscretion. While Caroline and her son—*his* son—had maintained their secret to protect his marriage and reputation, they'd embrace its disclosure when the time was right. Now, thanks to his unforeseen meeting with Eli Grainger, he'd finally located his elusive muse. Armed with names and

Chapter Forty

Longmire, Virginia
June, 2010

nning to feel like a man on a tightrope. While
l evidence of Grant Elliott's authorship of the
ngs was mounting, he still lacked definitive
her hand, he was growing increasingly uneasy
timacy of Marty Becker's ownership of the
by extension, his own. Could he secure the
hout imperiling his claim to the collection?

rry and Max had made substantial progress,
er and fewer leads to pursue. They agreed on
da item for the day: a visit to the former home
Brandon Blake.

arned of the location of Blake's studio from a
Grant Elliott Homestead. Unlike the latter, the
in which Blake had painted his masterworks
preserved as a shrine. It had been relegated to
disused outbuilding on the grounds of a private
upied by a family with a gaggle of children,
the jungle of toys, scooters, bicycles, and other
nile transport and amusement scattered about
yard.

ped the door knocker against the wooden front
was pounding a chicken cutlet. A woman
he sound of screeching children spilled from the
y. Clad in gym clothes and with her hair askew,

addresses, he could eliminate all uncertainty regarding the disposition of the Caroline Paintings, ensuring their long-delayed debut to the art world.

A black Lexus rumbled up the icy driveway and pulled into the clearing by the studio. Marty Becker was surprisingly punctual. Grant had telephoned the attorney, indicating his desire to update the letter of direction that would govern the distribution of the Caroline Paintings. Recognizing the artist's infirmities, Marty had offered to make a house call.

The lawyer barely recognized his client. In the year since their meeting in his office, the artist had deteriorated dramatically. Grant thanked Marty for agreeing to drop by, apologizing for the accumulated infirmities necessitating his visit.

Marty clutched his client by the elbow, helping him into the studio and out of the bulky parka into which he'd bundled himself for the slow, taxing trek from the house. The attorney's finely tailored gray pinstriped suit and silk tie belied the mounting difficulties that plagued his practice and personal life. "What can I do for you, Mr. Elliott?" he asked as they entered the studio.

Grant mentioned the letter of direction he'd furnished to Becker a year earlier, when he and Brandon had signed the trust papers. "I have a married name and current address for the beneficiary now," Grant explained, his voice frail and hoarse, "and an additional recipient to designate if the beneficiary's no longer living."

"I see," Marty said. "We can take care of that right now. I'll help you compose the letter and we can substitute it for the one you provided last winter."

Grant nodded. He shuffled to his worktable, pulled out the chair, and eased himself down. He fidgeted with the scrap of paper on which Eli had written the relevant information, placing it on the table alongside a clean sheet of paper. With Marty providing the guidance and mind-numbing legalese, Grant scratched out his revised letter of direction:

> Reference is made to the Trust Indenture dated March 4, 1994 between the undersigned as trustor and Brandon Blake as original trustee. I hereby provide that the artwork held under the provisions of such Trust shall be disbursed in full, upon the later to occur of my death and the death of my wife, Rebecca Turner Elliott, to Caroline McKellan Grainger, 3247 Davis Boulevard, Lincoln, Nebraska, if she shall then be living and, if she shall not then be living, to our son, Elliott Grant Grainger, 35 West Ontario Street, Chicago, Illinois.

Grant signed the letter and handed it to his attorney. His handwriting, borderline legible in better times, was nearly inscrutable. Marty read it aloud to confirm his client's intentions, tripping over the reference to "our" son.

"Don't you mean *her* son?" he asked.

"I meant what I said," Grant responded, fully aware that he was formally acknowledging Eli as his offspring.

"I see," his attorney said, restraining a snicker.

Marty bit his lip in contemplation. An idea flashed through his increasingly devious mind.

"Your handwriting," he said, pointing to the old man's scribbling, "is virtually impossible to read." Grant shrugged apologetically. "Let me make a suggestion," Marty said with a condescending grin. "Why don't you sign another blank sheet at the bottom, and I'll ask my secretary to type what you've

written right above it.
confusion arising from i

A sharper man with a
the peril inherent in N
accepted the recommen
placed before him.

"We're all set, then,"
sheets into his attaché
pleasure to see you aga
feeble right hand of the el
upon his lips as he exited

Jerry was
circumst
Caroline P
proof. On t
about the
paintings—
attribution

Althoug
there were
their first a
and studio

Max had
docent at t
restored ba
had not bee
the status o
residence
judging fro
forms of ju
the house a

Jerry thu
door like
responded.
open doorw

she was ill-prepared for an encounter with the diminutive Harvard professor and his jumbo Florida sidekick.

After introducing themselves, Max explained the purpose of their visit.

"Blake fans come here all the time," the young woman whined, "wanting to see where the 'Great Man' worked." Her facetious tone betrayed her annoyance. "Stroll the grounds like they own the place," she complained. "Look," she said, blowing an errant strand of hair from her face, "I just don't have time to escort another couple of Brandon Blake groupies around."

"We're sorry to drop by unannounced like this," Max said, "but we're not here to gawp. We're art sleuths trying to resolve a bit of a mystery." He turned his head to Jerry. "Show her the photos, Jerry."

Though harried, she was sufficiently intrigued to gaze at the photographs of Jerry's paintings.

"Do you recognize any of the backgrounds in the photos?"

She took the small stack from Jerry and flipped through them. "Sure," she said quickly, pointing to several in succession. "These were done in the barn over there, and this one," she said, referring to the painting called *Peonies*, "was probably painted on the side of the barn where there used to be a patch of peonies. It had pretty much reverted to nature by the time we moved in, so we plowed it all under and replaced it with sod."

Jerry became animated. "Would you mind if we took a peek inside the barn?"

"Sure," she huffed, "go ahead. The door's open." She brushed the hair from her eyes. "Now if you'll excuse me, I've got a houseful of screaming brats to look after." Her forceful closure of the front door put an emphatic end to the interview.

Jerry scurried toward the barn with Max in tow. "Eureka!" he exclaimed as he stepped inside. They immediately recognized the rough-hewn planks forming the walls that had been so meticulously reproduced by the artist in the background of his interior pictures. "Look at this window," Jerry cried out, waving one of the photos, "it's the same one behind the model in Elliott's reclining nudes!"

"So, now we know where the paintings were created," Max declared triumphantly.

"Yeah," Jerry confirmed. "Elliott could've done 'em here and his wife would've been none the wiser."

Next on the agenda (after a hearty lunch, naturally) was a visit to Mary Daniels, the former wife of Marty Becker. Initially reluctant to meet with them when Max had telephoned, she'd reconsidered when he revealed his Harvard affiliation. "My current husband went to law school there," she said with a hint of familial pride.

"We say *absolutely nothing* to suggest that the paintings were in Becker's possession when he croaked, okay?" Jerry said bluntly as he steered the SUV in the direction of Mary Daniels' house. "With a fucking Harvard lawyer as her current husband, I don't want them getting any ideas about worming in on the action." Max offered a perfunctory nod.

"So, what's my ex got to do with the art you're researching?" Mary asked the pair after she'd admitted them into her living room.

As Max opened his mouth to speak, Jerry interrupted. "We're trying to find some paintings done by Grant Elliott. We think Marty Becker may have done some legal work for the artist's estate but haven't been able to track down the paintings," he fibbed. "Thought you might be able to help."

Mary smiled, shaking her head. "Some guy came in here not two months ago asking the same questions. Something about some paintings of a young woman." She reached for the pack of Chesterfields resting on the side table, withdrew a cigarette, and lit up. "Damn interesting coincidence, wouldn't you say?"

Jerry and Max looked at each other. Jerry was turning pale. "Who was he?" he blurted out.

"Some big, handsome fella from the Midwest. Chicago, I think he said." She inhaled deeply before expelling a plume of smoke into the air. "Wait a minute. He left me his card." She deposited her cigarette in the ashtray and rose from the sofa. "Now where would I have put it?"

"Who the hell else would be sniffing around about this?" Jerry whispered to Max while Mary riffled through scraps of paper filling the pigeonholes of an old fall-front secretary in the back of the living room.

"I know I put it somewhere," she muttered. "Ah! Here it is!" Mary walked toward Max but Jerry lunged forward to intercept the card.

"Who the hell is Elliott G. Grainger, architect?"

"I guess you'd have to ask him," Mary said. "He never explained his interest in the paintings he was inquiring about," she said, stealing another puff, "and I didn't ask."

While Jerry smoldered, Max returned to the script. "Did your ex-husband have a relationship with either Grant Elliott or Brandon Blake?"

"His father was the attorney for the Elliotts for many years. Marty took over when his father died." She took one last puff before grinding the Chesterfield into the ashtray. "Some of it's coming back now. I remember him telling me he met with the two artists sometime in the mid-'90s, a few years before we divorced and he fled to Florida."

"*Fled* to Florida?" Jerry asked.

"Yeah. He'd made a mess of things, started drinking. I wouldn't have it, so I kicked him out. Divorced shortly after. Sky was falling in on him so he took a hike and never came back. Killed himself in a drunk driving accident down in Fort Myers maybe four years ago."

Max had surveyed the walls of the house for artwork when they'd come in. It was an occupational habit. You never knew where or when you'd make an important discovery. But there was little here but dusky old landscapes. Nothing to reflect a taste for the work of Grant Elliott. "Did your husband collect any of the work of either artist?"

Mary laughed before launching into a series of deep, raspy coughs. "I'm sorry," she said. "Marty wouldn't know a Grant Elliott from a Velvet Elvis."

"Thank you, Mrs. Daniels." Max said.

"Do you need this back," Jerry asked, waving the business card in his right hand.

"Nah, no reason to keep it, I guess. Go ahead and take it."

Jerry feigned a smile as they got up to leave.

Max and Jerry had their first major disagreement over dinner in the hotel that evening.

"You don't find it curious that the name on the card is *Elliott* Grainger? Or that the middle initial is G?" Max asked.

"So what?" Jerry shot back. "Elliott's a common name. Probably just a coincidence. Why read anything more into it?"

"Look, Jerry. I know what you're thinking. You can't bury your head in the sand. We need to understand this Grainger fellow's connection to the paintings. It could be the last piece of the puzzle."

"Yeah. It could also cost me my fucking paintings!"

"They're not yours to sell if they don't legitimately belong to you," Max insisted as Jerry huffed. "They're still unsigned, the attribution remains purely circumstantial, and you can't sell them as Elliotts without someone raising the same questions we've been raising."

Jerry ferociously devoured a rib eye steak, stewing along with every bite. He knew that Max was right. But he hadn't come this far to walk away empty-handed. And he wasn't looking to invite trouble.

"Okay, Jerry, look," Max said. "Why don't *I* call him. I can establish my art world credentials and tell him I'm tracking down paintings for a book. I can say I spoke to Mary Daniels in an effort to find paintings from Grant's estate and that she mentioned his visit. I'll ask him if he has any knowledge of the Caroline Paintings. We'll see what he volunteers, what his interest or angle might be."

"And what are you gonna say, Professor Holier-Than-Thou, if he asks if you know where they are?" Jerry was growing angrier.

"I can tell him I'm pursuing leads and could use his help. How's that?"

Jerry slammed his fork on the table. "Goddammit, Max! I don't fucking know *what* to do."

"Here's my suggestion: go back home and turn all those Marty Becker files in your garage inside out. See if there's an answer lurking somewhere among them."

Jerry let out a deep sigh. "Fine! I'll leave in the morning. What're *you* gonna do?"

"I'll fly back to Boston. I'll call Grainger. I'll let you know what he says and we'll plan our next move from there."

Jerry took out his frustrations on dessert.

Chapter Forty-One

Cambridge, Massachusetts
June, 2010

On the plane back to Boston, Max jotted down some notes. Questions he'd planned to ask Elliott Grainger. He'd also made a list of things *not* to say, in deference to Jerry.

While ownership of the Caroline Paintings meant little to Max, it meant everything to Jerry. Max owed his new friend a modicum of allegiance. Without his super-sized, sleuthing sidekick, he'd never have known of the paintings, the revelation of which could shake the foundations of the art world. In his daydreams, Max imagined himself introducing the Caroline Paintings to a captivated national audience; arranging an earth-shattering, multi-venue exhibition; penning a best-selling catalogue; appearing on The Tonight Show; hosting his own art-detective reality series. His fantasies were boundless.

Max put off making the call. He hoped Jerry would discover something among the files in his garage either supporting or negating his ownership of the paintings. Either way, he preferred to know where he stood before dealing with Elliott Grainger.

Max telephoned Jerry, seeking a progress report. But Jerry, too, was procrastinating, uneasy about upending his garage at the risk of discovering what he'd rather not find. "Haven't gotten to it yet," Jerry sniveled. "Haven't even finished unpacking my goddamn suitcase."

No longer able to rein in his curiosity—or his elaborate

fantasies—Max decided to proceed with his call to Elliott Grainger. A frantic search for the architect's business card ended with its discovery beneath a pile of books on the edge of his debris-laden dining room table. He punched the office number into his cell phone and asked for Elliott Grainger.

"He's tied up," a harried female voice responded. A stupid phrase, Max had always maintained, conjuring images of a hog-tied victim squirming to break free. The woman inquired curtly as to his identity and the purpose of his call.

"Max Winter, Professor Emeritus at Harvard," he said with assurance. "I'm doing research on the painter Grant Elliott." When she asked him to be more specific, he declined, requesting that she pass on the message as is.

"Fine," she sniffed, and hung up.

Operating at the boundaries of his kitchen competency, Max fired up the stovetop and plopped a slab of salmon into a pan. He poured himself a glass of red wine. As he lowered himself into his favorite chair, the phone rang. In a low, resonant voice, the caller identified himself as Elliott Grainger.

Grainger was reserved, cautious; wary, Max thought, of revealing his hand. Max glanced at his notes. "I'm doing some research on Grant Elliott," he began, citing his Harvard affiliation and ticking off his credentials. His introduction met with silence. "Uh . . . I'm trying to track down some paintings—"

"I'm an architect, Mr. Winter, not a collector. Why call me?"

Eli's tone was brusque. He was playing it coy, Max recognized. He'd have to reveal more.

"I had occasion recently to speak with a Mrs. Mary Daniels in Longmire, Virginia," Max said. He paused, hoping the reference would provoke a response. It didn't, so he plodded on. "She said you'd met with her recently about a similar subject," he explained, "so I thought I'd contact you to see if you might have some information relevant to my research."

Eli sighed audibly. While buoyed at the thought of a possible break in his ill-fated search for the Caroline Paintings, he couldn't help but be suspicious. Were they both on the same trail? Were they competitors or potential allies? Should he share information or withhold it? "What, precisely, are you looking for," he asked, "and why do you think I can help?"

Max fiddled with his notes briefly, then cast them into the general chaos of his living room floor. Might as well get to the point, he concluded. "I have reason to believe that Elliott produced some paintings of a young woman about forty years ago that remain hidden and unrecorded."

"I've seen the paintings," Eli said. "They're of my mother." Bingo! Max had found the missing link. And then the question Max had hoped to avoid: "Do you know where they are?"

Though he'd have preferred to answer the question directly, he declined to do so, in deference to Jerry. "I do," Max replied, "but I'm not at liberty to say."

The conversation slipped into uneasy silence until, unable to suppress his curiosity, Max blurted out: "Are you related to Grant Elliott?"

A brief silence, and then: "I'm not at liberty to say." Touché.

Neither party knew how to end the conversation. Max wanted desperately to gather all of the information he could about the Caroline Paintings. He wanted to interview Elliott Grainger and, if she were still alive, Caroline herself. But he realized he'd have difficulty in obtaining their cooperation if he continued to withhold information. Eli, on the other hand, wanted to stake his mother's claim to the art works, though he was wary of doing so prematurely.

Their awkward silence continued. Finally, Max broke the impasse. "I trust we'll speak again," he said.

"I'm sure we will," Eli replied icily.

As they hung up, each felt a flutter of excitement—and a gnawing sense of disquiet. Max's anxiety was exacerbated by the smoke emanating from the kitchen. He'd neglected the fish in the frying pan. Blackened salmon, anyone?

Chapter Forty-Two

Fort Myers, Florida
June, 2010

Jerry sat in a beach chair in the middle of his garage, staring at the boxes. Part of him wished he'd followed his initial impulse and chucked them all into the dumpster at KeepSafe Storage when he had the chance. Had he done so, he wouldn't be facing the moral and ethical dilemmas he faced right now.

Max had already regaled him with an account of his stiff but revealing conversation with Elliott Grainger. While it ended ambiguously, it confirmed what Jerry had hoped: that the Caroline Paintings were indeed the work of Grant Elliott.

As he poised for another crack at the files of Marty Becker, he considered the possible outcomes. Most likely, he'd find nothing even remotely relevant to the paintings. That result would leave him pretty much where he was now—the owner of a cache of artwork of unsettled, if dubious, provenance. At least it would ease his conscience. Unless someone could advance a superior claim to the art, he'd seek Max's blessing and, at the appropriate time, reap his windfall on the auction circuit. But the second possibility haunted him. What if he found incriminating evidence branding Marty Becker a thief? Would Jerry fess up and play the good Boy Scout? Or would he hunker down and destroy the offending proof? It troubled him to doubt his intentions when that moment of truth arrived—*if* it arrived. But whatever the result, one thing was for certain: there'd be room again in his garage for his beloved Chevy Blazer.

Though he'd sampled the files two months earlier, he hadn't known then what he was looking for. But he did now: anything connecting Marty Becker with Grant Elliott, Brandon Blake, or the Caroline Paintings. Finished with his procrastination, he dragged the first box of files to his chair, stopped at the mini-fridge for a Bud, yanked open the pop-top, and sat down to begin the tedious process.

Jerry awoke with a start. Where the hell was he? The room was pitch black. It took him several moments to realize that he'd dozed off in the beach chair in the middle of his garage. "Fuck me," he grunted, lifting himself from the chair, stumbling over a box of files as he fumbled for the light switch. Empty beer cans tinkled as they rolled across the floor. He flipped on the light and checked his watch. It was ten o'clock, twelve hours since he'd begun the ordeal of riffling through the files. Taking stock, he recognized he'd made it through a half-dozen boxes and a six-pack of Bud before the latter prevailed. The hours spent sifting through reams of paper produced nary a shred of anything relevant, which, of course, didn't entirely disappoint him.

What he did find among the flotsam and jetsam was hardly flattering to the already tarnished reputation of Marty Becker, Jr. Evidence of his negligence and incompetence was legion. One letter, written by an irate client, berated him for his failure to appear on the client's behalf at a court hearing. Another demanded the return of escrow funds that Marty had apparently held to facilitate a real estate transaction. "I've called you every day for the past two weeks," the client groused, threatening to report Marty to the state bar enforcement officials. There were letters from expert witnesses demanding payment for services rendered and from clients refusing payment for services Marty'd failed to render. One file contained a trio of empty whiskey nip bottles attesting to the source of Marty's woes.

Mustering his last ounce of strength, Jerry grabbed a handcart from its hook on the garage wall. One at a time, he hauled each of those first six boxes to the curb for recycling. He—and his Blazer—were halfway home.

Chapter Forty-Three

West Lafayette, Indiana
June, 2010

It was a two-and-a-half-hour drive from Chicago to West Lafayette. Eli's visit to his parents, on the weekend following his telephone call with Max Winter, was a welcome surprise. He'd called to say he was coming, but wouldn't say why.

Eli convened an impromptu family meeting in the living room. He sat in the same chair he'd occupied almost twenty years earlier, when he'd learned of his true father's identity. He'd been apprehensive that day, sensing that something significant was afoot. This time it was Caroline and Mike who bristled with anxiety.

"What is it that you couldn't discuss on the phone?" Mike asked, his eyes wide with concern.

He told them of his phone conversation with Max Winter. "He's an art professor from Harvard," Eli explained. He glanced at his mother. "Said he was tracking down information about the Grant Elliott paintings you posed for forty years ago." He smiled knowingly. "They're still out there, Mom," he declared, "and the professor knows where they are!"

Caroline gasped, her hands covering her mouth. "Really?" she squealed, shrugging off disbelief. She lowered her hands, revealing a wistful smile. Eli's mention of the paintings transported her to a time and place she'd thought little about for years. She'd resigned herself to the likelihood that the works would never emerge. Caroline assumed that the paintings had been destroyed, either because Becky Elliott found out, or to prevent her from discovering them. She couldn't have been more astonished to hear Eli report that the works still existed, and that he'd spoken to someone who knew where they were.

And if that weren't enough of a surprise, Eli's subsequent revelation, that he'd visited his father shortly before his death and had actually *seen* the paintings in Brandon Blake's studio, was even more of a shock.

"My God!" Caroline exclaimed. "I'm *naked* in some of those paintings!"

"You were beautiful, Mom," he smiled. "You still are!" It was a nice thing to tell your Mom, she thought, even if it was no longer the truth.

"Why didn't you tell us this years ago?" Mike asked him pointedly.

"I didn't know how either of you would react. And besides, Mom, telling you how feeble he looked wouldn't have pleased you.

"And there's another reason," Eli continued. "Something he told me during that visit. A promise he made that I was hesitant to believe." He rubbed his fingers across his chin. "A promise that hasn't been kept."

The drama was killing them. "Tell us, already!" Mike implored him.

Eli disclosed Grant's commitment to deliver the paintings to Caroline upon Becky Elliott's death. "I have no evidence of the promise," Eli conceded. "I was too awed—and maybe too naïve—to ask him for anything in writing."

Caroline's heartbeat accelerated. "I can hardly believe this," she said. "I hadn't communicated with him for decades. Why would he do something like that?"

"He was remorseful. Felt he'd let you down. Uprooted you. And still you protected him. Isn't that reason enough?"

"Still . . ."

Eli reached out for his mother's hand. "That's why I didn't tell you about it earlier. It seemed too good to be true. I didn't want to raise your hopes and see them dashed." He sat back, releasing his mother's hand. "When Becky Elliott died in 2005, I expected that you or I would hear from someone. But it didn't happen. Later, I began to ask questions." Eli told them of his fruitless inquiries, the troubling information he'd gleaned about the attorney Marty Becker, and his visit to Becker's ex-wife. "Everything led to a dead end," he said, "until this call, out of the blue, from Max Winter."

"He wouldn't tell you where the paintings are?" she asked.

"No. But he knows, I'm sure of it. He's covering for someone. Whether that person owns the paintings legitimately is not clear."

Mike listened to the conversation thoughtfully. "How can you be sure the old man wasn't just making an idle promise?"

"He wouldn't do that," Caroline protested.

"He was failing," Mike reminded them. "Maybe he never got around to it."

"He told me that he had a plan in place," Eli recalled.

"Then he probably did," Caroline said.

Mike looked to Eli. "Where'd you leave things with the professor?"

"We said we'd be in touch."

"What do you suggest we do?"

Eli leaned back in his chair. He'd obviously considered the matter at some length. "I suspect the professor's involved in some effort to unveil the paintings publicly. He'll seek your cooperation," he said, gesturing at his mother. "I need to know how you feel about that. You'd be identified as Elliott's model and—"

"And his paramour," Mike interjected.

"And he'd also be revealed as your father, Eli," Caroline added. She glanced at her husband. "And you, Mike, as the *un-father*." She couldn't help but giggle, although it was no laughing matter. By tacit agreement, the secret of Eli's paternity had remained within that room.

"I think the professor already figured that part out," Eli said. "He asked if I was related to Grant Elliott."

"What did you tell him?" Caroline asked.

"I neither admitted nor denied it."

"Should've been a lawyer," Mike chuckled.

"Speaking of which," Eli said, "I think we should consult one to see if there's a way to pursue a claim."

Caroline fidgeted. "This is too much, too fast." She stood up and strolled to the window, opening the blinds. "Let's let this sink in a while before we reach any conclusions. This could have a significant impact on all of us."

"Whether we cooperate or not," Eli reminded them.

For the rest of the day, Caroline thought of nothing else. Lying in bed that night, she recalled her precocious desire to serve as Elliott's muse. She remembered the modeling sessions, the heady thrill of inspiring a legendary artist. How young and foolish she'd been to seduce him! And how reckless he'd been to respond! She'd loved him, in a way she could never fully articulate. He'd been there for her when her parents weren't. She'd abandoned her life in Longmire partly to protect him, but the life she'd found was far superior to the life she'd forsaken. She was happy.

Once, she dreamt of the day that the world would finally see the Caroline Paintings. She'd imagined reveling in the glow of her role as the ultimate muse. She no longer craved that attention. She was fifty-eight now, a shadow of the physical specimen she'd been at sixteen. She'd aged well, people said, but the decades had taken their toll. Would she embarrass herself in the eyes of the public, her friends, and her family?

As she thrashed beneath the covers, she realized that it really didn't matter what she thought. The story would be too big—and too titillating—to control. The facts would come out. She'd never been ashamed of what she'd done. Why fear the truth now?

Chapter Forty-Four

Fort Myers, Florida
June, 2010

This was it, Jerry swore to himself. The last fucking day he'd glue himself to that old beach chair sifting through cartons of files. There were six boxes left. By the end of the day, they'd be sitting on the curb and his Blazer would be restored to its place of honor in his garage.

If Grant Elliott was a master of the art of painting, Jerry was a master of the art of procrastination. To avoid resuming his examination of the files, he ate a slow breakfast (three bowls of cereal instead of the usual two), wiped down the kitchen counter, cleaned out the refrigerator (for the first time in years), ran a wash, exercised (five sit-ups, a half-dozen push-ups, and a squat that ended badly), read the newspaper (the whole thing, not just the sports section), ran the dryer, and made his bed (for the first time since his wife passed away three years ago). When he'd run out of excuses and diversions, he prepared a second pot of coffee, filled the thermos, grabbed his old transistor radio (a relic from the Seventies), and trudged to the garage.

Jerry flipped on the local oldies station, turned up the volume, and plunged into the first box of files. It was late afternoon when he opened the last. Though bored senseless, he took comfort from his failure to find anything damaging to his cause. His search yielded more of the same—miscellaneous legal files, letters from angry clients, past-due creditors' notices, another couple of nips of whiskey, even a half-empty bottle of Ballantine's Scotch (a bit too raunchy to salvage).

He'd made it halfway through the final box when he noticed something odd: a lone red file lying flat across the bottom of the carton. The remaining files had been vertically arranged above it. Had it slipped through or been intentionally hidden? His curiosity piqued, he yanked it out from beneath the others. There was no identifying label. He opened the file. Inside he found an unmarked, nine-by-twelve manila envelope and a business envelope with the words "Letter of Direction" printed neatly across the front.

He opened the manila envelope first. Inside he found a document bearing a date of March 4, 1994 with the title "Trust Indenture." He'd encountered dozens of similar instruments buried within the rubble of Becker's career. He was poised to discard it until he spied the two names cited in capital letters in the opening paragraph: GRANT ELLIOTT and BRANDON BLAKE.

Jerry repaired to the mini-fridge for a beer to help him focus. He opened the can, took a gulp, and stared at the document with trepidation. He began to read. Amid the cascade of whereases and wherefores peppering the first page was a reference to "certain items of artwork, hereinafter referred to as 'The Cornelia Paintings,' as set forth on Schedule A attached hereto." Holding his breath, he flipped to the end of the document. There it was: "Schedule A—Artworks Subject to Trust." It was two pages long. He ran his finger slowly down the initial page. Twelve paintings numbered consecutively, each identified as tempera on canvas, with titles and dimensions. He glanced quickly at the titles: *Grief, Peonies, Lady Liberty, Reading, Soon,* and seven others. His heart skipped a beat. Everything matched. On the second page was a reference to "Sixty-four (64) drawings and watercolors constituting studies for the aforementioned paintings, Nos. 1-12."

Jerry's forehead erupted in puddles of perspiration. His hands trembled as he forced himself to read the entire document. Sandwiched between incomprehensible phrases of legal gobbledygook was a passage whose import was terrifyingly clear:

> *As soon as practicable following the later to occur of the decease of Grant Elliott and Rebecca Elliott, the artworks subject to this Trust shall be distributed by the Trustee to the person(s) and/or institution(s) set forth in a letter of direction executed by the Grantor and delivered to the Trustee making reference to this Trust Indenture.*

Flipping back to the first page, he confirmed that Grant Elliott was the "Grantor" and Brandon Blake the "Trustee." Several pages ahead was a paragraph captioned "Successor Trustee." It provided that "upon the death or resignation of the original Trustee, Martin S. Becker, Jr., if he shall then be living, shall become the successor Trustee."

Everything was suddenly clear as day. Marty Becker was in possession of the Caroline Paintings legitimately, as the successor trustee to Brandon Blake. It meant he didn't steal them—or did it?

Jerry guzzled the balance of his Budweiser. He slipped back inside his condo. On the desk in the bedroom was a file containing the probate records for Marty Becker that he'd copied at the Justice Center in May. He opened the file and noted the date of Becker's death: March 11, 2006. He opened his computer and googled Rebecca Elliott's date of death: September 11, 2005. Six months had elapsed and Marty still had the paintings. Did he know of her death? If so, what was he waiting for?

Returning to the garage, he picked up the smaller white envelope marked "Letter of Direction." Shaking, he opened it. Inside were two one-page documents. One was handwritten, the other typed. Both were signed illegibly. One could shatter his dreams; the other revive them.

He studied the one in longhand first. The words were nearly indecipherable. Line by line, he struggled to decode the shaky script. "I hereby provide that the artwork . . . shall be disbursed in full . . . to Caroline McKellan Grainger . . . if she shall then be living and, if she shall not then be living, to our son, Elliott Grant Grainger."

The document was dated February 12, 1995. In context, the signature could only be Grant Elliott's. "Fuck me," he moaned.

He turned his attention to the second document, which bore the same signature. Captioned "Bill of Sale," it was dated April 20, 1995, two months *after* the first letter and, if his memory was correct, just a month before the artist's death. Like a sailboat buoyed by a fresh gust of wind, his demeanor suddenly brightened.

"For good and valuable consideration," the instrument recited, "the receipt and sufficiency of which is hereby acknowledged, the undersigned, Grant Elliott, does hereby sell and convey to Martin S. Becker, Jr., the artworks described on Schedule A hereto." The attached Schedule A was a comprehensive list of the Caroline Paintings. It was the same Schedule A attached to the Trust Indenture. What did it mean? Jerry massaged his temples vigorously. Did Becker *buy* the Caroline Paintings? In exchange for . . . what? What the hell was "good and valuable consideration"?

Jerry put down the file. The beach chair groaned as he

arose. He walked past the mini-fridge. Another beer wasn't the answer. He didn't know whether to mourn or celebrate. Re-entering the condo, he grabbed a glass from the kitchen and opened the liquor cabinet in the dining room. Scotch. Straight. He stepped into the living room and sat down. He took a long swig and began to think.

Chapter Forty-Five

Cambridge, Massachusetts
and
Chicago, Illinois
June, 2010

Max sat at his dining room table surrounded by open books. An indefatigable researcher, he relished the prospect of compiling the definitive catalogue of the Caroline Paintings. "Secret Muse: Elliott Grant and the Caroline Paintings" he'd call it, and it would accompany a national touring exhibition by the same name. A brilliant analytical essay by Max Winter would garner him accolades, make him the toast of the art world.

Spread before him was Becky Elliott's catalogue raisonné and the exhibition catalogue for Brandon Blake's retrospective at the Pennsylvania Academy. Max scribbled notes onto a yellow legal pad while a Beethoven violin concerto trilled in the background.

Two of the principal mysteries surrounding the Caroline Paintings had been solved. Grant Elliott was clearly the artist and Caroline McKellan Grainger the model. What remained was to unravel the circumstances of their execution and concealment—a narrative that was potentially captivating and salacious—and to orchestrate their introduction to the art world.

But while he'd plotted it all out in his imagination, reality lagged behind. To proceed, Max needed the cooperation and support of all of the relevant parties: Jerry, Elliott Grainger, and most importantly, Caroline McKellan Grainger, if she were still living.

Over the past three days, Max had telephoned Jerry at least a half-dozen times. By now, he'd have certainly completed his review of the Becker files. Each call was rerouted to his answering machine. Max left messages, sent emails. Still, no response. Was Jerry avoiding him, and if so, why? Had he found something damning or had he suddenly gone rogue? By the fourth day, frustrated and itching to move forward, Max left one last message, advising Jerry of his plans to arrange a meeting with Elliott Grainger and (he hoped) Caroline McKellan Grainger, to begin to unearth the story behind the paintings. He urged Jerry to participate. "The train's about to leave the station," Max declared, "where the hell *are* you?"

Eli sat at a table in the back corner of The Speakeasy, an upscale Chicago bar in a trendy underground space that had housed a thriving speakeasy during Prohibition. He'd arrived early, nearly finishing his bourbon and water by the time Rachel strolled in.

"Sorry, Eli. Conference call ran over," she said, panting, embracing Eli with the restrained warmth befitting a former fiancé. "Let me buy you another while I try to catch up." She signaled a waiter, ordering herself a wine cocktail and another bourbon for him.

She looked good, Eli thought, her dark eyes gleaming beneath precisely clipped bangs. But she still had that harried look accompanying that 24/7 drive, the all-out ambition that made her a great lawyer but a dubious choice for a mate. "To what do I owe the invitation?" she asked.

"Free legal advice," he said presumptuously, "and an excuse to touch base."

Rachel smiled. Their engagement had dragged on for years before she'd agreed to a wedding date—with a qualification: she didn't want kids. She'd never said never before, but she did then. He wasn't surprised. Her devotion to her practice left little room for family. Their subsequent break-up was amiable and they'd remained friends—and at times more than friends. Deep down, he knew he still loved her.

It had been six months since she'd last seen him. She asked how he'd been. "Got a steady?" she asked with a grin.

"Nope," he admitted. "You?"

"No time," she said. He'd figured as much.

She rattled off courtroom achievements while he responded in kind, citing a bevy of architectural commissions that had recently come his way. It all felt hollow to him.

"So, what kind of trouble have you gotten yourself into?" she asked, assuming her litigator's mien.

"It has to do with my mother," he began. He shared the whole story, from his mother's fateful reign as Grant Elliott's muse through his meeting with the artist in 1994. He told her about Elliott's unfulfilled promise, his efforts to locate the paintings, and his suspicions about Marty Becker. And he described his telephone conversation with Harvard Professor Max Winter. Eli revealed everything except the most explosive fact: Grant Elliott's paternity. For now, at least, he preferred to keep that to himself, more for his parents' sake than his own.

Rachel listened intently, thoroughly intrigued. "Your mother's beautiful," she said, "but who'd've guessed . . . posing for someone like *Grant Elliott* . . . and at *sixteen*!" She shook her head. "You never told me any of this. I was your fiancée, Eli."

"I knew nothing of this myself until I turned twenty-one. My mother had her reasons for maintaining her secret. She expected I'd do the same, and I've honored her wishes."

"It won't stay secret if the paintings are revealed."

"She's prepared for that."

"And you've no clue who has them?"

"No, but the professor obviously knows."

"How can I help?" Rachel asked.

Eli sipped his bourbon. "How can we pursue a claim for the art on behalf of my mother?"

Rachel polished off her cocktail and signaled the waiter for a refill. "From what you've told me, you have nothing more than an oral promise. The promisor is deceased and you've got no witnesses. Did you tell anyone about this at the time?"

"No."

"Not even your mother?" she asked incredulously.

"I didn't want to inflate her hopes in case it never materialized."

"She knows now?"

"Yes. This could all become suddenly public. I didn't want her to be blindsided."

"You've searched for documentation?"

"Becker's law firm dissolved. There are no files, so far as I know."

Rachel sipped thoughtfully at her second wine cocktail. "I think we need to know the basis for this other party's claim of ownership before devising a strategy," she said. "But I'm not gonna kid you, Eli, there's not a lot to work with here."

"I thought as much," he said, frowning.

"Have you considered what your next step might be?"

Eli nodded. "The professor is legitimate and well-respected, at least from what I've gathered online," he said. "His interest, I think, is primarily academic." He selected an olive from the small plate the waiter had delivered with the last round of drinks. "I'm sure he'll want to talk to my mother about the paintings," he said, massaging the olive between his thumb and forefinger. "My thought is to insist on full disclosure on his end before offering cooperation on ours."

Rachel puckered her lips as she thought, an endearing habit he'd witnessed on countless occasions in the past. "That would seem your best leverage at the moment," she acknowledged. "And for now, until you know more, I'd withhold any suggestion that you might pursue a claim of ownership."

"Makes sense," he said, flipping the olive into his mouth.

"You'll let me know what happens next?"

He flashed a suggestive smile, letting the bourbon take charge. "I know what *I'd* like to see happen next."

His message was loud and clear. Rachel's wide grin telegraphed her concurrence. They were evidently still exes with benefits. "Your place or mine?"

"Yours is closer," he said with a smile.

Chapter Forty-Six

Fort Myers, Florida
June, 2010

The red light flickered on the answering machine on the kitchen counter. Another message from Max, Jerry feared. Must have called a half-dozen times. Jerry'd ignored them all. "Give it a rest!" he groused at the machine. He had to think.

What he'd found in that little red folder had changed everything. Or nothing. It was up to him to decide. How could he reconcile the artist's letter of direction with the bill of sale just two months later? Did the latter overrule the former, effectively negating the Trust? On the face of it, the answer was yes. Or was it?

Jerry paced the kitchen floor. He opened and closed the refrigerator door three times. Something didn't add up— something beyond the remarkable fact that he failed to grab something to eat. Why on earth, Jerry puzzled, would Grant Elliott sell a cache of paintings to his lawyer, especially paintings as sentimentally meaningful at the Caroline Paintings? How could Becker have afforded them? He died nearly penniless. And why would Becker have sought them? Max and Jerry had already confirmed that he wasn't a collector. Was it an investment? A settlement for money Grant owed Becker for legal or other services ("good and valuable consideration")? And why would Grant sell *those* particular paintings? Could it have been *because* they were secret?

Jerry's mind turned somersaults. Maybe it *wasn't* a straight economic transaction. What if Marty Becker was *blackmailing* Grant Elliott, threatening to reveal the existence of the paintings to Mrs. Elliott? Maybe the bill of sale was a forgery. Jerry was no handwriting expert, but it looked to him that if the first signature was legitimate (and why wouldn't it be?), then the second signature was also. Did Becker trick the old man into signing the latter document? Or sign it in blank, perhaps, like a blank check for Marty to fill in? Had he meant to *steal* the paintings? And if the bill of sale superseded the letter of direction, why did Marty retain them both?

Back to the refrigerator, this time for a beer. The more Jerry ruminated over the multitude of possible explanations, the more flummoxed he became. His head began to pound. He popped the top and took a long gulp.

And then he had an epiphany. He remembered Max's parting words over dinner on their last night in Longmire. "Go back home and turn all those Marty Becker files in your garage inside out," he'd charged Jerry. "See if there's an answer lurking somewhere among them." In search of Max's singular "answer," he'd discovered a slew of them. Even if Jerry had his suspicions, how could he possibly know, much less prove, which of the competing explanations constituted the truth? No one alive actually *knew* what had happened, so why shouldn't *he* control the narrative?

Jerry raided the pantry cabinet, emerging with a half-consumed bag of Cheetos. He sat at the kitchen table and began to snack. Crunching Cheetos became the soundtrack to his contemplation.

In the end, Jerry concluded, it really didn't matter what Marty Becker did or intended to do. The Trust Indenture, the letter of direction, and the bill of sale were all in Jerry's possession, along with the Caroline Paintings. He'd bought the

Caroline Paintings fair and square. He'd paid for them. He'd done his research. He'd traveled to Miami, Cambridge, and Longmire to establish their origin, authenticity, and value. He *deserved* them.

Jerry polished off the Cheetos and drained what remained of his beer. Taking what he'd found at face value, *he* was the owner of the Caroline Paintings. To conclude otherwise would be to dismiss the bill of sale as a forgery, a fraud on the artist, or both. In the absence of irrefutable evidence, he was unwilling to do that.

Jerry pressed the button on the answering machine. He checked the last call. "I plan to arrange a meeting with Elliott Grainger and his mother, if she's still in the picture, to uncover the story behind the paintings," Max had said in his message. "The train's about to leave the station, where the hell *are* you?"

Jerry lifted the receiver and dialed Max's number. He was glad to go directly to voicemail. "Set up the meeting," he said. "Tell me where and when. I'll be there."

Chapter Forty-Seven

Cambridge, Massachusetts
July, 2010

Max played Jerry's message. A dozen words, but nary an update or explanation. Had Jerry found anything in Becker's files? Max called again to find out. This time, Jerry's answering machine was full. "Damn him!" Max growled, slamming the receiver into its cradle.

To Max, Jerry's obstinacy was a growing concern. The planets had begun to align: the paintings were now firmly attributable to Elliott Grant, his muse had been identified, and Max was homing in on a meeting with the man he surmised was their son. But what had become of the guy with the pictures? Though Max had grown fond of the big galoot, Jerry had suddenly become a wild card, a variable Max couldn't control. Could he rely on his friend to cooperate in the research, planning, and implementation of the rollout of the Caroline Paintings? Or would Jerry sabotage Max's efforts with a stubborn defense of his dominion over the artworks? The answers, Max suspected, would soon be revealed.

Max telephoned Eli Grainger. While continuing to withhold Jerry's identity, he proposed they convene at the professor's Cambridge apartment on the following Thursday afternoon.

Eli was miffed by the professor's persistent opacity. But he calculated that more could be accomplished by attending the meeting than by withholding cooperation. He'd finally learn who possessed the paintings and how they'd been obtained.

Armed with that information, he and Rachel could formulate a suitable plan of action. "We'll attend," Eli said tersely, and with a studied hint of reluctance.

Max heard only the plural pronoun. "*We* meaning you . . . and your *mother*?" The professor was fairly salivating. Until now, he'd yet to establish that Caroline was even alive.

"Yes," Eli confirmed.

Max let out an inelegant whoop of relief. "That's fantastic!" he gushed. Nothing, he realized, would contribute more to the glitz and glamour of the debut of the Caroline Paintings than the first-person account of the elusive Caroline herself!

Jerry answered the phone when Max called to inform him of the upcoming meeting. Max pounced on him. "Why don't you return my calls?" he grumbled. "I called you at least four times!"

"Six," Jerry replied.

"Okay, then, six!" His frustration was palpable. "What on earth is going on, Jerry?"

"Been busy."

"What, washing your hair?"

Jerry chortled. "I'm a nut about personal hygiene."

Max groaned, then got to the point. "I thought you were gonna review those files in your garage."

"Finished that."

"Found nothing, I assume?"

"Not exactly."

Max asked him to explain. Jerry told him about the little red file. He revealed the contents of the Trust, the letter of direction, and the bill of sale. He offered no analyses, arguments, or apologies. While he laid out the facts dispassionately, he was clear about his conclusion. "So," he said, "the bill of sale would seem to seal the deal."

Max listened patiently and then exploded. "Jesus Christ, Jerry! Don't you find that even a *little* bit fishy?"

"Why should I?"

"Marty Becker's a rogue."

"He was a drunk. Surely negligent. Likely incompetent. Does that make him a fraudster?"

"Certainly increases the probabilities," Max opined.

"Look," Jerry shot back, "I'm not an idiot. I thought about it. You can spin all the sinister theories you want, but you can't prove any of them. Accepting the documents at face value cements my right to the paintings. That's my position," Jerry insisted, "and I'm sticking to it."

"It's none of my business," Max conceded. "But I'm not gonna lie for you."

"Never asked you to, Max."

Max sighed, but offered no comment.

"See you in a few days," said Jerry dismissively as he hung up.

Max puckered his lips and exhaled. Even if he couldn't have imagined the donnybrook to come, his hopes and expectations for his highly anticipated meeting were rapidly plummeting.

Chapter Forty-Eight

Cambridge, Massachusetts
July, 2010

It was a sweltering afternoon in late July. Max flitted about his apartment like a hummingbird on coke, reversing a decade's worth of disorder. The impending arrival of the Graingers had him on edge. While buoyed by the prospect of unraveling mysteries, Max was apprehensive, fearful that Jerry's prickliness would exacerbate Eli's distrust.

Jerry was the first to arrive. Averse to the indignities of modern commercial aviation and unwilling to entrust his art to the whims of baggage handlers, he'd elected to drive, hurtling up the East Coast in a whirlwind two days.

Max greeted him as he emerged from his Blazer. Drenched with perspiration, he clutched a bubble-wrapped painting in his meaty right fist.

"Fuckin' air conditioning broke down in South Jersey," Jerry complained, patting his forehead with a soggy handkerchief. "But it's nothin' a little deodorant can't fix." Max winced.

While Jerry retired to the bathroom to "freshen up," Max unwrapped the canvas he'd brought with him. It was *Peonies*, Max's favorite. It would make a splendid impression on the Graingers, Max anticipated, even if Jerry didn't.

Jerry returned from the bathroom reeking of deodorant. From the center of the living room, he surveyed the professor's apartment. He barely recognized the place. Gone were the piles of papers, the unshelved books, the random stacks of unhung artwork. "What'cha do, hire a SWAT team to clean the place?"

"Actually, I did it myself," Max revealed with a hint of pride.

"Discover any long-forgotten Wyeths or Pollocks?"

"Just a moldy sock and an old pair of underwear," Max laughed, content to play along. His quip induced guffaws and a bear hug. Whatever tension that may have arisen between the pair had quickly dissipated.

As Jerry and Max traded barbs, the Graingers arrived at the front door—two of them at least. Max hurried over to greet them. Eli introduced himself first. "And this is my dad, Mike Grainger."

Though identified as his father, Max was under no illusion as to Eli's paternity. Eli looked nothing like the gaunt and bespectacled Mike Grainger; to the contrary, he was the spitting image of a young Grant Elliott. Although he hadn't anticipated Mike's presence, Max was quick to welcome him.

"Sorry, Caroline's fiddling with something back in the car," Mike said. "She'll join us momentarily."

After Max introduced Jerry to Eli and Mike, Caroline entered the apartment. There was no mistaking her still shapely figure, strawberry blond hair, and riveting blue eyes. "Caroline Grainger," she announced, reaching out to shake their hands. Max and Jerry were enthralled. She was as graceful as she was beautiful, even forty years after she'd last posed for Grant Elliott.

Having dispensed with the pleasantries (including Caroline's comment on the appeal of Max's quarters, the first such compliment he'd heard in at least a decade), Max directed them toward the dining room table, on which he'd placed the painting *Peonies*.

"Oh . . . my . . . God!" Caroline gasped, her eyes bursting with emotion. Unable to articulate her surprise and elation, she broke down instead in tears. Mike smiled, placing his arm around her shoulder, squeezing her tightly. Eli grinned with satisfaction. "I remember it like it was yesterday," she whimpered, catching her breath. "We were walking outside the studio when I was drawn by this magnificent stand of peonies. Without thinking, I bent down to inhale their fragrance," she remembered. "Grant nearly screamed at me, deciding on the spot that *this* was the perfect pose. And I remember..." Caroline hesitated, recalling her exchange with the artist over his inclusion of the scars on her wrist. She shook her head, withdrawing a handkerchief from her pocketbook to wipe her eyes. "I'm sorry," she apologized, declining to reveal her brush with suicide.

"No need to apologize," Eli said, squeezing his mother's hand as she took a seat at the table. While the others followed suit, Max repaired to the kitchen to fetch refreshments. It was then that Eli began his interrogation of Jerry.

It began innocently enough: routine questions about his background—where he'd grown up, what he'd done for a living, the pastimes he pursued in retirement. Jerry spoke of his career with the IRS, his late wife, his residence in Fort Myers, his love for baseball and, more recently, antiques and art. When Max returned with a pitcher of cold drinks and a quintet of glasses, Eli bore down.

"How'd you obtain the paintings?" he asked Jerry pointedly.

"Bought 'em in the sale of the contents of a storage locker in Fort Myers," he said calmly. "Belonged to a lawyer who'd passed away."

Jerry had spent the last two days preparing for his inevitable interrogation. He'd decided to be direct and assertive, to exude confidence. Don't pussyfoot around the details, he admonished himself, and for God's sake don't show any weakness or doubt. The paintings are yours, he'd assured himself, and they're going to remain yours.

Eli was just warming up; the real game was about to begin. "Was the lawyer Martin Becker, Jr., by any chance?"

"The very same," Jerry replied with a smirk.

"And how did Mr. Becker obtain the art works?"

"Grant Elliott signed them over to him in April of '95," Jerry explained. Eli's raised eyebrows registered his surprise at Jerry's revelation.

Sitting at the head of the table, Max watched anxiously, his head shifting back and forth from Eli to Jerry as the inquisition gained steam.

"How do you know this?" Eli's eyes were as piercing as his mother's, but in a more ominous way.

"Got a bill of sale to prove it."

Eli snorted in disbelief. "Have it with you?"

"Sure do," Jerry said with an edge. "But let me ask *you* something. Why is this any concern of yours?"

"Because," Eli snapped, "Grant Elliott promised those paintings to my mother, just six months before his death. He made the promise to me, in person, in his studio, in November of '94. He told me that plans were already in place, that they'd go to my mother when his wife passed away."

Jerry reached into his pocket, extracting a folded document. "Well, here's the bill of sale," he said blankly. "Dated April 20, 1995, five months *after* his meeting with you. Apparently, he changed his mind," Jerry insisted. "Or maybe he never really intended to follow through." He unfolded the bill of sale, pushing it across the table for Eli's inspection.

Eli was livid. Caroline sat beside him, her face tinged with disappointment. She reached over and grasped Eli's forearm.

"Calm down, Eli," she whispered. "We can discuss this later."

Ignoring her advice, Eli scrutinized the document. Jerry, showing no emotion, stood his ground. While Mike frowned, Max fretted. "What in God's name is 'good and valuable consideration'? This is *bullshit!*" Eli roared. "And you *know* it's bullshit!" he said, pointing an accusing finger at Jerry. "Becker was a scoundrel," he protested, "and worst of all, a thief!"

Max lowered his face into his hands in exasperation. "Gentlemen," he pleaded, "let's—"

"I'm afraid we have nothing more to say," Eli declared. "Mom, Dad, let's go."

Max sprung to his feet, pleading for them to reconsider. The Graingers rose in unison, shrugging off the professor's entreaties and heading toward the door. Eli turned to Max. "You know how to reach me," he said.

And then they were gone.

Chapter Forty-Nine

Cambridge, Massachusetts
and
New Jersey Turnpike

July, 2010

"Goddammit, Jerry!" Max cried as the front door slammed shut. "What the hell were you thinking?"

While sympathetic to Max's profound disappointment, Jerry was unapologetic. "I answered his questions. Honestly. Every damn one of them. What did you want me to do, roll over and surrender what's rightfully mine?"

"What makes you so goddamn sure they're *rightfully* yours? You heard what he said. The paintings were promised to Caroline. You had the proof of that right there in your goddamn little red file!"

"Look, Max, calm down. We've been over this. I can't deny that Grant Elliott may have once intended to transfer the paintings to Caroline. But, as you're well aware, the bill of sale bears Elliott's signature too, as well as a later date. For whatever reason, he changed his mind. He had every right to do so."

"You didn't even acknowledge the *existence* of that letter of direction!"

"Why the fuck should I? And besides, he never asked."

Max was beside himself, shaking his head repeatedly, circumnavigating the living room like a madman. "They'll never cooperate. In fact, they'll probably sue your ass!" he whined. "Shit," he said, before uncharacteristically launching into a stream of epithets that would have embarrassed a sailor.

Jerry tried his best to be conciliatory, but to little avail. "Look, Max, I'm sorry about how it turned out." Max ignored him, continuing his living room walkabout while Jerry observed from Max's favorite armchair. "Who knew they had an agenda?" he muttered. "But if you think I'm gonna help you achieve your dreams by sacrificing mine, you've got another guess coming."

Back in their Cambridge hotel, the Graingers commiserated among themselves. Of the three, Eli was by far the most despondent. "I brought you all the way out here," he told his parents, "hoping for an impossible result. I should never have done that. I'm so sorry to disappoint you."

Caroline sought only to console him. "The trip was worth it," she insisted, "if only to see *Peonies* again after forty years. It brought back wonderful memories, Eli."

"It just galls me," he continued, his face reddening, "to watch that bastard sit there smugly, claiming ownership through a thief. He knows that document is bogus. For all we know, he created it himself!"

"Let's give old Jerry the benefit of the doubt," Mike interjected. "What would *you* do if you'd stumbled upon the paintings along with the bill of sale. Would you have given *us* the benefit of the doubt?"

"Look, honey," Caroline said. "What does it really matter? All I ever wanted was to see the paintings revealed one day to the public. Until you told us of Grant's promise, I'd never given a moment's thought to actually owning one—much less all of them. What on earth would we do with them, anyway?"

"They're worth millions, Mom. It could set you up for life."

"We're blessed with the life we have. We're happy. We wouldn't trade it for anything," she assured him.

"For what it's worth, I support your mother on this," Mike said.

"And since we've come all this way," Caroline added, "why not do what *I* came here to do—to make certain that when the paintings are revealed to the public, our story will be told honestly and accurately." She smiled, reaching out to touch each of their hands. "The professor seems like a decent guy. You tell me he's got the credentials," she said, eyeing Eli. "He wants to tell our story. Why don't we help him to do that?"

While his parents dressed for dinner in their hotel room, Eli made a phone call from his.

"How'd it go?" Rachel inquired.

"A disaster." Eli elaborated, furnishing a blow-by-blow account of his brief but explosive encounter with Jerry Deaver.

"That's not all bad news," Rachel opined. "We've now got a handle on the basis for his claim of ownership—and it's far from invulnerable. There are chinks in his armor. At the very least, I think we can mount a respectable challenge if you're willing to entertain the possibility."

Eli sighed. "My mother claims it doesn't matter to her . . . that she never considered actually owning the paintings anyway. Says she's ready to tell her story. That's apparently what's most important to her," he said, his voice betraying his frustration. "And Dad fully supports her."

"You need to talk to her—and to Mike. Make them understand that it's not just her legacy she'd be dismissing. It's yours as well." She paused. "And that of the family you could have some day."

Eli thought he detected a tinge of longing in Rachel's last sentence. But he quickly dismissed it as wishful thinking. "She wants to meet with the professor to tell her story," he continued. "Doesn't that impact our leverage?"

"It doesn't have to, Eli," she said. "Prevail upon her to get him to sign an NDA."

"A what?"

"A non-disclosure agreement, agreeing that he won't disclose any of the details she reveals without her written permission."

"Where am I going to get an NDA?" he asked impatiently.

"Relax, lover," she laughed. "I'll fax you one." She hadn't addressed him that way for ages. "Text me a fax number for your hotel. I'll have it for you in a couple of hours."

"What if the professor won't sign it?"

"He'll sign it," she said confidently. "And by doing so, you'll position him to lobby this Jerry character for some sort of compromise."

"I owe you, Rachel."

"Yes, Eli, you do," she giggled. "Your place or mine?" Her mischievous signals were perplexing. Was she just teasing him, he wondered, or was something else brewing? Mike rapped on the door before Eli could further explore her intentions.

"My parents are ready to head out to dinner. I'll talk to them," he promised her. "I have to go."

Jerry turned up the radio as he sped down the New Jersey Turnpike. With his windows open to counter the Blazer's failed air conditioning, he endured the rumble of countless tractor-trailers while nearly swooning from the olfactory assault of swamp gas and refineries.

As disagreeable as this stretch of the journey was, it was no more so than his abortive meeting with Max and the Graingers. His tense exchange with Eli Grainger had dashed the professor's plans for a carefully orchestrated rollout of the Caroline Paintings with the cooperation of the artist's most compelling muse.

As he hurtled past the factories and garbage dumps, Jerry reevaluated his position. Even without the participation of Caroline Grainger, he sat on a gold mine. He knew far more about the Caroline Paintings now than he'd known several months earlier, when he hauled his unattributed artwork to Landrigan's in Miami. Would Max deny Jerry his formal endorsement of the paintings as Grant Elliott's simply because he'd stuck to his guns on the matter of ownership? Could Caroline Grainger credibly deny her identity as the model? Would she even want to? Not likely, Jerry calculated. So, while Max's dreams of a fancy exhibition with a cool catalogue and the enthusiastic cooperation of Grant Elliott's supermodel might have faded, Jerry's cache was still a precious commodity on the auction block.

As the stench of the armpit of New Jersey receded, Jerry's cell phone rang. Maybe Max was calling with a Plan B. Jerry glanced at his phone. Area code 239: Fort Myers. He didn't recognize the number. Never blessed with a large coterie of close friends—except maybe for Gus—he dismissed it as a random solicitation, a golden opportunity, perhaps, to replace all of his condominium windows at a one-time, rock-bottom price. He declined to answer.

Ten minutes later, the phone rang again. Same number. This time he answered. The voice on the line was trembling. "Jerry?"

He recognized the voice of Gus's wife. "Audrey, is that you? What's wrong?"

"Jerry, Gus . . ." The words caught in her throat. "Gus passed away last night."

Jerry wondered if he'd heard her correctly; the connection wasn't ideal. "Did you say that Gus died last night?"

The sorrowful sound she emitted in response was his confirmation. Jerry pulled over to the shoulder. Their conversation was brief. There was little to say: his friend had died in his sleep. Gus was seventy-two, just a year older than Jerry. The funeral would take place in two days.

"Would you perhaps say a few words . . . at the funeral?" she asked.

"Well, I . . ." Jerry was no public speaker. He hadn't even spoken at Blanche's funeral. He didn't want to do it. "Of course, Audrey," he said, biting his lip.

Sure, Jerry thought after he'd hung up, Gus could be a pain in the ass. But so was Jerry. Despite that, Gus had been a loyal friend since the day Jerry and Blanche first arrived in Fort Myers. And now he was gone.

Chapter Fifty

M ax took refuge in his favorite chair after breakfast, still in his pajamas, sulking as if his dog had died. Not that he had one, but his aspirations for the Caroline Paintings were as close to his heart as man's best friend. Jerry's emergence on the scene two months earlier had ignited a spark in Max's life—a life grown dull with its own obsolescence. He'd borne the label of professor emeritus like an albatross around his neck. Buried in a basement office, shorn of teaching responsibilities, and devoid of passion for anything but art (and baseball), he'd been simply marking time. Yesterday, the Caroline Paintings were his deliverance. Today, he had nothing but shattered dreams.

And then the phone rang.

Max recognized the resonant voice of Eli Grainger.

"Professor," he said, in a tone that was markedly conciliatory, "my mother's decided that she would like to tell her story after all."

The words to Max were like a shot of adrenaline. "By all means!" he panted. "I'm all ears. Ready whenever you are!"

The Graingers arrived an hour later—an hour in which Max got himself dressed, restored his apartment to respectability, and ran to his neighborhood bakery for a boxful of pastries. Beaming, he welcomed his guests, seating them at the dining room table amid a spread of baked delicacies and a pitcher of iced tea.

"I'm sorry about yesterday," Caroline said. "I don't really care how your friend found the pictures. Point is, he found them. One way or another, they'll go public," she acknowledged. "I'd like you to tell their story properly."

Max asked permission to record their interview. Before his mother could respond, Eli spoke up.

"My mom is willing to talk with you on the condition that you sign a non-disclosure agreement." He reached into a small leather portfolio and withdrew a four-page document.

Eli had discussed the matter with his parents during dinner the previous evening.

"I told you I don't care about the paintings," Caroline had reiterated to him between courses.

"But I do. This is a family legacy, Mom," he'd told her, echoing Rachel's advice. "It means something to me and it might mean something to your grandchildren someday. Don't dismiss it so cavalierly."

Caroline's ears had perked up. "What's this about grandchildren? Is there something we should know? Are you and Rachel—"

"No, Mom, no," he'd interjected, slightly flustered. "But who knows? I'm not a confirmed bachelor yet."

By the arrival of dessert, Mike had endorsed Rachel's plan, securing Caroline's acquiescence.

Eli slid the agreement across the table. Max, taken aback by the formality, scanned its contents warily.

"My mother is willing to speak freely, Professor, and you're welcome to record it, but the agreement provides that her written consent will be required before you're authorized to disclose any of the information she provides you today."

"I see," Max mumbled, cowed by the sudden avalanche of legalese. He flipped through the pages, his eyes glazing over. "What will it take," he asked, gazing up at Caroline, "to obtain your consent?"

Again, Eli interjected. "A satisfactory settlement with respect to the ownership of the paintings."

"Hmm." Max now recognized that the issue had been joined. Jerry would be livid. While the hurdle the Graingers had imposed was understandable, it severely complicated Max's pursuit of his objectives. To achieve his goals, he'd have to broker some kind of agreement between Jerry and the Graingers. Though his earlier euphoria had been tempered, he was nonetheless brimming with questions and flush with curiosity. He'd concern himself with the legal niceties later.

Max signed the NDA, pressed the *record* button, and plowed ahead. "Tell me how you first came to model for Grant Elliott," he urged.

Caroline poured herself a glass of iced tea, took a sip, and began reminiscing. "I overheard him ask my father if he could paint me," she said, recalling a conversation following a dinner hosted by her parents. "It was something I'd wanted to do for a long time. The answer," she chuckled, "was a resounding no, but I had other ideas." Flashing a mischievous grin, she described her unannounced visit to the painter's studio, her brazen persistence in the face of the artist's resistance, and Grant's reluctant decision to sketch her. "He did it to shut me up, I think, but he liked what he'd drawn too much to dismiss the thought of doing it again."

"How old were you?"

"Sixteen," she said sheepishly.

"Is that why it was secret?"

"It was secret because my parents forbade it. They denied

Grant's request that night at dinner and I wasn't going to ask them again."

"Maybe they were right," Mike chuckled. "After all, you did wind up getting pregnant."

Caroline smiled while Eli winced. "Fair enough, but there was another reason."

"What was that?" Max asked.

"Grant had had an affair a few years earlier with a young model from town. It came out and embarrassed Becky. She wouldn't let that happen again. She didn't want even the *appearance* of impropriety."

"How did you manage to keep your modeling sessions a secret?"

"Both Grant and I had strong reasons for maintaining our silence. We were careful. I told my parents I was doing an after-school activity on Thursdays—that was the day we usually met—and they never bothered to check up. I think I told them it was art club." She laughed at the irony. "Brandon Blake—it was in his studio that we had all of our sessions— was the only other person who was privy to our arrangements. He and Grant were extremely close and he wouldn't have dreamed of betraying his friend."

"Or revealing his own complicity in the matter," Max suggested.

"I suppose so," she acknowledged.

Caroline recounted their first real modeling session. "He asked me to wear something meaningful to me," she remembered fondly. "So, I brought my brother's beat-up, old sweater." Her explanation of its significance yielded the first of many tears she'd shed revisiting her long-forgotten memories. She sighed deeply when Max showed her an image of the painting *Grief* on his computer.

Over the next several hours, prompted by Max's well-organized inquiries and photographs of each of the remaining paintings (which he displayed to her in numerical, and hence chronological, order), Caroline detailed the evolution of her relationship with Grant Elliott, both professionally and personally, from the first painting to the last. Mike and Eli sat quietly, their expressions manifesting a range of emotions, from surprise and admiration to discomfort, even shock.

Not surprisingly, the most awkward moments arose when the images of the nudes appeared on Max's computer screen. Blushing ever so slightly, Caroline playfully raised her hands to cover Eli's eyes. While Eli felt understandably conflicted about staring at his mother naked, Mike, hardly unaccustomed to such tableaus, reveled in the experience.

"When did you first pose naked for Grant?" Max asked her. "And how did it come about?"

Caroline couldn't help but laugh. "I remember it so vividly! It was June of 1970. School had just ended. I usually came to our sessions dressed as I was for school, but this time I arrived in shorts and a halter top." She crinkled her lips puckishly. "I knew, for a long time, that Grant wanted to paint me nude, but he hesitated. I'd volunteer, but he'd say something like, 'You're sixteen, for God's sake' or, later, 'You're barely seventeen!' So, on that afternoon, I decided to have some fun with him. I complained it was too hot to wear clothes. And before he knew it, I'd slipped out of everything." Caroline laughed, Mike smiled, and Eli grimaced. "I remember humming a striptease while twirling my panties from my index finger, teasing poor Grant until he had little choice but to relent."

"God, Mom, you were incorrigible!" Eli couldn't help but join in the laughter.

Max struggled with the next question, its delicacy flustering him. "How . . . how," he stuttered.

"I know where you're going, professor," Caroline said. Eli and Mike did, too, and weren't so sure it was a good idea.

"Mom, you don't have to—"

"It's okay. I want to. I don't want there to be any misunderstanding." She refilled her glass with iced tea.

"Maybe something stronger?" Max suggested.

Caroline smiled. "Not necessary." She took a sip from her freshly refilled glass. "To me, in the beginning, it was just a game. I was modeling for a famous artist. That was extraordinary—ego boosting, to say the least. We got along famously. I couldn't talk to my parents, but I could talk to Grant . . . about anything. And the more comfortable I became, the more I delighted in teasing him, even seducing him, I suppose. But I didn't give much thought to how it was affecting him." She paused for another swig of tea. "In time, after he began to paint me in the nude, I became more forward. I loved Grant, but it was the love of an immature teenager for a world-famous artist. And once I convinced myself that I wanted him, he was toast."

"Still, Mom, he shouldn't have—" Eli interjected.

"Of course he shouldn't have, Eli! But what you have to understand is that I *wanted* it to happen. It happened only once—he was too ashamed and embarrassed to do it again. He regretted it immediately, but I didn't." Caroline sighed. "Well, I guess I did regret it when I learned I was pregnant. But once you came along, Eli . . ." Her voice trailed off. Caroline hugged Eli, even as he shook his head. It was awkward to hear your mother discussing your conception.

"What did he say when he found out?" Eli asked his mother.

"When he eventually noticed I was pregnant, I denied it was his."

Her answer surprised Eli. "Why?"

"Because I was worried about what he might do. I cared for him. I didn't want to shatter his marriage or his career. I figured we'd both be better off if he didn't know the truth."

"But you told him later."

"Right, Eli. But you already knew that. I wrote Grant a letter on the night I left home," she said. "I always wanted him to know, and by then I thought it was safe, as long as he didn't know how to find me."

Max found Caroline's revelations fascinating.

Seeing the paintings after forty years unlocked in Caroline a flood of memories, some jealously guarded, others long forgotten.

"Why hadn't you told us this before?" was a frequent refrain from both Mike and Eli.

"The urges and desires of an immature young woman are hardly appropriate for one's son, especially when they relate to his biological father," she told Eli. To Mike she said: "You were my lover, and then my husband. I didn't want to hurt you or embarrass myself."

Eli had never understood the genesis of the breach between his mother and her parents. He was horrified to learn of their treatment of Caroline, both before and after her pregnancy. He'd never truly appreciated his mother's courage in abandoning home in order to keep her son, or the serendipity of Mike's intervention at the Truck Stop Café.

The interview went on for four hours. No one even thought to break for lunch. For Caroline, it was a long-delayed catharsis; for Eli and Mike, it was a revelation, a tale of excitement and heartbreak, a chance to clarify the hazy picture they'd harbored of Caroline's earlier life, and a reason to admire her more.

And for Max, it was an art historian's mother lode.

Chapter Fifty-One

J erry sat anxiously on the aisle in the second row of pews awaiting the minister's signal. Judging from the overflow crowd at the First Presbyterian Church, Gus Schmidt had a boatload of friends. Why select Jerry, of all people, to deliver the eulogy, he'd asked Gus's widow, Audrey. "Because he could count on you," she said.

His brief sermon finished, Pastor Davis nodded to Jerry. Slowly, he stood up, wresting his ample frame from the pew and climbing the steps to the podium. From his pocket, he withdrew a crumpled piece of paper on which he'd hastily scribbled a jumble of notes.

Jerry surveyed the assemblage of mourners. Most, like him, were retirees. Each, like him, was a wayward clot or a diabolically multiplying cluster of cells removed from the fate of his friend. Were he the victim, he imagined with a shudder, there'd be no overflow crowd. In fact, there'd be neither a church nor more than a handful of mourners—assuming it didn't rain.

"We've lost a friend," Jerry mumbled into the mike, the static feedback blasting the eardrums of his audience, amplified through hearing aids dialed up for the occasion. "Gus was a generous cuss," he continued, his voice quaking as he broke into a cold sweat, "who cared more for others than he did for himself. He had his quirks," he acknowledged, "but in the end, his friendship enriched us and his kindness made the world a better place."

Those words, and the observations that followed, were a fitting paean to Gus. At the same time, he realized, they were a savage self-indictment. How, over his seventy-one years, had Jerry made the world a better place? Sure, he'd snagged a few tax scofflaws, but no one would recall him for that. To whom had he been generous, giving, or selfless? How would *he* be remembered, if remembered at all?

Jerry paused at the podium, directing his gaze at the crowd. Tears flowed freely among the mourners. He thought of Marty Becker, for whom no one had shed a tear. A forgotten man, he'd died without notice, leaving behind little more than an abandoned storage locker. Though its contents were worth millions, he'd shared his windfall with no one. And worse, Jerry feared—though stubbornly refused to acknowledge— he'd probably pirated his booty from the eminently more deserving Caroline Grainger.

Jerry muddled through the eulogy in serviceable fashion. He told a few anecdotes, shared a few memories, recounted acts of generosity and compassion. He omitted any mention of the millions in artwork old Gus had unwittingly bestowed upon him for the princely sum of $600. He'd never divulged to Gus the extent of his good fortune, much less offered to share even a speck of that bounty with the friend who'd "pushed the envelope" to facilitate it.

Concluding his remarks, Jerry descended from the stage, his head bowed. Resettling in his pew, he continued his descent into despair. That he was no Gus Schmidt was troubling enough, but the parallels between Marty Becker and himself were especially disturbing. In succeeding to Becker's spoils, was he not willfully acceding to his culpability? Jerry's inaction, his dismissal of the conclusions suggested by the evidence in that little red file, made him no less guilty than Becker. For the IRS, he'd spent decades chasing cheaters and rogues. He knew how they thought—the law was unjust, they were oppressed, they were entitled to shirk the rules that applied to everyone else. Was that who he was? And if Caroline was Becker's victim, wasn't she Jerry's as well?

What would he do with the fruits of his perfidy? He didn't really need the money. Would he buy a villa on the Riviera and live out the rest of his life in luxury? Not likely. And if he died tomorrow, the ultimate irony would prevail: his cache of paintings would languish in a KeepSafe storage locker—he'd stowed them with Gus before travelling to Cambridge—until his ne'er-do-well nephew, his only living heir, stepped into his tainted shoes, enabling the vicious cycle to repeat.

Chapter Fifty-Two

J erry found a message on his answering machine when he returned from the funeral. "You'll never believe what happened," he heard Max say. "Caroline decided to tell me her story . . . for *four fabulous hours!* The background, the narrative behind each of the pictures, even the story of her affair with Grant Elliott! Call me!"

Great news, but Jerry was hardly in the mood to endure the chatter of the euphoric Professor Winter. He'd just lost a friend—one he'd taken for granted—as well as his bearings. He'd disappointed Max as well, but the harm, it seemed, had proven fleeting. Max now had the fodder for his catalogue, but he needed Jerry's pictures for his exhibition.

Until now, Jerry had given only lip service to Max's lofty ambitions for a major exhibition of the Caroline Paintings. Preoccupied with authenticating them and securing their ownership, he'd given little consideration to the next step. Now, thinking it through, he began to have qualms. The public splash accompanying the introduction of the Caroline Paintings would place him in the spotlight—or was it the crosshairs? Would his fifteen minutes of fame be a dream or a nightmare? People would wonder how a retiree from Florida, a mere dabbler in the world of art, wound up with a fortune in clandestine Grant Elliotts. Some enterprising reporter would start digging, poking at the soft underbelly of the narrative: the

Marty Becker connection. Eli Grainger would reveal the promise his father had made. The proverbial feces would hit the fan.

Caroline Grainger was beautiful, credible, and charming. Impregnated by the artist as an impressionable seventeen-year-old, she'd defied the odds, making a life for herself and her son while selflessly preserving the artist's scandalous secret. Who'd credit the claim of an overweight, retired IRS agent over that of the supercalifragilisticexpialidocious heroine? He'd be a laughingstock.

Anxious to preserve one of his few remaining friendships, Jerry returned Max's call. He bit his lip as Max rhapsodized about Caroline Grainger. "You couldn't ask for a better heroine," the professor gushed. "America will absolutely adore her!"

Jerry listened patiently, though his head was bursting. "That's great, Max," he said with feigned enthusiasm.

"So, let's talk about the exhibition," Max said. Jerry responded with dead silence. "I've got a million ideas," he continued. "I'll contact curators at Harvard, the Art Institute of—"

"Can it, Max."

"What?"

"I said, *can* it!"

"What in God's name—"

"I've been thinking," he growled. Jerry proceeded to articulate the fears that had begun to consume him. "I'll be grilled and eaten alive," he fretted.

It was the first time Max had heard Jerry use a food metaphor to his detriment. This was serious, Max realized.

"I'm thinking I should send the paintings to auction," Jerry said.

Max's gulp was audible. "You can't be serious."

"That way, I can sell them anonymously. No one has to know—"

"But our research! The exhibition!" Max interrupted, turning frantic. "It can only add to the value of the paintings!"

"I'd rather have a few less bucks than become America's piñata," Jerry grumbled.

"You can't do this! *Please* don't do this."

"I have no choice."

"You *do* have a choice. You've *always* had a choice."

"Yeah, right."

Max remained silent for what seemed like an eternity. Finally, he let out a deep sigh. "Uh, Jerry . . . there's one more thing you should know," he said haltingly.

"What's that?"

"The Graingers, I think, plan on making a claim to the paintings."

"What the hell are you talking about?"

"Eli Grainger forced me to sign an NDA—a non-disclosure agreement—prohibiting me from using the fruits of my interview until Caroline grants her written consent."

"Which depends on what?"

"That's what I asked."

"Impressive, Max," said Jerry sarcastically. "So great minds do think alike. Big fucking deal! So, *I repeat*, dependent upon what?"

"On a satisfactory settlement regarding the ownership of the paintings."

"Goddammit!"

"And, from the looks of that NDA, I think they've already gotten themselves a pretty good lawyer."

Jerry stiffened. "Well, I'll go get myself a fucking lawyer too!" he exploded.

Max waited for Jerry to calm down. "Look, if you go to an auction house, things will only get worse. The Graingers would probably sue to block any sale until the matter of ownership is resolved. I think everyone would be better off if you just agreed to some kind of compromise."

Jerry muttered a few choice four-letter words before fashioning his epithet-laden response. "What the fuck kind of goddamn compromise are you talking about?"

"I don't know, Jerry," Max whined. "That's up to you. But I'm willing to host another meeting at which both sides can sit down to discuss the matter civilly."

"Yeah, well, fine. But I gotta go get myself a fucking lawyer now, Max, don't I!"

"Might be a good idea, buddy."

"Yeah. Right."

"Think it over, Jerry, and call me back in a few days."

"Sure, Max. Whatever you say." With that, Jerry hung up, picked up his telephone, and flung it across the room.

Chapter Fifty-Three

Chicago, Illinois
July, 2010

It happened again. He called her to formulate a strategy for reclaiming his mother's artistic legacy, she met him at The Speakeasy for a couple of drinks, and they wound up at his place, making love. And, unless he was seriously misreading her signals, they'd ratcheted it up to a level not experienced since the peak of their relationship four years earlier, before they'd reluctantly cancelled their engagement.

"What's going on here?" Eli asked during the rapturous lull following their second coupling of the evening.

"I've been thinking," Rachel mused, brushing her hand softly across his chest.

"About?"

"Life," she murmured wistfully, "the choices I've made, the opportunities I've squandered."

Eli held his tongue. She'd broken his heart once; he'd steeled himself against any recurrence. They'd gone their separate ways, each enjoying serial companionship but nothing even remotely approaching the relationship they'd mutually abandoned. Up until now, he concluded, their occasional post-engagement trysts were little more than a form of commiseration, a way to ease the pain of their subsequent romantic disappointments.

"I'm going out on a limb here," she muttered into the teeth of his silence.

"I'm not gonna climb out with you if you're planning on sawing it off," he answered tersely, straining her metaphor.

"I get it," she said. "What I'm trying to say here is that I still love you, Eli. You were right to break it off. I wanted a career more than I wanted a family." She fixed her eyes on his. "But that was then and this is now. I'm thirty-five. It's not too late to rearrange my priorities."

The hints were all there. He'd sensed them during his telephone conversation with her from Cambridge. Eli would've liked nothing more than to rekindle their relationship, but was understandably gun-shy.

"What would you say if I told you I wanted to start a family. With you, Eli."

"I'd wonder if you were truly committed or just lonely."

"Sure, I'm lonely," Rachel acknowledged. "I've missed you a lot over these last four years. Every time we've done ... *this* ... since then," she said, "I've felt an emptiness afterwards, a regret I've never quite been able to shake. Thing is," she added, breathing deeply, "I've achieved what I sought in my career, but I'm not fulfilled. My friends have spouses, children. They complain, of course, but I can sense their happiness. I think about what it might've been like if we'd gotten married and had an ankle-biter or two tripping about the house. I find myself longing for another chance at that particular storyline. And I want it to be with you, if you'd have me after all I've put you through."

Eli smiled, albeit tentatively. "Was that a proposal?"

"An offer, perhaps," she giggled. "Do you have a response?"

Eli's lips quivered with the hint of a smile. "As you lawyers say, I'm going to have to take it under advisement."

She nodded hopefully, then shifted gears. "Shall we try for a trifecta?"

Jerry fished out the dog-eared copy of the Yellow Pages from the bottom shelf of his bookcase. Few people used it anymore, but he was unapologetically old school. He flipped to the attorney listings. He shuddered when, under the B's, he found the name of Martin Becker, Jr. "Fuck this," he grunted, tossing the dated volume into the trash can and switching on his computer instead.

What was he looking for? Some Florida attorney he could drag to a meeting in Massachusetts, all expenses paid, on top of outrageous hourly fees? That didn't compute. A Boston area lawyer made more sense, he concluded. Someone who's been around the block and can sit there at a meeting looking ferocious enough to put the fear of God into the Graingers. He recalled an old acquaintance from Medford, a neighbor of his and Blanche's, who was an attorney somewhere in Boston. He'd be in his sixties by now, clearly "around the block." Jerry googled him on the internet, found an office number, and placed a call.

Jimmy O'Toole recalled his old neighbor. "How's Blanche?" he asked.

"Dead," Jerry said.

Jimmy offered his belated condolences and asked how he could be of assistance.

"You can attend a meeting and cover my ass," Jerry said.

"What's this all ab—"

"I'll fill you in on the details later."

"Well, I—"

"Good," Jerry snapped. "You're hired. Goodbye."

"Whew," Jerry sighed, relieved to have lawyered up. Jimmy O'Toole, on the other hand, had no clue what he was getting into.

Chapter Fifty-Four

Cambridge, Massachusetts
September, 2010

Like prizefighters entering the ring with their seconds, the combatants filed into Jerry's apartment, taking their respective positions on either side of the dining room table. On one side sat the Graingers: Caroline biting her lip, her discomfort evident; Mike at her side, expressionless; Eli with a look of steely determination. Sitting between Caroline and Eli was an attractive woman with short, dark hair, smartly dressed in a navy-blue blazer and matching slacks. "This is our attorney, Rachel Rosner," Eli announced with a mingling of pride and confidence.

Sitting alongside Jerry on the opposite side of the table was a balding man with Coke-bottle glasses, approaching Jerry in both age and weight, wearing a thin, rumpled gray suit with an unfashionably wide olive-green tie. "And this is *my* attorney, Jimmy O'Toole," Jerry countered with unfounded conviction.

Max stood at the head of the table like some family patriarch preparing to carve the Thanksgiving turkey. He introduced himself to the newcomers and welcomed his guests. Selecting his words cautiously, he invited both sides to express their positions frankly in hopes of finding common ground. "The Caroline Paintings are an artistic treasure," he pronounced stiffly. "They can trickle into the art world in fits and starts, or be introduced with honor and sensitivity through a cooperative effort of all concerned. A series of exhibitions accompanied by a scholarly catalogue would, in my estimation, best serve the art community and each of you sitting at this table." As Jerry rolled his eyes, Max continued his professorial monologue. "I invited you all here in an effort to encourage you to—"

"Enough, Max," Jerry interrupted. "We get it." Max shut up and sat down. But before Jerry could say anything further, Rachel claimed the floor.

"As you all know, Grant Elliott made an unambiguous promise to my clients sixteen years ago. He committed unequivocally to gift to Caroline Grainger what you, Professor Winter, refer to as The Caroline Paintings. His motive was obvious: he respected my client deeply and was the father of her son." Pausing, she poured herself a glass of iced tea from the pitcher Max had strategically placed at the center of the table. "Martin Becker, Jr., was Grant Elliott's attorney and, by all accounts, his fiduciary. There is no other plausible explanation for his possession of the paintings. And there can be no denying Becker's history of negligence, malpractice, and breaches of client responsibility and trust. The paintings, Mr. Deaver, are not yours to keep. Absent a mutually satisfactory agreement today, we are prepared to bring action in Federal court to establish Mrs. Grainger's ownership of the Caroline Paintings and to block any effort on your part to sell or otherwise dispose of them."

Jerry listened calmly and without interruption, offering only an occasional eye roll in response. Jimmy O'Toole, huddled beside him, nervously studied his notes.

Sitting up straight in her chair, Rachel stared into Jerry's eyes. "We appreciate where you come from in this matter and hesitate to attribute to you any wrongdoing or ill will. And for that reason, Mrs. Grainger has expressed a willingness, in exchange for your relinquishment of claims to the Caroline Paintings, to permit your retention of a small portion of the artwork as a gesture of good faith."

Jerry smirked, nudging his lawyer. Jimmy flinched, lurched forward, shuffled a few papers, and began to speak in a thick Boston accent.

"Uh... r—right," he stuttered. "I hold in my hands a document signed by, um, Grant Elliott, conveying these... um... this artwork"—he pronounced it *aht-work*—"to Martin Becker, Jr., now deceased. This sheet of paper," he said, waving it in the air as if he were hailing a cab, "is, as you might say, Ms. Rosner, equally unequivocal. And moreover, the operative principle in this case, as I'm sure you'll recognize, Ms. Rosner, is, um, that my client acquired these, um, paintings as a..."

Jimmy paused mid-sentence, lifting the pitcher of iced tea and pouring it largely onto the table, almost completely missing his glass. The participants rose abruptly, rescuing notepads, cellphones, and papers from the torrent of tea surging like a tsunami across Max's dining room table. Caroline lunged forward with a napkin as Max retreated to the kitchen in search of paper towels.

Several minutes later, the crisis quelled, Jimmy resumed his presentation. "Uh, right, where was I?" he muttered sheepishly. "Oh... yeah, as I was saying, the law recognizes my client here as, um, a *bona fide purchaser* of this... um... these paintings." Jerry rubbed his eyes in exasperation. "Your client, Ms. Rosner," he continued, "bases her, um, claim on an alleged oral promise witnessed by no living person. Well, what I mean, of course, is no person *now* living. Um, except for her son, I mean." Again, he paused, winding up for the final thrust. "Anyway, I submit that it will take a great deal more than that to convince a court to deprive poor Mr. Deaver here of what he legitimately acquired as an, um, *bona fide purchaser* in a properly conducted, um, foreclosure sale."

The lawyers sparred incessantly for the next thirty minutes in a bout of elegance against earthiness, landing and ducking arguments like punches. Jerry sat hunched over the table, his hands supporting his drooping head while each of the Graingers wore grimaces borne of frustration and fatigue. Max's repeated efforts to broker a compromise were universally ignored.

Finally, Caroline placed her hand on Rachel's arm to silence her. "This is going nowhere," she conceded. "I'd like to speak with Jerry privately if I might."

Jerry raised his head hopefully, transmitting his willingness to accede to her suggestion. The lawyers accosted their respective clients, admonishing them against proceeding with discussions in the absence of counsel. Eli, too, expressed his unease with his mother's suggestion. Caroline shook her head, stood up, and beckoned Jerry to join her in Max's study.

Jerry shadowed Caroline into the study and shut the door. Caroline sat at Max's desk, nearly obscured by mountains of books and paper, while Jerry pulled up a chair.

"Look, Jerry. You seem like a decent, honest person. I can understand how this must make you feel. You've gone through a lot to get here and you don't fancy giving it up." Jerry nodded, allowing Caroline to continue. "These paintings mean a great deal to me. I've waited over forty years for their reappearance. I'm not interested in rehashing with you all the legal mumbo jumbo. We both have reasonable arguments. Can't we work something out?"

Jerry genuinely liked this woman, but was wary of surrendering what he'd labored so hard to retain. "What do you have in mind?"

"What I'm proposing is that half of the artwork goes into a foundation my family will establish to preserve the art and make it available to loan to museums. Or we might choose to gift some of the paintings outright to one or more of those institutions. You, Jerry, get to keep the other half, which you can sell, but which we hope you'd make available first for the kind of exhibition the professor has his heart set on."

As Caroline gazed at him with those mesmerizing blue eyes, Jerry felt his resistance melt away. He leaned back into a thoughtful pose, rubbing his hand across his cheek and chin. His mind wandered to the day of Gus's funeral, a day on which he obsessed over doubts about the legitimacy of his bounty and his personal fears of worthlessness. With the proceeds of the sale of even *half* of the paintings, he could live like a king—if he wanted to. Why be a prick and hold out for twice as much? Sure, Eli Grainger's aggressiveness had rubbed him the wrong way, but the poor kid—the poor bastard, as it turns out—was only protecting his mother. And this Rachel woman (was there something going on, he speculated, between her and Eli?) was, if nothing else, formidable. She'd eat Jimmy for lunch in a courtroom, for sure, and hiring a competent lawyer instead would cost him everything he had—and with no assurance of ultimate success.

Caroline sat patiently as Jerry pondered her offer. The fact that he'd listened and failed to immediately object was heartening. Loath to interrupt his consideration, she remained silent and hopeful.

Finally, Jerry rose from his chair. "If we stay in here much longer," he quipped, "your husband'll wonder what's goin' on." He stepped forward and held out his hand. "You've got a deal, Mrs. Grainger."

"Caroline, *please*! And thank you, Jerry," she said, smiling broadly. "I appreciate it from the bottom of my heart."

Back in the dining room, the five others were growing fidgety, subsisting on meaningless small talk and banalities. When the door to Max's office opened, all five turned around in unison, seeking an omen, like Catholics anticipating the puff of white smoke heralding the election of a pope. The smiles on the faces of Caroline and Jerry were a harbinger of reconciliation, though each side worried what the other might have surrendered.

Jerry, smiling smugly, announced that he and Caroline were running away together. "Just kidding," he chuckled.

Caroline spoke up. "We're happy to announce a compromise," she said, beaming. "Each of us will receive half of the paintings."

Max sprung from his chair crying "Whoopie!" like a six-year-old with a new bike. The others were more restrained, a sign, perhaps, that each was equally impacted by a deal that was inherently fair. Slowly, taking their cue from the principals, they extended their hands in congratulations.

Max stood there glowing. The rest, he understood, was up to him. His dream, nearly dashed on the rocks of discord, was back on the road to fruition.

Chapter Fifty-Five

Max orchestrated it like an impresario. Sitting regally behind the jurists' bench of the Ames Courtroom at the Harvard Law School, beneath the elaborate oak panels in chairs traditionally occupied by judges, he was flanked on his left by muckety-mucks from Harvard University, the Art Institute of Chicago, and the Los Angeles County Museum of Art, and to his right by Jerry Deaver, Caroline Grainger, and Mike Grainger. In the several rows before him sat a handful of invited guests and a clutch of journalists, drawn like flies by Max's artfully crafted press release. Brief yet tantalizing, it announced the discovery of a secret cache of paintings, dubbed the Caroline Paintings, created by the illustrious Grant Elliott. "The paintings," teased the release, "were hidden away for forty years, their existence known only to a precious few, including the artist's protégé, the late Brandon Blake, and his model, Caroline Grainger, with whom the artist bore a son."

The last clause of the press release had been the subject of much internal debate. Eli had opposed it, considering it salacious, but Caroline changed his mind. "I've always been proud of your heritage," she told him, "and you should be, too." Mike had his misgivings, but deferred to his wife.

"It'll be obvious right off the bat," Max told Caroline. "Anyone who even glances at Eli will see the uncanny resemblance, and anyone doing the math will confirm it. Better to reveal it up-front, to acknowledge your willing participation—despite your tender age—rather than invite the narrative of your victimization." They were walking a fine line, Max conceded, but it was all for the best.

Max began the press conference by introducing the representatives of the three museums. With a self-satisfied grin, he announced the agreement of the institutions to collaborate on a major exhibition of the Caroline Paintings to open in Chicago in 2012, and to travel to the other museums thereafter. A definitive catalogue would be produced, he added with particular pride. Then, with fanfare not usually associated with staid old Harvard, a cadre of white-gloved art handlers paraded between the bench and the gathering, displaying a small but choice sampling of the collection. Onlookers gasped and murmured; cameras clicked and flashed. Their appetites whetted, Max proceeded to introduce Jerry and Caroline. Max called on Caroline—Jerry having declined to comment—to say a few words, all of them well-rehearsed.

"I'm thrilled to be here," Caroline began, "to witness the first public revelation of these wonderful paintings, each of which has such incredible meaning to me. Lest anyone think otherwise, I revered Grant Elliott. Together, we kept two very important secrets, the existence of this treasure trove of art, and the paternity of our son. I'm proud to have been the subject of these works of art, and prouder still—"

"Was your liaison consensual?" shouted a reporter in the front row, rudely interrupting her.

"How old were you when he—" piped another.

"How could you countenance . . ."

Within a matter of seconds, what began as a carefully choreographed press briefing had devolved into bedlam.

Reporters stood up, shouting over each other, jostling each other as they competed for attention. Max grabbed the microphone, pleading for order, but to no avail.

Then, just as abruptly, Jerry rose from his chair, grabbing the mike from Max's trembling hands. He placed his left thumb and index fingers between his lips and emitted an ear-splitting whistle, the kind he'd long ago perfected in the grandstands at Fenway Park. "Enough!" he shrieked. A shocked and eerie silence ensued. Emboldened, Jerry rattled on. "We invited you here to see something extraordinary and to meet a woman whose love and perseverance are deserving of the greatest admiration. *That's* what you should be writing about," he chastised the offending reporters, "not the scandalous crap you're prattling on about!" The look on his face was murderous and the reaction instantaneous. In a surprising concession to propriety, the reporters reclaimed their seats.

After a few moments of awkward silence, the art critic for *The New York Times* spoke up. "Tell us about this painting," she urged Caroline, "the one in which you're wearing what appears to be a moth-eaten sweater." Jerry returned the mike to Caroline, who calmly and eloquently described the heart-rending story behind the painting, *Grief.* Another journalist asked her what it felt like to see the paintings again after four decades.

"I'm humbled," she responded, "by Grant Elliott's sensitivity and skill . . . and by the pounds and gray hair I've added since." Laughs filled the room. They were back on track.

The display of the painting *Peonies* elicited questions and answers that revealed much about the mutual respect between the artist and his model. To avoid a repeat of the line of questioning which had threatened to derail the proceedings, Caroline spoke frankly, unprompted, about her relationship with Grant Elliott, admitting to a single, ill-advised liaison for which she bore at least as much responsibility, in her eyes, as the artist. She recounted the origins of their collaboration and their reasons for maintaining over forty years of secrecy. She described, in brief but poignant terms, her life after Longmire.

"Mr. Deaver," shouted a reporter for *The Boston Globe*, "can you tell us how you discovered these paintings?" Max leaned toward Jerry, goading him to respond. Reluctantly, he accepted the microphone from Max.

"I bid on the contents of a storage locker at a foreclosure auction in Florida," he stated, fully aware that morsel of information would provoke a cascade of additional questions. With rare restraint, Jerry offered his version of the story—the one in which Marty Becker "somehow" acquired the paintings from the artist and died, tragically, while they remained in his possession. To shield Jerry from speculative inquiries about Becker's role and the manner in which the attorney had obtained the Caroline Paintings, Max quickly reclaimed the microphone.

"We are continuing to research the provenance of the collection," the professor asserted, "and will provide any further information when and if it becomes available." Jerry heaved a sigh of relief.

With that particular line of inquiry foreclosed, the reporters refocused their attention on Caroline, who answered each of their questions with uncommon patience and candor. Her responses revealed her to be as charming and remarkable as the art that portrayed her.

The newspaper accounts and magazine articles emanating from the press conference generated a deluge of excitement about the Caroline Paintings and a renewed interest in the art and life of Grant Elliott. But the country's fascination with Caroline far exceeded expectations. She received book and movie proposals, fielded interview requests, even shared her story on *Oprah*. The brash teenager's adolescent dream—to become a famous muse—had become a reality.

Chapter Fifty-Six

Cambridge, Massachusetts
February, 2011

After years of comparative irrelevance, Max was the center of art world attention. Long forgotten colleagues congratulated him on his coup. His inbox was flooded with messages, from museum directors making last-ditch pleas for inclusion in the travelling exhibition schedule to collectors angling for a chance to acquire a Caroline Painting for their collections. Of course, he still got email solicitations for sexual performance enhancers and an occasional offer of easy profits from a Nigerian prince. But one email particularly intrigued him. It was brief:

Dear Professor Winter—

I just read the article in Time Magazine about the newly discovered Grant Elliott paintings. I was surprised by the article's mention of Marty Becker. I was his legal secretary for about two years, until he fired me in 1995. Although I didn't fully appreciate it at the time, the reason for my firing would seem particularly relevant to your study of the ownership history—I think you call it provenance—of the "Caroline Paintings." If you care to reach me, my number's below.

(Mrs.) Gladys Taylor
Longmire, VA
540-555-0126

Max stared at the email, rereading it several times as he debated the wisdom of responding. The ownership dispute between Jerry and the Graingers had been amicably resolved. The exhibition arrangements had been set, and his catalogue was in progress. Why tempt fate by soliciting information that could inject new and possibly nettlesome issues into the mix? On the other hand, he didn't want to be blindsided by anything damaging, and his curiosity was tormenting him like a chronic hemorrhoid.

Max dialed the number in the email. The voice on the receiving end was middle-aged, with a hint of prissiness amplified by a decidedly Southern accent. Max introduced himself, inviting Mrs. Taylor to elaborate on her email.

Gladys Taylor disclosed that she'd worked for Becker & Becker from 1990 until February of 1995. "I was secretary to Martin Becker, Sr.," she explained, "until he passed suddenly in 1992. Such a fine man," she recalled mournfully. "After his death, I began working for his son, Marty." She emitted a throaty harrumph. "Marty was a disaster. Had no idea what he was doing and little interest in doing it. Well," she conceded, "that's neither here nor there."

Though unsure where her ramblings were headed, Max urged her to proceed.

"Well, anyway, one snowy day in early 1995, Marty left the office to meet with Grant Elliott at his studio."

"Was Elliott a client?"

"Well, yes. He'd come in with another well-known local artist, Mr. Blake, a year or so earlier to set up a trust. I remember it, because I typed up the trust myself and found it curious."

"How so?" Max inquired, his interest piqued.

"I'm probably not supposed to reveal things like this, but as all of the parties are now deceased . . ."

"*Please*, Mrs. Taylor, continue," he implored her.

"Yes, well, it had to do with a group of Mr. Elliott's paintings. Mr. Elliott and Mr. Blake were pretty important people in town, so I took particular note of the paragraph that called for Mr. Elliott to designate, in a separate letter if I'm not mistaken, who'd get the paintings after both he and his wife passed away. I didn't really understand why these paintings were treated so specially, but it wasn't my place to ask . . ."

"Can we get back to that snowy day in ninety- . . ."

"Five. Yes. Well, as I said, Junior—we called him that sometimes, rather derisively, I'm afraid—anyway, he visits the artist and returns to the office with a letter in longhand signed by Mr. Elliott and another sheet, blank but for Mr. Elliott's signature at the bottom." She paused, as if anticipating a response.

"And then?" Max asked impatiently.

"A few days later, Marty gives me a sheet from a yellow legal pad on which he'd written out a bill of sale. And what really surprises me," she said, her voice lowering to a whisper, "is that it's a bill of sale from Mr. Elliott to my boss! He tells me to type it onto the blank sheet, above the signature, but to make sure it fits as if it was always supposed to be there. And to copy the list of paintings from the trust and attach it to this new bill of sale. Well," she said with a huff, "I thought that sounded a little bit suspicious, you know? So, I take a look back at the file, at the letter from Mr. Elliott that I'd filed when he'd returned from the artist's studio. Well, Mr. Elliott's letter said the paintings were to go to Caroline McKellan. I recognized the name," she added in passing, "because I belonged to the same church as her parents. And now Junior's telling me to type this bill of sale transferring those very same paintings to him!"

"Did you discuss this with Mr. Becker?"

"I'm getting to that," she insisted.

"I'm sorry. Please go on." Max anxiously awaited the conclusion of her compelling, if tedious, account.

"Well, I'd heard—we'd all heard—these rumors about Marty. That he misapplied client funds, failed to show up for hearings, stuff like that. So, I'm thinking that maybe I was really supposed to be retyping that longhand letter from Mr. Elliott on the blank sheet instead of a bill of sale turning the paintings over to Junior! So, I go up to Marty and I tell him I think something doesn't make sense here, and he just *explodes* at me! Tells me to mind my own... well he uses a rather colorful word... business. And when I hesitate to do what he says he just up and fires me on the spot."

"So, it was your impression that Mr. Becker was committing a fraud on Mr. Elliott with that bill of sale?"

"Very much so! He was an *awful* man. Alcohol on his breath almost all of the time. Fighting with his wife over the phone. A miserable human being, the exact opposite of his father."

Max sighed. This was the missing part of the story, the narrative that lent context to the dueling documents in Jerry's little red file.

"Well, Ms. Taylor, I thank you very much for sharing your recollections with me. I appreciate your candor."

"I just thought you'd want to know," she said before the line went dead.

Now that he knew, he wasn't sure he wanted to.

Chapter Fifty-Seven

Seven Miles Over
Knoxville, Tennessee
and West Lafayette, Indiana
March, 2011

Jerry gripped the armrests tightly, sweating profusely, his frame scrunched uncomfortably into the middle seat. He'd have preferred a colonoscopy to a commercial airline flight. Another brutal hour to Indianapolis and then a two-hour bus ride to West Lafayette.

But in one way, he was glad he'd chosen to fly: he couldn't turn back. He'd cursed at Max for relating the story he'd gleaned from that telephone call with some woman named Taylor. "Jesus, Max," he'd groused, "why'd you have to go and ruin my day by telling me that goddamn story?" He'd surrendered his claim to half of the Caroline Paintings because he'd finally accepted the premise that Caroline's view of the facts was as defensible as his own. But now this old biddy pops out of the woodwork and alleges, with some pretty damning testimony, that Becker was indisputably a thief. Jerry's contention that the bill of sale at least *might* have been legitimate had now lost all credibility. And though Caroline was pleased with their settlement, and Jerry insulated by its finality, his conscience was churning again. He knew now that his claim to even *half* of the windfall lacked what his late, self-righteous, Bible-thumping grandmother used to call "moral rectitude."

"I gather you don't like to fly." The voice was that of the young lady in the aisle seat to his right.

"Fucking hate it," he said, scowling.

"My mom is like that," she said, smiling sympathetically. A polite half-smile was all Jerry could summon in response. He regarded his seat mate curiously. She was blonde, attractive, and not much older, he figured, than Caroline Grainger had been when she abandoned Longmire forty years earlier, pregnant and without prospects. Her tale of hitching a ride with a trucker, spending the night in a truck stop motel, and being rescued, fortuitously, by her eventual husband, was already a staple of talk shows and late-night television. "It's a far better story than I can muster," he grumbled to himself, assessing his comparatively lame saga of storage locker serendipity.

"Excuse me?" said the young woman, glancing up from her in-flight magazine.

"Sorry, just thinking out loud."

Caroline's resiliency was, indeed, remarkable and admirable. He held that thought for the final hour of the flight.

His taxi pulled up to the modest but well-groomed bungalow at 31 Parkland Street, in a charming residential neighborhood not far from the Purdue campus. It was six o'clock, later than he'd anticipated. Jerry strolled up the walkway to the front porch and rang the doorbell.

Mike Grainger did a double-take as he opened the front door. "Jerry?" he sputtered, as if doubting his capacity for facial recognition. "Hey, hon, it's Jerry Deaver!" he announced, having dismissed the possibility of hallucination.

Caroline interrupted her dinner preparations and scampered to the door. "Well, invite him in, Mike!" she ordered, equally dumbfounded by Jerry's appearance.

"Sorry to arrive unannounced," he said, entering the threshold, a sheepish grin on his face. "I came on a whim," he added, offering no further explanation for his presence.

"You must be hungry," Caroline speculated, "having come all this way. Mike," she said, turning to her slack-jawed husband, "why don't you set another place at the table."

Never one to refuse a meal, Jerry accepted their invitation. "Don't mind if I do."

While Caroline improvised in the kitchen, stretching their dinner to accommodate their unexpected guest, Mike asked the obvious question. "What brings you to West Lafayette, Jerry?"

"I've got something to show you." But as Jerry began to reach into his pocket, Caroline arrived from the kitchen with a heaping bowl of spaghetti and meatballs.

"Dinner!"

Jerry withdrew his hand. "It can wait," he muttered to Mike, making a beeline to the dining room table.

"Looks wonderful!" Jerry bellowed as he watched the steam curl up from the bowl.

"Dig in!" Caroline commanded. So, he did, transferring fully half of the pasta and two of the three meatballs onto his plate. His hosts were as stunned by his appetite as they were by his presence.

"This is fabulous!" Jerry opined, processing his first mouthful while spearing a meatball.

Neither Caroline nor Mike knew quite how to begin the conversation. Why was he here, having travelled more than a thousand miles? Their settlement had been signed, sealed, and delivered. And yet here he sat, ensconced at their dining room table, gleefully devouring more than half of their dinner.

Caroline broke the silence. "Mike and I have been wondering about your plans for your share of the collection." The two of them stared at Jerry with a mix of anticipation and apprehension, waiting for him to suspend his chewing long enough to answer.

Jerry slurped down another forkful of spaghetti before surrendering his utensil to the tabletop and formulating a response.

"That's what I've come here to discuss," he replied. "That storage locker that included the paintings also contained a dozen boxes of Marty Becker's legal files," he explained, continuing to chew. "That's where I'd found the bill of sale I brought to Max's." He looked at the Graingers, gauging their reaction. Had he detected any hint of hostility, he might have changed course right then and there, but he didn't. Nor had he expected to. Mike and Caroline looked at him kindly but anxiously. "Well, I took another pass at the files," he lied, adjusting the timeline to save face, "and found something else."

Jerry reached into his pocket and withdrew a creased sheet of paper. He handed it across the table to Caroline before harpooning another meatball.

With Mike leaning over her shoulder, she studied the document. While struggling with its legibility, she immediately grasped its tenor. "So, Eli was right! Grant *did* plan to ..." Her voice trailed off. She glanced at Jerry, tears in her eyes. "But what about the—"

"The bill of sale?"

"Yes, the bill of sale."

"Ever hear of a lady from Longmire named Gladys Taylor?"

"Sounds vaguely familiar," Caroline mused. "Might've belonged to our church way back when."

"Well, this Mrs. Taylor was secretary to Marty Becker in the mid-1990s. After reading about the paintings, she contacted Max last week." Jerry relayed the story Max had told him about Becker's use of the sheet signed in blank to concoct a bill of sale. "She was reluctant to help him do it, so he fired her."

"So, your bill of sale was fraudulent?" Mike asked.

"Just as you probably anticipated," Jerry said with a smirk.

Caroline and Mike looked at each other. Why would Jerry reveal this, they wondered? Had he come to gloat over his ill-gotten gains while hijacking their dinner?

"I know what you're probably thinking," Jerry said. "And that brings me to why I came." The Graingers sat transfixed, even as Jerry sprinkled another spoonful of grated parmesan over his rapidly dwindling mound of spaghetti.

"I'd like to donate my share of the Caroline Paintings to your foundation," he said, his face displaying a smug smile over a smudge of tomato sauce.

Caroline gasped.

"Are you *serious*?" Mike asked, his head spinning.

"I am. I have what I need," he said soberly, "except for my late wife, Blanche. Money won't bring her back, but I think she'd be kinda proud of me right about now, and that's enough for me."

Caroline leapt from her chair and hugged Jerry, planting a grateful kiss on his cheek even as he eyed the last strand of spaghetti on his plate. He pointed to Caroline's dish. "You gonna finish that?" he asked. "If not, do you mind—"

"Help yourself!" Caroline laughed. "It's the least we can do."

Jerry reached over, grabbed her plate, and dug in.

Chapter Fifty-Eight

Fort Myers, Florida
September, 2019

Athrong of several thousand descended upon City of Palms Park, the former spring home of the Boston Red Sox, on a clear, mild Saturday morning. "A beautiful day for a ball game," Jerry might have crowed. Dressed in shorts, bright tee shirts, and sundresses, they filed past the welcoming palm trees, beneath the broad marquee, and through the main gate, quietly populating the roped-off section of box and reserved seats along the first base line, well below the grandstand seats Jerry had occupied in springs past.

There were strings pulled, to be sure, to arrange for the use of the old ballpark as the venue for a memorial. But then the late Jerry Deaver wasn't your typical ordinary guy.

Though Caroline Grainger and her son received the lion's share of media attention when the Caroline Paintings were revealed to the public eight years earlier, a handful of more enterprising reporters turned to Jerry, the overweight, baseball-loving, beer-guzzling, Everyman Florida retiree; witty, charming, and cantankerous, the man who stumbled onto a fortune in art and gave it all away. They never knew the crises of conscience he endured, the ethical quagmire he traversed, or the demons he battled before deciding to donate his windfall to the foundation established by the Graingers. In the succeeding years, the foundation had lent Caroline Paintings to dozens of institutions, while donating nearly half the collection to museums across the country, large and small, metropolitan and rural, assuring the continuation of the artist's legacy and the model's remarkable story for generations to come. When the eyes of the public finally focused on Jerry Deaver, they discovered a man to whom everyone could relate, the ordinary guy who displayed an extraordinary generosity of spirit. Who *couldn't* relate to the slovenly-clad average Joe, the man whose idea of epicurean delight was a Fenway Frank slathered with mustard, chopped raw onions, and (on special occasions) a dollop of sauerkraut?

The man who eschewed attention got more than he'd bargained for, but rose to the occasion. Jerry became a celebrity in his own right, appearing on *The Tonight Show* with Jay Leno, and later doing the rounds with Jimmy Kimmel, Seth Meyers, Jimmy Fallon, and Stephen Colbert. "If only Blanche were here to see this," he told himself repeatedly, pinching himself to confirm his suddenly altered reality.

And speaking of reality, nothing was more improbable than Jerry's stint as a reality show superstar, appearing as a guest host on *Storage Wars* and, his most famous gig, hosting his own program on The Food Network. "In Search of the Perfect Hot Dog with Jerry Deaver" scoured the country—and dozens of ballparks—for what he unabashedly termed "the finest fuckin' frank imaginable" (it was cable TV).

And when cancer struck in 2018, Jerry shouldered on, even as he approached his eightieth birthday.

Among his biggest fans was Caroline Grainger. Enamored of his authenticity, transparency, and love for life, she developed a genuine affection for the sometimes crabby but always reliable co-director of the Deaver-Grainger Foundation—she'd insisted his name appear first, if only for alphabetical integrity.

But it was Max Winter who became Jerry's closest friend. Jerry routinely checked in with him as the professor wrote the definitive catalogue of the Caroline Paintings and organized their ambitious trans-American exhibition schedule. Jerry cared little about the details, but endured, unfailingly, Max's long-winded progress reports on marathon telephone calls made tolerable by the six-packs Jerry would consume through their duration. And when baseball season arrived in the spring, Jerry would host his buddy for the entirety of the Grapefruit League schedule in March, the pair attending nearly every Red Sox spring training game at City of Palms (and later JetBlue) Park. They made an odd couple, annoyed each other unceasingly, but mutually treasured their friendship. It was Max, using his Harvard connections, who arranged for his friend's memorial service to take place at City of Palms Park (which Jerry preferred over the newer park, deeming the latter "a tad too corporate for my taste").

Jerry would've been proud of the guidelines Max had set for the service. "Dress casually," he wrote in the press release announcing the memorial observance, "like you would for an actual ball game. The sloppier, the better," Max insisted. "Wear any baseball cap you want," he added, "as long as it bears a Red Sox logo." The third suggestion: "Bring peanuts, popcorn, or Crackerjacks . . . or better yet, all three."

Max never anticipated the turnout. Fans of Jerry's reality show wore tee shirts with the words "Finest Fuckin' Frank Imaginable" stenciled across their chests. Max wore his Kevin Youkilis tee shirt in honor of the day they met. Eli Grainger, a lifelong Cubs fan, abandoned his Cubbie paraphernalia for the David Ortiz replica jersey Jerry had presented him as a wedding gift. His wife, Rachel, and their twins—Caroline and Mike's beloved grandchildren—donned child-sized versions of the Finest Fuckin' Frank tee shirts, with asterisks superimposed over the final five letters of the second word.

While several speakers extolled the virtues—as well as the quirks—that characterized the late Jerry Deaver, Caroline's recollections were the most poignant. After recounting his generosity, she related the story of his unannounced visit to her Indiana home eight years earlier and his unabashed appropriation of the lion's share of their spaghetti-and-meatball dinner. She thanked him for bringing the Caroline Paintings back from forty years of obscurity, allowing her to realize a long-deferred dream. When her remarks ended, and without her prior knowledge, Max arranged for the public address system to play a recording of Neil Diamond's *Sweet Caroline*, traditionally played prior to the home half of the eighth inning at Fenway Park. "In honor of Jerry, symbolic both of his eighty years and the end of his game," Max told the crowd. "And in this particular case, in honor of his association and cherished friendship with sweet Caroline Grainger."

Jerry would have enjoyed the heartfelt tribute on this glorious day. Nine years earlier, when he delivered a eulogy for his friend Gus, the man whose invitation to bid on the contents of a storage locker would change his life in ways he'd never have imagined, he despaired of ever deserving, much less receiving, a comparable sendoff. In the end, he got what he deserved.

When the memorial observance concluded, Max reclaimed the microphone for one final announcement: "Please join us at the concession stand for a Fenway Frank with all the fixings!"

—The End—

Acknowledgments

It was the so-called 'Helga Pictures' by Andrew Wyeth, a secret cache of more than 240 paintings featuring the artist's neighbor and model, Helga Testorf, revealed (with considerable hullabaloo) to the art world in 1986, which afforded the initial inspiration for *The Caroline Paintings*. What developed from that kernel of an idea is the product of my own twisted mind, although credit is due to the characters themselves, who, whether serendipitously or perversely, directed me how the story should proceed.

Though writing may seem like a solitary endeavor, no book can reach fruition without the contributions of trusted, diligent, and perceptive readers. I am truly fortunate to have coaxed several to endure the indignities of earlier drafts and improve them with their thoughtful comments. My special thanks to Tim Neely, whose plot suggestions carved a creative path through a maze of possibilities; to Ken Brooks, who delivered me from my inadvisable excesses; and especially to Gary Null, who rescued me on countless occasions from plotting inconsistencies, erroneous usage, grammatical quicksand, and other literary debacles.

And special thanks to my wife, Peggy, whose support and encouragement has made it all possible.

Finally, I thank you, my readers, for taking time out of your busy lives to read what I've written. If the spirit moves you, please consider posting a review online (e.g., on Amazon, Goodreads, or other social media) and/or share your thoughts by contacting me through my author website, www.hittnerbooks.com. Your input and support is nectar to independent authors and is sincerely appreciated.

About the Author

ARTHUR D. HITTNER is the author of three critically acclaimed books: **Artist, Soldier, Lover, Muse** (Apple Ridge Press, 2017), a novel about an emerging young artist in New York City during the late Depression and prelude to World War II; **Four-Finger Singer and His Late Wife, Kate: A Novel of Life, Death & Baseball** (Apple Ridge Press, 2019), a dark, romantic comedy that transcends mortal boundaries, and **Honus Wagner: The Life of Baseball's Flying Dutchman** (McFarland Publishing, 1996), recipient of the 1997 Seymour Medal awarded by the Society for American Baseball Research for the best work of baseball biography or history published during the preceding year. He has also written or co-written several art catalogues, a biography and catalogue raisonne on the artist Harold J. Rabinovitz, and articles on American art and artists for national publications including *Fine Art Connoisseur*, *Antiques & Fine Art* and *Maine Antique Digest*.

A retired attorney, Hittner spent nearly thirty-four years with the national law firm now known as Nixon Peabody LLP, resident in the firm's Boston office. He served as a trustee of Danforth Art (formerly the Danforth Museum of Art) in Framingham, Massachusetts and the Tucson Museum of Art in Tucson, Arizona. He was also a co-owner of the Lowell Spinners, a minor league professional baseball team affiliated with his beloved Boston Red Sox.

Married with two children and three grandchildren, Hittner currently divides his time between Oro Valley, Arizona and

Natick, Massachusetts. He is a graduate of Dartmouth College and Harvard Law School.

For additional information about the author's other books, please visit www.hittnerbooks.com.

mine?" he asked tentatively, his voice quavering.

Caroline hesitated. She'd been poised to tell him the truth, but her resolve abruptly faltered. Her relationship with Grant Elliott hung in the balance. If she confirmed his responsibility, their further interactions, if any, would be governed by his fears: fear for his marriage, his reputation, even criminal conviction. The fact that he asked her the question—*is it mine?*—struck her as an affront to her character. He'd offer her money—for her silence or the abortion her parents forbade her—and their collaboration would come to a screeching halt. She didn't want his money; she wanted his friendship, respect, and, yes, even his love, if that were possible. But in that moment, she knew that it wasn't.

"No," she heard herself mutter. "It's not yours." She had all she could do to keep from bawling, straining to maintain the falsehood she believed would protect him and preserve their relationship.

"How do you know?"

"I had my period after we made love," she lied again.

"Who's the father?" he asked, his heartbeat calming.

"I'd rather not say."

"What will you do?"

"I don't know," she said.

"I'm here for you," he avowed, though she no longer truly believed it.

And then, it was as if nothing had happened. Grant found her condition intriguing, artistically inspiring, and drew her that day, and over the succeeding months, as she swelled with pregnancy, heartbreak, and fear.

Chapter Sixteen

Longmire, Virginia
March, 1970

Becky informed him at lunch. Grant was wolfing down an egg salad sandwich, eagerly anticipating his afternoon session with Caroline at Brandon's studio.

"Alice McKellan dropped by this morning," Becky told him. "Said Caroline left for school yesterday and never came home."

Grant nearly choked on his sandwich. "What do you mean never came home?"

"Ran away, it seems. Some clothes were missing, including an old sweater of her brother's that Alice said she cherished."

The color drained from Grant's face. "Did they call the police?"

"The police say there's nothing much they can do. Kids run away all the time, they told her."

"My God!" Grant shuddered. "Shouldn't we all be out looking for her? She's pregnant, for God's sake!"

Becky was surprised by the intensity of her husband's reaction. But even more so regarding Caroline's pregnancy— and Grant's awareness of her condition. "What? Since when?"

Grant realized he'd spoken without thinking. He needed a plausible cover for his potentially explosive gaffe. "I, uh, heard about it sometime last month," he sputtered. "Brandon mentioned it."

"Brandon? How the hell would he know?" Becky wrinkled her forehead as she peered at Grant.

"He met her a couple of years ago when she barged into the studio asking me to paint her. You remember, don't you? Sees her walking home from school from time to time. Asked if I knew she was pregnant." Beads of sweat were forming on his forehead.

"How would he even remember her?"

"It's hard to forget a young woman like Caroline."

Becky smirked. "Why the hell didn't you tell me?" she said with a look of exasperation.

"Sorry, Beck, I guess I just forgot. You know how things slip my mind when I'm working." Grant breathed a little easier, sensing he'd dodged a bullet. But he was deeply shaken by the news. "Why'd she leave?"

"Alice didn't offer any explanations. Besides, since she never even *mentioned* her daughter's pregnancy, there's probably a lot more going on over there than they're willing to share."

"Is there anything we can do?"

Becky shook her head. "No. I already offered. They're hoping she'll call but not particularly optimistic."

Having partially regained his composure, Grant finished his sandwich. "I'm going over to see Brandon," he said.

Grant drove to Brandon's studio. He hoped, by some miracle, to find Caroline sitting on the studio porch astride her backpack, waiting patiently for his arrival. He knew, of course, that she was unhappy at home, particularly after her parents had learned of her pregnancy, but he'd failed to recognize the depths of her desperation. He felt he should do something— look for her, perhaps. But where would he look?

There was no sign of Caroline at the studio. Since she'd never missed an appointment, he decided, against all logic, to wait. He felt he'd let her down, though he wasn't sure how. She'd confided in him, trusted him, but now she'd abandoned him. His emotions spanned the spectrum from hurt to guilt to desolation. He tried to distract himself by painting, but most of his canvases were works in progress for which she had posed. Studying her image just heightened his despair. He put down his brush and returned home.

Over the next several days, Grant found painting impossible. He moped about in his studio, unable to concentrate. On the fourth day, Brandon paid a visit. Grant had already informed him of Caroline's disappearance.

"This arrived this morning," Brandon said, handing Grant a small, white envelope. "Thought you'd want to see it right away."

Grant stared at the envelope. Addressed to him in a feminine hand, it bore an Indianapolis postmark but no return address.

"Gonna open it or what?" Brandon prodded him.

Biting his lip, Grant reached for the letter opener on his worktable and slit the envelope open. He withdrew its contents: a three-page letter scribbled on paper torn from a spiral-bound notebook. Unfolding it, he began to read.

Hey Old Man,

> *If you're waiting for me at the studio, you're out of luck. As you've probably heard by now, I've flown the coop. I'm sorry I couldn't say goodbye. I miss you already.*

> *I could no longer bear living at home. How can you live where you're constantly despised and ridiculed?*

addresses, he could eliminate all uncertainty regarding the disposition of the Caroline Paintings, ensuring their long-delayed debut to the art world.

A black Lexus rumbled up the icy driveway and pulled into the clearing by the studio. Marty Becker was surprisingly punctual. Grant had telephoned the attorney, indicating his desire to update the letter of direction that would govern the distribution of the Caroline Paintings. Recognizing the artist's infirmities, Marty had offered to make a house call.

The lawyer barely recognized his client. In the year since their meeting in his office, the artist had deteriorated dramatically. Grant thanked Marty for agreeing to drop by, apologizing for the accumulated infirmities necessitating his visit.

Marty clutched his client by the elbow, helping him into the studio and out of the bulky parka into which he'd bundled himself for the slow, taxing trek from the house. The attorney's finely tailored gray pinstriped suit and silk tie belied the mounting difficulties that plagued his practice and personal life. "What can I do for you, Mr. Elliott?" he asked as they entered the studio.

Grant mentioned the letter of direction he'd furnished to Becker a year earlier, when he and Brandon had signed the trust papers. "I have a married name and current address for the beneficiary now," Grant explained, his voice frail and hoarse, "and an additional recipient to designate if the beneficiary's no longer living."

"I see," Marty said. "We can take care of that right now. I'll help you compose the letter and we can substitute it for the one you provided last winter."

Grant nodded. He shuffled to his worktable, pulled out the chair, and eased himself down. He fidgeted with the scrap of paper on which Eli had written the relevant information, placing it on the table alongside a clean sheet of paper. With Marty providing the guidance and mind-numbing legalese, Grant scratched out his revised letter of direction:

> *Reference is made to the Trust Indenture dated March 4, 1994 between the undersigned as trustor and Brandon Blake as original trustee. I hereby provide that the artwork held under the provisions of such Trust shall be disbursed in full, upon the later to occur of my death and the death of my wife, Rebecca Turner Elliott, to Caroline McKellan Grainger, 3247 Davis Boulevard, Lincoln, Nebraska, if she shall then be living and, if she shall not then be living, to our son, Elliott Grant Grainger, 35 West Ontario Street, Chicago, Illinois.*

Grant signed the letter and handed it to his attorney. His handwriting, borderline legible in better times, was nearly inscrutable. Marty read it aloud to confirm his client's intentions, tripping over the reference to "our" son.

"Don't you mean *her* son?" he asked.

"I meant what I said," Grant responded, fully aware that he was formally acknowledging Eli as his offspring.

"I see," his attorney said, restraining a snicker.

Marty bit his lip in contemplation. An idea flashed through his increasingly devious mind.

"Your handwriting," he said, pointing to the old man's scribbling, "is virtually impossible to read." Grant shrugged apologetically. "Let me make a suggestion," Marty said with a condescending grin. "Why don't you sign another blank sheet at the bottom, and I'll ask my secretary to type what you've written right above it. Then there'll be no possibility of confusion arising from illegibility."

A sharper man with all his faculties might have recognized the peril inherent in Marty's suggestion. Grant, however, accepted the recommendation, signing the blank sheet Marty placed before him.

"We're all set, then," Marty announced, depositing both sheets into his attaché case and snapping it shut. "It was a pleasure to see you again, Mr. Elliott," he said, shaking the feeble right hand of the elderly artist. A villainous smirk played upon his lips as he exited the studio.

Chapter Forty

Jerry was beginning to feel like a man on a tightrope. While circumstantial evidence of Grant Elliott's authorship of the Caroline Paintings was mounting, he still lacked definitive proof. On the other hand, he was growing increasingly uneasy about the legitimacy of Marty Becker's ownership of the paintings—and by extension, his own. Could he secure the attribution without imperiling his claim to the collection?

Although Jerry and Max had made substantial progress, there were fewer and fewer leads to pursue. They agreed on their first agenda item for the day: a visit to the former home and studio of Brandon Blake.

Max had learned of the location of Blake's studio from a docent at the Grant Elliott Homestead. Unlike the latter, the restored barn in which Blake had painted his masterworks had not been preserved as a shrine. It had been relegated to the status of a disused outbuilding on the grounds of a private residence occupied by a family with a gaggle of children, judging from the jungle of toys, scooters, bicycles, and other forms of juvenile transport and amusement scattered about the house and yard.

Jerry thumped the door knocker against the wooden front door like he was pounding a chicken cutlet. A woman responded. The sound of screeching children spilled from the open doorway. Clad in gym clothes and with her hair askew,